Hurricane Hole

10

Hurricane Hole

John Kerr

ROBERT HALE · LONDON

ISBN 978-0-7090-9905-5

Robert Hale Limited
Clerkenwell House
Clerkenwell Green
London EC1R 0HT

www.halebooks.com

2 4 6 8 10 9 7 5 3 1

For my wife and children

Typeset in 10.75/14.75pt Sabon
Printed in Great Britain by the MPG Books Group,
Bodmin and King's Lynn

PROLOGUE

Nassau, The Bahamas
February, 1955

TOM HAMILTON TURNED from the glittering sea beyond the window and surveyed the room, as though he might never see it again. The only sound was the lazy hum of the ceiling fan. He examined an intricately carved jade figurine on the bookshelf, feeling a pang of sadness and regret, and glanced at the headline on the British racing sheet: SIR PHILIP SASSOON DIES – FOUR EPSOM DERBY WINNERS. Hamilton smiled at the photograph of Sir Philip and visualized him in his favorite chair, surrounded by his cherished Kipling, looking rakish despite his age and infirmity.

'Tom....'

Hamilton turned toward the stairs. 'Hello, Marnie,' he said with an affectionate smile. 'You've caught me.' He stared admiringly at her.

'Yes,' she said. 'I've caught you. After all these years, you haven't changed. Never could stand a crowd.'

'Well, not that crowd.'

'I suppose you're right. All the local higher-ups and their dreadful wives. Here to pay their respects and, if they're lucky, get their names on the society page.'

Hamilton stared at her, thinking how little she'd changed in the decade since the war. From a distance, she still had film-star looks, though she was well over forty, but, as she came closer, he could see that years of constant exposure to the sun had taken their toll. He slipped off his jacket and tossed it over the back of a chair. 'Marnie,' he said, 'I could use a drink.'

She walked to the stairs and called down, 'Henry ... Mr Hamilton would like a drink. You remember?'

'Yes, ma'am, for sure.' The voice that drifted up was velvety smooth, in the distinctive Bahamian accent.

'And I'll have a Bellini,' she added. Lady Sassoon – 'Marnie' to Hamilton since the day they'd met in 1942 – walked back to him, stopping within inches and gently taking his hands. 'Tom,' she said softly, gazing up into his eyes. 'With Philip gone ... it's going to be so lonely here. If only you'd stay for a while. For old times' sake.'

He briefly studied her face, thinking that her sadness accentuated the wrinkles at the corners of her eyes and mouth. 'You'll be all right,' he said at length. 'Don't worry. I'll be back to visit.'

She lightly squeezed his hands. 'Well,' she said with a shrug. 'What was I thinking?'

An elderly black man with close-cropped silver hair ascended the stairs carrying a polished salver with slightly trembling hands. 'Here you are, Mr Hamilton. Martini with two olives.' He handed a fluted glass of a sparkling peach concoction to Lady Sassoon, as Hamilton lifted his drink from the tray. 'Mighty nice havin' you back, Mr Hamilton,' said the old man.

'Thanks, Henry,' said Hamilton. 'It's good to be back.' He slumped down on the rattan sofa. 'God, Marnie,' he said with a sigh, 'it's hard to believe Sir Philip's really gone.' She stared at him, biting her lower lip and holding her glass as though unsure what to do with it. He took a sip of the ice-cold martini and said, 'Mmm, that's good. What is it about taste and smell that brings back memories?' He leaned forward, resting his arms on his knees. 'So many memories.'

She tilted back her head and took a sip of her drink. 'You know, Tom, I used to think ...' A blush radiated across her tanned face. 'Oh, God,' she said, her voice breaking as she turned away and walked to the window. 'I used to think,' she began again, 'that if something happened to Philip, we might ... there might be a chance for us.' She stood with her back to him, staring at the turquoise sea. As he rose from the sofa, her eyes shifted to his reflection in the glass. 'But now that he's gone ...'

He walked over and placed one hand on her shoulder.

She spun around and beamed at him. 'It's going to be all right, isn't it?' she asked.

'Of course it is.' He tenderly placed a hand on her cheek and brushed away a tear.

She buried her face on his shoulder. 'Oh, Tom,' she murmured. Breaking away, she said, 'You're not leaving? Not now, I mean?'

'I'm sorry,' he said. 'My plane's waiting at the airfield.'

'You won't even stay for dinner?'

'No.' He stood with his hands on her shoulders. 'Marnie,' he said softly, 'I'm sick I didn't get to see Sir Philip again. I've always had this feeling there was something he never … well, something he knew that he never told me.'

She blinked uncomprehendingly into his intense grey eyes. 'What? Not about Sir Harry and de Marigny and all that?'

He let go of her and walked to the window. 'Well, not exactly,' he said. 'But what about de Marigny?'

She uttered a short laugh. 'Living the good life in Cuba, I suppose. But wait, what were you thinking Philip might have known?'

'About Evelyn,' said Hamilton.

'No,' she said simply. 'You're wrong. Philip didn't know anything. She's gone, Tom. And it was a long time ago.'

'Yes,' he said. 'A long, long time ago.'

CHAPTER ONE

GLANCING UP FROM his newspaper, Tom Hamilton stared out the windshield of the twin-engine Cessna at the flat expanse of the Caribbean, patches of deep blue amid shades of turquoise, sparkling under the strong noonday sun. 'How much longer?' he asked.

The pilot, a young navy lieutenant wearing a denim shirt and a wrinkled pair of khakis, glanced at his watch. 'Twenty minutes, maybe,' he replied. 'Just a short hop from Miami.'

Hamilton glanced down at the shimmering water and asked, 'What sort of depth is it here?'

'Let's take a closer look.' The pilot made a slow banking turn, descending to an altitude of 500 feet. 'There,' he said, 'the water's so clear you can see the sandbanks.'

'What do you figure? Thirty feet?'

'Yeah,' said the pilot. 'I haven't looked at the charts.'

'Not much room for a sub to operate,' observed Hamilton.

'Not on this side of the island,' said the pilot. 'They steer clear of the flats. The deep channel's on the northern side. Up toward the Abacos, and from there it's a clear shot to Florida.'

Hamilton turned back to his Miami paper. After ten minutes passed with no sound but the drone of the engines, he said, 'Look at this.' He jabbed his finger at the newsprint. 'Almost the whole page is war news. *"Marines Gain on Guadalcanal." 'Russians Fall Back in Mid-Caucasus"*.'

The pilot glanced at him through aviator sunglasses. 'Yep,' he agreed. 'And some of it good for a change. There she is,' he added, pointing toward a patch of light brown and green on the horizon. 'New Providence Island.'

Hamilton peered out as the small plane crossed the boundary from sea to shore. The sandy coral soil was covered with a thick blanket of pale green vegetation; sea-grape, banyans, palms, and the taller Australian pines. Passing low over a brackish pond, he observed a cluster of shanties where a knot of nearly naked black children was pointing up at the plane. Throttling back the engines, the pilot angled the nose straight for the ribbon of runway and within seconds the tyres bumped and the plane rolled smoothly toward a Quonset hut. A Union Jack fluttered above a sign with the words: OAKES FIELD – NASSAU. Hamilton observed the fences topped with silvery concertina wire and a row of RAF Spitfires parked in a recently built hangar. 'Looks like they've been busy,' he commented.

'You should have seen what was here before,' said the pilot. 'This guy Oakes is supposedly worth a fortune, and he built this airfield for the local authorities.'

'Very generous,' said Hamilton as the engines sighed to a stop. 'Yes, I know about Harry Oakes. Richer than Croesus. And though he's as much an American as you or me, he managed to acquire a British title.' The pilot gave him a puzzled look. Hamilton grinned. 'Sir Harry,' he explained.

'I get it,' said the pilot, though he didn't. 'At any rate,' he added, 'they've just upgraded this field into a training base for the RAF. Built the whole thing with US dollars under Lend-Lease.'

'How long are you staying?' asked the pilot, as Hamilton opened the door.

'That remains to be seen. But if anyone should ask, this is *my* plane and you're *my* pilot.' Hamilton jumped down on the tarmac and reached for a bulky duffle bag and suitcase. 'OK, Lieutenant,' he said. 'Thanks for the lift.' By the time he reached the Quonset hut, a damp stain had formed on the back of Hamilton's shirt. He dropped his bags and mopped his brow.

'Your passport, please,' said a plainly bored British official.

'Hamilton,' he said, studying the passport. 'What brings you to Nassau?'

'Business. And a little pleasure, on the side.'

The official arched his eyebrows. 'What sort of business?'

'Real estate. And I was hoping to do a little fishing—'

'There's a war on,' interrupted the official.

'So I hear.'

'Goddamned American,' said the official under his breath. He slapped a stamp on the passport and said, 'There you are. I trust you'll enjoy your stay.'

'Thanks,' said Hamilton with a smile. 'How can I get a ride into town?'

'If you're lucky, you'll find a jitney outside.'

When Hamilton walked up to the sole taxi, the driver, whose tattered straw hat was pulled low over his face, was sound asleep. Hamilton examined the windowless British car, of indeterminate age with a fringed canvas top. 'Excuse me,' he said. Hamilton gave the man's shoulder a shake. 'Sorry,' he said in a louder voice. 'Could you—?'

'Hah, hah,' laughed the driver as he sat bolt upright, his hat falling back to reveal a round, cheerful face. 'You surprised me, Cap'n.'

'I was wondering—'

'Hop in. Wherebouts can I take you?'

Hamilton tossed his bags in the back and said, 'The British Colonial.'

In a cloud of dust, the jitney lurched down a narrow road that merged with a two-lane highway. As they sped along in the open air, Hamilton admired the graceful homes along Cable Beach, with manicured lawns and matchless views of the crystal Caribbean. Within fifteen minutes Nassau lay before them, Government House and the old stone fortifications at the top of a hill overlooking neat rows of buildings and a long wharf. Conspicuously above the rest was a tall pink structure with white awnings above the waterfront. Observing Hamilton's inquisitive stare, the driver said, 'Pretty, ain't it?'

'The town, you mean?' said Hamilton.

'The Colonial. Your hotel, Cap'n.' As the driver manoeuvred around a mule-drawn wagon, it dawned on Hamilton that they were driving on the left, British-style. Once they entered the town, he noticed the British constabulary on the corners, in starched white uniforms and hats trimmed in gold. The driver sailed past pale-pink and yellow buildings, turned on Georges Street, and drove neatly up under the hotel's portico.

'Good afternoon, sir,' said a uniformed bellman in a pleasant accent. 'Welcome to Nassau.' He reached into the back for Hamilton's bags.

Hamilton reached into his pocket for a roll of bills. 'Sorry,' he said, 'but I forgot to change my money.'

The driver grinned and said, 'Your dollars will do jus' fine.'

From his balcony Hamilton enjoyed a panoramic view of the city centre and waterfront. He checked his watch, debating whether to call his contact. First things first, he decided, stepping inside and snapping open the clasps of his suitcase. After unpacking his shaving kit and putting away his neatly folded shirts, he unzipped the duffle bag and reached inside for his .25 Beretta, wrapped in a soft chamois. Hamilton checked the action of the nickel-plated pistol and then placed it underneath his shirts in the dresser. Dressed in a sea-island cotton shirt and charcoal slacks, he stood before the mirror running a comb through his damp hair. Like his late father, he was turning prematurely grey in his mid-20s, with a touch of silver at his temples and a shock of white in the dark cowlick. With an otherwise youthful face, the salt-and-pepper hair and dark eyes had a striking effect. Securing the comb in the bristles of his hair-brush, Hamilton walked out on the balcony and surveyed the layout of the town and waterfront, bathed in the evanescent light of the gathering dusk. After a few moments he went inside and took a slip of paper from his wallet and picked up the telephone. After giving the operator the number, he listened to the distinctive British double ring.

'Sassoon residence,' answered a man in a pleasant Bahamian accent.

'May I speak to Sir Philip?' said Hamilton.

'May I say who's calling?'

'Tom Hamilton.'

After a few moments, a woman's voice came on the line. 'Hello, Mr Hamilton,' she said in a soft Southern drawl. 'Philip and I were hoping you could join us for dinner.'

Hamilton hesitated. He expected the first contact would be a discreet, private meeting. 'Sure,' he said after a moment. 'And where should I—?'

'We'll send a car. Seven-thirty, at your hotel.'

'Fine. I'm staying at—'

'The Colonial. We'll see you shortly, Mr Hamilton.'

Hamilton scratched his head, wondering what else Sassoon might have confided to his wife. Judging from his dossier, Philip Sassoon was a rich, elderly Englishman, confined to a wheelchair, an amateur as far as espionage was concerned. Hamilton knotted a regimental tie, slipped on a blue blazer, and, with a final glance in the mirror, let himself out.

The evening was pleasantly cool and the air perfumed with the fragrance of tropical blossoms. Listening to the rustling of palm fronds, Hamilton checked his watch just as a cream-coloured Bentley convertible swung into the hotel drive. A tall Jamaican wearing a dark suit climbed out, idling the engine, and walked around to open the passenger door.

'Mr Hamilton?' he said.

Hamilton nodded and got in. He leaned back on the soft leather upholstery and glanced at the driver as he sat behind the wheel. 'You work for Mr Sassoon?' he asked.

'Sir Philip,' the driver corrected him with an easy smile as he started down the drive. 'My name's Carter.' He turned and accelerated up toward Government House, the neo-classical columns of which were brightly illuminated against the evening sky. As they drove along in silence, Hamilton stared at the burled walnut dashboard, his face faintly illuminated by the glow of the instruments and his hair tossed by the wind. Leaving the town, he turned to the driver and said, 'Where are we headed?'

'Cable Beach.' The driver pointed to the lights of the ocean-front houses sparkling in the distance. 'Another half-mile and we'll be there.' He slowed and then turned into a gravel drive with a hand-painted sign that said 'Eves'. The large house at the end of the drive was partially obscured by tropical shrubbery and tall palms. The driver switched off the ignition and said, 'Follow me, Mr Hamilton.' The house was a modern design, white with plate-glass windows, a contrast from the distinctive colonial architecture in Nassau. Standing in a pool of yellow lamplight, Carter rang the bell, and a Bahamian woman, wearing a black uniform with white lace collar, answered the door.

'Annie will show you in,' said Carter, following Hamilton inside.

'Thanks for the lift,' said Hamilton, as he started down the hall, aware of the sound of men's voices. On the far side of a spacious, blue-tiled living room, a silver-haired gentleman in a dinner jacket was engaged in conversation with a distinguished-looking man seated next to him, while a blonde in a black cocktail dress lounged against a bar.

''Scuse, me, Sir Philip,' said the maid. The men looked up. 'Your guest has arrived.'

Hamilton walked quickly across the room, certain that the man seated in a wheelchair was Sassoon. 'Hello,' he said, extending his hand. 'I'm Tom Hamilton.'

Sir Philip gave Hamilton a vigorous handshake. The blonde appeared at Sir Philip's side, placing an arm on the back of his chair. Hamilton glanced briefly at her deeply tanned face and bare shoulders. 'Lady Sassoon,' said Sir Philip.

'Marnie,' she said, in the same Southern accent Hamilton remembered from the phone.

'And my friend Geoffrey Hopwood,' said Sir Philip.

'How do you do,' the older gentleman said solemnly, giving Hamilton a limp handshake.

'Let's get you a drink, Mr Hamilton,' suggested Marnie. 'You've come a long way.'

'How long?' asked Hopwood.

'All the way from Texas,' explained Sir Philip.

Hamilton followed Marnie to the bar, where a broad-shouldered Bahamian in a coffee-coloured jacket was standing with an expectant smile. 'What can I fix you?' he asked.

'A martini,' said Hamilton. 'On the rocks, with a couple of olives. Now,' he said, turning to Lady Sassoon, 'if you'll call me Tom, I'll call you Marnie.'

'Fair enough,' she said with a smile.

'Tell me, Marnie, where did that Southern accent come from?'

'Tennessee,' she said. 'Cleveland, Tennessee, to be exact.'

'Here you are, sir,' said the bartender, handing Hamilton his drink.

Hamilton followed Marnie over to Sir Philip's side. 'This is quite a place,' said Hamilton.

Sir Philip nodded. 'I built it in '36 when I moved out from London. For the climate,' he explained. 'After my illness, I couldn't tolerate the cold and damp.'

Hamilton studied the elaborate wheelchair, upholstered in green leather, and noticed the slackness of Sir Philip's trousers. Above the waist, he was powerfully built, with wide shoulders and a thick chest. He wore a thin moustache that reinforced a certain rakish impression with his tanned face and dark hair streaked with grey. 'Pull up a chair, Mr Hamilton,' said Sir Philip, 'and tell us what brought you to Nassau while we wait for our other guests.'

Hamilton made momentary eye contact with Sir Philip, searching for a clue but finding none. Marnie settled on the sofa, crossing her long, shapely legs, while Hamilton chose a rattan armchair. 'Well,' he began, 'I thought I'd combine some business with a little pleasure.'

'What sort of business?' asked Hopwood, who remained standing.

Hamilton glanced from Sir Philip to Hopwood. 'Real estate,' he replied. 'Developing a resort hotel.'

'We've more than enough hotels,' said Hopwood. 'And most of them are empty.'

'The war won't last forever,' said Hamilton with a shrug. 'And I've got something a little different in mind. A hotel with a casino. After all, Nassau's just a hop, skip and a jump from Miami.'

'Where were you thinking of placing this hotel?' asked Sir Philip. Hamilton detected the slightest suggestion of a knowing look.

'On Hog Island,' said Hamilton. 'I understand there's nothing there, and it's right across from town.'

'Well, I should have thought a young man like yourself,' said Hopwood, 'could find something, well, more *productive* to do, what with the war on. And not going very well, I might add.'

The maid reappeared and said, 'Sir Philip ... the other folks are here.'

'Show them in, Annie,' Sir Philip called out. 'Let's take our drinks on the terrace.' Marnie rose from the sofa and grasped the handles of his wheelchair, swivelling it toward the open French doors. Hamilton politely waited for her to roll her husband out on the terrace and then followed the couple outside. Hurricane lamps flickered along the border of the terrace, and the boom of the surf was carried along on the breeze from the darkened sea. The sound of dance music came from somewhere in the distance. Hamilton turned around just as a man and woman entered the living room. Like Marnie, the woman was tall and striking, in a pale-blue chiffon dress that accentuated her trim figure. She smiled briefly and began walking toward them with her companion, a short man with a dark moustache and slicked back hair. Like Hopwood, he was wearing a dinner jacket, a degree of formality Lady Sassoon's offhand invitation had failed to suggest.

'Hello, Evelyn, my dear,' said Sir Philip as the pair stepped outside.

'Mrs Shawcross,' said Hopwood with a slight bow.

'Evelyn,' said Sir Philip, 'let me introduce an American visitor, Mr Thomas Hamilton.' Turning to Hamilton, he added, 'And the Marquis de Videlou.'

Hamilton shook the man's hand. 'Hello,' said Hamilton, turning to Evelyn Shawcross. 'A pleasure.' In the faint light of the lamps he was struck by her deep-blue eyes, dark hair and soft, pale skin that must have been shielded from the Caribbean sun. She briefly looked in his eyes and smiled.

'Good evening, Mr Hamilton,' said Georges de Videlou in a thick French accent. 'Welcome to Nassau.'

CHAPTER TWO

IN CONTRAST TO the rest of the modern house, the dining-room at Eves was richly appointed with an antique walnut table, matching sideboard, and high-backed Chippendale chairs. An eighteenth-century silver tea service gleamed beneath an oil painting of a coal-black thoroughbred stallion. Sir Philip, elegant in a white dinner jacket, smiled at his guests and signalled to the servants to begin serving. Annie ladled soup from a porcelain tureen, which Henry, the genial butler, served the dinner guests.

'You were saying, Mr Hamilton,' said Hopwood, 'you're in the *oil* business?'

Hamilton nodded. 'That's right. Along with cattle ranching.'

Evelyn, placing her fingertips together at her chin, smiled and said, 'You don't fit my idea of a Texas oilman.'

'Maybe I should have turned up in boots and a ten-gallon hat,' said Hamilton with a smile.

'All the same, Tom,' said Marnie, 'you're a damned sight more refined than the other Texas oilmen *I've* run across.' She lifted her spoon and took a first sip of soup, an act the others had been dutifully awaiting. Sir Philip motioned to Henry to pour the wine.

'*Magnifique,*' said de Videlou, holding his spoon aloft. 'The finest sea turtle soup in the Bahamas.'

'Perhaps, Mr Hamilton,' suggested Sir Philip, 'you acquired your polish from an Eastern education.'

'That's the usual American approach,' said Hamilton. 'You make your money and then send your kids back East for a proper education. In my case, Exeter and Yale.'

Hopwood arched his eyebrows imperceptibly.

'Sort of the American equivalent of Eton and Oxford,' Hamilton explained.

'I see,' said Hopwood, dabbing a linen napkin at his chin. During the ensuing lull, the only sounds were the clink of china and silverware and murmured requests for salt and pepper.

Finished with his soup, de Videlou lifted his wineglass and stared across the table at Hamilton. 'Tell me,' he said, 'why have you not rushed off to fight in this war like the rest of your countrymen?' In the awkward silence, all eyes were on Hamilton.

He gave de Videlou a tight-lipped smile. 'Seems like a funny question for a Frenchman to ask,' he said. 'Maybe I'm yellow. Or maybe I've got better things to do.' De Videlou glared back.

'Mr Hamilton is planning to build a hotel,' said Hopwood, stifling a yawn. 'And a casino.'

'Oh, really?' said Evelyn. 'Here in Nassau? What a peculiar notion.'

'Peculiar?' said Hopwood. 'I should say so. With the shipping losses to these dreadful U-boats, and the rioting in June, the economy is in a shambles.'

'Well, I'm thinking about it,' said Hamilton. 'That's what brought me to this quaint little outpost of British civilization.'

'You got that right,' said Marnie in an aside.

'Anyway,' Hamilton continued, 'the war's not going to last forever—'

'On that point I would agree,' interjected de Videlou.

'And when it's over, a first-class hotel with a European-style casino, just a short boat ride from Miami, could be a huge success.'

'Mr Hamilton makes an excellent point,' said Sir Philip. 'And now I suggest we leave our poor guest alone and enjoy the main course, some excellent grouper from this morning's catch.'

'I have one last question,' protested de Videlou with a slight wave of his hand. 'Where are you are thinking of building this hotel?'

'On Hog Island,' said Hamilton. 'In fact,' – he briefly caught Sir Philip's eye – 'I'm planning to take a look at the site in the morning.'

'But virtually all of Hog Island belongs to Monsieur Ericsson,' said de Videlou.

'Almost,' said Hamilton, 'but not quite.'

'OK,' said Lady Sassoon, as Henry appeared at her elbow with a large platter of sautéed grouper accompanied by rice and English peas. 'Enough business talk. Let's enjoy dinner.'

Later, after another carafe of wine had gone around and the local gossip had died away, Sir Philip invited his guests to take coffee or cordials on the terrace. Opting for coffee, Hamilton strolled down from the terrace to a low seawall with a view of the beach and narrow pier that disappeared out of sight into the black water. Content to be alone, he sipped his coffee and then closed his eyes and deeply inhaled the fresh breeze, fragrant with gardenias. He was soon aware of another, more subtle fragrance, which after a moment he was able to name. Opening his eyes, he turned and saw Evelyn Shawcross at his elbow. '*Pois de Senteur,*' he said. 'From Caron.'

'I'm impressed.' The blue of her dress was barely perceptible in the moonlight. 'They're few men on this island who would recognize that perfume, and it happens to be my favourite.'

'Mine too,' he said.

She took a step closer and placed her palms on the smooth tiles on top of the wall, staring out at the surf. 'It's lovely here,' she said. 'So peaceful.'

'Yes,' he said, leaning against the wall.

'I'm sorry about what was said earlier,' said Evelyn. 'That was terribly rude.'

'Oh, you mean that crack from the Frenchman? I forget his name.'

'De Videlou. He can be dreadfully obnoxious.'

'I take it you're not his, ah ...'

'Not on your life,' she said with a soft laugh. 'He's the sort of conceited Frenchman who expects every woman to swoon at his feet. I merely took Sir Philip's suggestion for a dinner partner.'

Hamilton studied her face in the dim light. 'It's Mrs Shawcross, isn't it?' he asked.

'Yes, it is. My husband's in the army. Stationed in North Africa.'

'I see. And what brought you here?'

'To this quaint outpost of British civilization?' she said with another laugh. 'I'm afraid I'm here for the duration. Of the war, that is.'

'Why Nassau?'

'Daddy sent me,' she said with a shrug. 'After the blitz – we had a bit of a close call – he thought it best I leave London. We have a winter home here. That's where I'm staying. Greycliff.'

'Greycliff,' he repeated.

'Yes. You must come for a visit. If your schedule permits it, that is.'

'I'd be delighted.'

'Well, Tom,' she said, unexpectedly reaching out to shake his hand, 'I should be going.'

'Goodnight, Evelyn.' He watched as she walked up to the terrace, spoke briefly with her hosts and disappeared inside. Once he was satisfied that the other guests had departed, he strolled to the terrace where Sir Philip and Lady Sassoon were seated with their drinks.

'That was an interesting crowd,' said Hamilton. 'I imagine by tomorrow morning everyone in town will know what I'm supposedly doing here.'

'That was the general idea,' said Sir Philip.

'Oh ... I see. Well, when do you think we might have a private chat...?'

'I would suggest tomorrow afternoon,' said Sir Philip. 'After you've had a look at the goings-on at Hog Island. I'll be keen to hear your report.'

'If you gentlemen will excuse me,' said Marnie, 'I think I'll turn in. Tom, it's been a pleasure.'

'Carter is standing by to drive you to your hotel,' said Sir Philip, once they were alone. 'We should plan to meet here for tea, at say, four. I should be able to illuminate a few things.'

'Good,' said Hamilton. 'They could use a little illumination.' He noticed Carter in the shadows. 'Well, Sir Philip, thanks for dinner. It's been a long day.'

'Good evening, Mr Hamilton.'

By the time he arrived at the hotel, Hamilton had made up his mind that Sir Philip Sassoon had handled the dinner party brilliantly while he had arrogantly spent the better part of the evening in bored agitation, resenting the fact that he'd been the object of so much attention. Yes, he concluded, as he let himself into his room, he had underestimated Sir Philip, who had orchestrated events to ensure that by morning it would be generally known in the proper circles that a wealthy American playboy, dodging the draft, had arrived in Nassau with the intention of pursuing a risky hotel scheme. Precisely the cover his superiors at OSS had decided upon. Hamilton flung his jacket on the bed, loosened his tie, and opened the door to the balcony. As the cool sea breeze washed over him, carrying the faint strains of a calypso steel drum, he felt suddenly wide-awake and energized. Walking outside, he thought about Lady Sassoon and Evelyn Shawcross, two of the most attractive women he'd encountered in a long while. A blonde and a brunette, one deeply tanned and the other with the complexion of a Geisha, both tall with terrific figures. And both married. A shame, he considered, for though not overly burdened with scruples, he drew the line at married women unless the marriage was clearly in the process of dissolution. Marnie seemed a strange match for the far older Sir Philip – he'd have to get to the bottom of that story. But Evelyn excited stronger feelings, far beyond mere sexual attraction. An aura, a mystique, perhaps having to do with her obvious intelligence or her upper-class British manners. And who was de Videlou, and why had Sir Philip invited him? For that matter, who, really, was Sir Philip? Standing at the railing, Hamilton considered that in the morning there would be much to learn.

*

He awoke with the sun and ordered juice and coffee, which he sipped on the balcony in the cool air. After shaving and a shower, he dressed in an old pair of dungarees, a polo shirt and rubber-soled shoes. Tucking the Beretta in his waistband, he slipped on a light-weight jacket and, with a quick glance in the mirror to make certain the pistol was well concealed, let himself out. He walked briskly past the storefronts and seedy bars that catered to sailors or the cheaper class of tourists and then abruptly encountered the burnt-out ruins of buildings that had been torched by the mob in the June riots, when more than a thousand Bahamians went on a sponta-neous rampage in the centre of town, sparked by a protest over the low wages paid on the massive construction project at Oakes Field. Something about the war, Hamilton considered, as he inspected the blackened hulks, had breathed freedom into the air, inspiring the poor Bahamians to rise up in a way that their colonial masters had never thought possible. A special commission empanelled by the Duke of Windsor – appointed Governor General shortly after the fall of France – investigated the uprising, leading to a bitter clash between the Colonial Office in London and the local authorities who had brutally quelled the riots, with devastating effect on the already weakened economy.

Ahead lay Rawson Square, where even at the early hour, Bahamian women in colourful garb were setting up stands to hawk their straw baskets, hats, and trinkets. On an impulse, Hamilton approached a heavy-set woman with large, gold loops dangling from her ears, and purchased a simple straw hat, the sort he supposed a man out to catch fish would wear for protection from the sun. He hurried on to Prince Georges Wharf, past the docks where rusting fishing vessels were berthed next to a Royal Navy patrol boat with a five-inch gun turret. With the stench of rotting fish and bunker fuel assailing his nostrils, he arrived at the long wharf at precisely 8:00 a.m.

At first Hamilton failed to recognize the tall black man lounging against a stack of lumber, wearing an old pair of shorts, a cotton shirt and worn-out sandals. But then he made contact with the intel-

ligent eyes beneath a long-billed fishing cap and identified Sir
Philip's man, Carter. As Hamilton walked up, Carter smiled and
said, 'Mornin', Mr Tom. Ready to go?'

'Hello, Carter,' said Hamilton. 'Didn't recognize you for a
second.'

Carter reached for a canvas bag and motioned toward the end of
the wharf. 'The boat's down this way,' he said, as he began walking.
Hamilton followed him to a slip where a sleek powerboat was
bobbing in the clear turquoise water.

'She's a beauty,' said Hamilton, gazing at the satiny wooden hull
as Carter climbed on board.

'And she's fast,' said Carter, letting the canvas bag drop with a
thump. 'A Chris Craft utility cruiser, with a 275-horsepower V-8.
And with a hundred gallon tank, we can make it from here to the
Abacos and back in a day.' He turned the ignition and backed the
boat out of the slip as Hamilton peered at the wharf above them,
satisfied that no one was paying them any attention. Within
moments they were cruising at ten knots toward the open sea.
Carter pushed down the throttle and the boat surged forward,
planing across the calm, blue water. 'I'll make for the north-east
channel,' Carter called to Hamilton, who was standing beside him
with one hand grasping the windshield and the other holding down
his hat, 'before swinging back around to Hog Island.' Hamilton
looked at the uninhabited island that was separated from New
Providence by only a few hundred yards, directly across from
town. As Carter lowered the throttle, the water turned from
turquoise to dark azure, the deeper waters that run north to Grand
Bahama and the Abacos. Once they were far out of sight from the
shore, Carter steered toward the west, arcing around the northern
tip of Hog Island. Hamilton glanced at the dashboard, noting their
cruising speed of 40 m.p.h. Carter turned toward him and smiled.
'In a few more minutes,' he said, 'we'll run in for a quick look at
Shangri-La.'

'Shangri-La?' repeated Hamilton.

'The place the Swede bought and fixed up for himself.' He pulled out a pair of binoculars and handed them to Hamilton. 'Take a look,' he said.

Hamilton squinted through the lenses at a large colonial style home set back from the beach. 'Shangri-La,' he said softly, following the outline of the pale-yellow villa with graceful arches and a red tiled roof, noting the manicured grounds and a high fence that disappeared into a thick stand of trees. 'I can't make out any kind of pier. How the hell do you get there?'

'Around to the left there's a channel,' explained Carter, as he abruptly turned to head back out to sea. 'You take that into a big marina the Swede's building. They call it Hurricane Hole.' He lowered the throttle and the Chris Craft surged forward with a powerful roar.

'Why Hurricane Hole?' asked Hamilton.

'They say he's building it strong enough to take a direct hit from a hurricane....'

'Or a bomber,' said Hamilton almost to himself.

'Anyway,' Carter continued, 'there's no way to get close enough for a good look. The Swede has armed patrol boats, and they mean business. Shot at a fishing boat last week.' He steered the boat toward the far tip of the island barely visible above the flat expanse of sea.

'Where are we headed now?' asked Hamilton.

Carter smiled, the sunlight reflecting on his dark, smooth face beneath the bill of his cap. 'We're gonna take a little swim, Mr Tom. And then see if we can get a look at the project.'

Hamilton decided to wait before asking any more questions, but said, 'I didn't bring a suit.'

'There's an extra,' said Carter, pointing behind his seat. 'You can put it on while I find my spot.' Within five minutes they were anchored in twenty feet of crystal water no more than a hundred yards from a desolate beach. Wearing a faded swimsuit, Carter sat on the transom stretching a flipper over his heel as Hamilton scanned the shoreline. 'Ready to go?' asked Carter, strapping the binoculars in a waterproof case over his shoulder. Hamilton nodded with a thumb's-up, and both pulled on diving masks and splashed backwards into the sea. They immediately surfaced and began swimming. Though he'd captained the Yale swim team, Hamilton struggled to keep up with Carter, a powerful swimmer with long, muscular arms and legs. A sandy beach loomed ahead, and they rose to wade in the final yards through the gentle surf. Hamilton tore off his mask and followed Carter across the beach to a sandy path that disappeared into the scrub vegetation. 'We'll leave our gear here,' said Carter, tossing his mask and flippers behind a bush and starting down the path.

Not more than a hundred yards inland they reached a small, muddy stream and a dilapidated wooden dock almost hidden by dense, overhanging foliage. Hamilton swatted at the swarms of mosquitoes as Carter knelt on the bank and reached for a low boat concealed under the dock. More a pirogh than a canoe, the gunnels scarcely cleared the turgid water as Carter climbed into the stern. Hamilton climbed in after him, balancing on the thwarts and lowering himself into the bow. Producing a single paddle, Carter expertly turned the pirogh and paddled along the shallow stream further inland. As they slowly glided along, Hamilton, searching the undergrowth, was startled by a sudden disturbance and flash of motion. He looked back at Carter, who smiled and said, 'Feral hog. I used to hunt 'em all over the island.' After another ten minutes, Carter steered the craft to a muddy landing place. 'Almost there,' he whispered, as he balanced on the gunnels and nimbly leapt from the rocking boat. He offered a hand to Hamilton and then tied the painter to a branch. Standing on the sandy bank with sweat dripping down his torso, Hamilton panted in the heat like a dog and slapped at the mosquitoes on his neck.

'Here,' said Carter, taking a vial of clear liquid from his pocket. 'Put this on.'

Hamilton poured some of the pungent solution into his palm and smeared it liberally over his face and shoulders. 'OK,' he said, handing the repellent back to Carter, 'lead on.'

Pointing down at the bank, Carter whispered, 'Be careful.'

Hamilton's heart skipped a beat as a water moccasin, thick as a man's forearm, slithered from a branch and disappeared into the murky water. They started down another sandy trail in a low crouch. After snaking along for another five minutes, they heard the sound of men's voices, shouting and laughing, from a nearby clearing. Carter, never looking back, pressed on, dropping to his hands and knees to crawl through the dense undergrowth, with Hamilton following.

Through a gap in the brush, they could see a number of men, stripped to the waist as they toiled in the intense sun in a line that reached across a wide clearing, some wielding picks and shovels, others loading barrows and dumping them into mule-drawn carts. 'Some sort of excavation,' whispered Hamilton. Carter nodded. 'On a huge scale,' added Hamilton, estimating as many as 300 labourers. Tall wooden towers overlooked the work site, with platforms shielded from the sun by corrugated tin roofs. Hamilton motioned for the binoculars, and, resting on his elbows, trained them on the nearest tower. A guard, clearly European, lounged against the railing, wearing a khaki uniform and military cap, with an insignia of some kind on the collar. The guard cradled a carbine with a scope, which he unexpectedly swung to his shoulder and ranged across the area where Hamilton and Carter were hiding. 'Let's get the hell out of here,' muttered Hamilton as he backed away. 'That's all I need to see for now.'

'And so, in your estimation,' said Sir Philip Sassoon as he leaned back in his rattan armchair, an unlit briar pipe in his hand, 'military guards are overseeing the project?'

'Well,' said Hamilton, relaxing in Sir Philip's upstairs study, 'they were wearing uniforms, with military-style caps and insignias. Maybe Nils Ericsson has his own private army.'

'Perhaps. Ah, Henry. Our tea.'

Henry placed the tray on a coffee table and poured two cups. Hamilton waited until Henry served both of them and disappeared down the stairs.

'At any rate,' he said, after taking a sip, 'he's involved in one hell of an excavation. Looks like he's hired every available labourer in Nassau.'

'Rumour has it,' said Sir Philip, 'he's digging a canal across the island.'

'Along with this hurricane-proof marina,' said Hamilton. 'Called Hurricane Hole.'

'Well, Mr Hamilton,' said Sir Philip, 'what's your assessment?'

'According to his OSS dossier, Ericsson is one of the wealthiest men in Europe. He emigrated from Sweden to Nassau, acquiring the estate on Hog Island, ostensibly to avoid income taxes and devote more time to his passion for yacht racing. We believe he has extensive holdings in Mexico and South America. And well-known ties to the Nazis, particularly Goering, whose first wife was a Swedish baroness. Lastly, he's an outspoken advocate for peace with Germany.'

'All true,' said Sir Philip, putting aside his tea and reaching for a square of shortbread.

'With the Nazi submarine offensive in the Caribbean,' said Hamilton, 'my orders are to find out what Ericsson is really up to on Hog Island.'

'The submarine attacks appear to have abated,' said Sir Philip.

'For the time being,' agreed Hamilton. 'But Doenitz has thirty U-boats in the Caribbean, and they've sunk dozens of ships, mainly tankers hauling gasoline and diesel from refineries on the Gulf coast and Trinidad.'

'Fuel that was eventually destined for Great Britain,' said Sir Philip, 'where we're facing a critical shortage. Less than two months' supply.'

'The problem for the Germans,' said Hamilton, 'is the lack of a base, someplace to refuel and refit their subs. Everybody's worried about Martinique, but the French are too nervous to risk that. And it's damned inefficient to run a Caribbean U-boat fleet from a home base in Brittany.'

'What are you suggesting?'

'That Nassau is the perfect site for a German submarine base. You've got a first-class airfield, thanks to Uncle Sam, and a deep-water port with all the facilities. All that's lacking are bomb-proof pens for the U-boats.'

Sir Philip smiled and stroked his chin. 'Hurricane Hole,' he said. 'And a channel across Hog Island.'

Hamilton abruptly stood up and walked to the window, leaning his hands on the sill and staring out at the sea. 'Can you imagine,' he asked, turning to face Sir Philip, 'what havoc they could cause to the East Coast of the US? A large percentage of our fuel and other critical war supplies is shipped out of the Gulf through the Florida straits. A hundred miles north-west of where I'm standing. A well-protected U-boat base in Nassau would be an Allied disaster.'

'Intriguing,' said Sir Philip. 'But pure conjecture.'

Hamilton leaned down to pour himself another cup of tea. 'And what about you, Sir Philip?' he asked, holding out the pot to freshen the older man's cup. 'Where do you fit into the picture?'

'Well, Mr Hamilton, the secret intelligence service has given me a rather curious assignment. Keeping an eye on His Royal Highness.' Hamilton shot him a puzzled look. 'The Duke of Windsor. Governor of the Crown Colony of the Bahamas.'

'No kidding,' said Hamilton, reclining back on the sofa. 'What on earth for?'

'It so happens,' said Sir Philip, 'that the former king, like your man Ericsson, is known to have pro-Nazi sympathies, having visited Hitler in Berlin shortly before the outbreak of the war. As a matter of fact, at the moment when Britain was facing her greatest peril, immediately after the fall of France, a clique in London favoured a negotiated peace with Hitler. Chief among them was Halifax, the Foreign Secretary and, you may recall, Churchill's rival for PM. After all, they argued, it would be suicide for Britain to continue the fight, alone, against a vastly superior German foe.

'The Duke of Windsor,' Sir Philip continued, 'embittered by his forced abdication, was living in Paris.' He paused to take a sip of tea. 'Well, Whitehall was able to hustle the duke and his American wife to Madrid before the goose-stepping Huns arrived at the Arc de Triomphe. But there the Nazis – to whom Franco extended the widest courtesies – approached him with an extraordinary proposal: assist in their efforts to secure a negotiated peace, and, in return, resume his rightful place on the throne.'

'Wait a minute,' said Hamilton. 'You're saying this actually happened?'

'Correct. Our agents in Spain obtained proof of the parley. As soon as Churchill learned of it, he immediately offered the duke the governorship of the Bahamas, an unprecedented office for a member of the Royal Family.'

'An offer he couldn't refuse,' said Hamilton, 'which would get him out of the way.'

'Precisely,' agreed Sir Philip. 'Along with Halifax, who was promptly dispatched to Washington as ambassador. But ...' Sir Philip paused and gazed intently at Hamilton. 'The sentiments of these two powerful men favouring a negotiated peace with Hitler are still very much alive. And will only burn hotter if the Soviets collapse under the Wehrmacht onslaught in the Caucasus. Hence my job is to keep a very sharp eye on our governor and those in his inner circle. Which happens to include Nils Ericsson.'

'Hmm,' said Hamilton. 'Is there anything I can do to help?'

'As a matter of fact there is. A cousin of Lord Halifax happens to be here in Nassau. And she's on very close terms with the duke and duchess.'

'And who might that be?'

'Evelyn Shawcross,' said Sir Philip. 'I should like you to get to know her.'

CHAPTER THREE

Westbourne, a sprawling mansion on Cable Beach, was the Nassau home of Sir Harry Oakes, reputedly the wealthiest man in the British Empire. Like many men with immense fortunes, Oakes was obsessed with avoiding taxes, and chose to reside in the Bahamas, which, like its sister colony Bermuda, levied no taxes on the income of its residents. Establishing residency in the Bahamas marked the end of a long and circuitous path of shifting nationalities for Sir Harry, beginning with his humble birth in Maine in his native America, thence acquiring citizenship in his adopted Canada, where he made his fortune, and on to Great Britain, where he managed to acquire the hereditary title of a baronet – the result, it was rumored, of a gift of £50,000 to St Georges Hospital in London. He arrived at last in Nassau at the age of 63, purchased 10,000 acres, a full one-fifth of New Providence Island, acquired Westbourne, and soon became the most powerful, and possibly the most feared and disliked, figure in the Bahamas. Oakes had been living almost alone at his ocean-front estate during the fall of 1942, as his Australian wife Eunice, who detested the tropical heat and humidity, chose to remain in the rambling Oakes summer cottage overlooking the rocky Maine coastline at Bar Harbor with three of the couple's five children. Fourteen-year-old son Sidney was with his father at Westbourne, and a daughter, Nancy, resided in her own house on Victoria Street in Nassau with her thirty-seven-year old husband, the infamous Count Alfred de Marigny, with whom she had scandalously eloped at the age of eighteen.

Seated in a leather armchair in his study, Sir Harry stifled a yawn. He had few real friends but was long accustomed to dispensing favours to chosen business associates who were happy to reciprocate by staying as house guests of the temperamental tycoon, partnering in doubles at tennis and playing tedious games of Chinese checkers or backgammon late into the sultry evenings. One of these cronies was Sherwood Bascomb, a real estate agent in Miami known to his friends as Woody. Nearing the end of a week-long stay, Woody Bascomb was growing weary. Sir Harry withdrew a gold watch from his pocket, gave it a glance and pressed a buzzer on the table. A few moments later, Jenkins, the portly English butler, appeared in the doorway.

'Sir?' he said, his nose in the air like a bloodhound.

'I need a drink,' said Sir Harry. 'Woody, how 'bout a drink?'

'Sure, Harry, you bet,' said Woody, putting aside the day-old Miami paper.

'Bring us a couple of those rum punches, Jenkins,' commanded Oakes. 'And use that Mount Gay dark rum.'

'Yes, sir,' said Jenkins. 'Right away, sir.' He turned and disappeared.

'Anything interesting in the papers?' asked Oakes.

'Oh, I don't know,' said Woody. 'The usual war news. The Germans are beating the crap out of the Russians. Makes you wonder how long those poor bastards can hang on.'

'I couldn't care less for the goddamn Russians,' said Sir Harry. 'But if they're out of the war, we're in a helluva fix. And it worries me what could happen to this little island.'

'How do you mean?' Woody sat forward, resting his fat, sunburned arms on his knees.

'All it would take for the Germans to knock over this place is a U-boat, a destroyer maybe, and a couple of hundred storm-troopers.'

'But what about that brand new RAF base at Oakes Field?' Both men looked up as the butler, who seemed uncomfortably warm in his black wool tailcoat, entered the room.

'There you are, sir,' he said, handing Sir Harry his drink. 'And Mr Bascomb.'

'Tell the cook,' said Oakes, 'to whip us up a couple of those roast beef sandwiches. And some baked beans.'

'Yes, sir,' said Jenkins. He nodded and withdrew.

'What were you saying?' asked Oakes. He took a sip and then said, 'Oh, yeah. The RAF base. Hell, that's nothing but a training field. What about sabotage? The security's so lax around here, it's bound to be crawling with Germans. And what do we have to defend us? One little company of Cameron Highlanders with their fancy kilts. Hell, they were hiding in their barracks when the natives went on that rampage.' He snorted and took another long swallow.

Sir Harry's guest nodded and smiled agreeably, having heard these somewhat paranoid discourses a number of times over the course of his stay.

'Say,' said Oakes, 'did you hear about this fellow from Texas who showed up last week?'

'No,' said Woody, 'I don't think so.'

'With a lot of money from the oil business. My sources tell me he's looking at buying a piece of Hog Island across from town and building a hotel and casino.'

'Not a bad idea,' said Woody. 'Do you know the guy?'

'Nah,' said Sir Harry, 'but I knew his old man. A famous wild-catter from Oklahoma. My kind of man. Started with nothing, and then brought in a tremendous oilfield near Tulsa, during the last war. Biggest in the world, at the time.'

'Something like your Lake Shore strike?' suggested Woody, refer-ring to Oakes's fabled discovery of the world's largest gold mine, an event he never tired of discussing. Having gone broke staking gold mines in North America and Australia, Oakes had seized on a hunch, according to legend, following a Chinaman off a Canadian Pacific train in northern Ontario, where he stumbled upon the Kirkland Lake gold deposits, giving him a net worth estimated at $200 million.

'You might say so,' said Sir Harry with a smile. 'On a smaller scale. Anyhow, this boy Hamilton may be in for a little surprise if he pursues this casino idea.'

The butler appeared with a tray of sandwiches and a steaming dish of Boston baked beans, Sir Harry's favourite, which he placed on an inlaid card table. 'Anything else, sir?' he asked.

'No thanks,' said Oakes.

As they rose from their chairs and walked to the table, Woody said, 'I thought Hog Island belonged to that Swedish fellow. What's his name?'

Sir Harry tucked his linen napkin in his collar. 'Nils Ericsson,' he said irritably. 'The sonofabitch *wishes* he owned all of the island. But there's a little strip on the Nassau side that happens to belong to an investment syndicate.'

'Oh, yeah?' said Woody, perking up with his interest in real estate.

'Yeah. What Hamilton doesn't know, or anybody else, is that I hold the mortgage on it.'

Woody smiled and said, 'You're the sly one, Harry. Like I always said.'

Oakes took a large bite of his sandwich, followed by a forkful of beans. 'Mmm,' he said, 'the way I like 'em. Anyhow, this boy will have to deal with me if he wants that strip of swampland. And I'm having my people keep a sharp eye on him, just like they are on Ericsson.' At the sound of footsteps on the hardwood floor, he turned to see Jenkins in the doorway.

'You have a visitor, sir,' said the butler.

'A visitor?' said Oakes sceptically.

'Yes, sir. Monsieur de Marigny,' said Jenkins disdainfully.

'De Marigny?' said Oakes. 'Goddamn nerve. Dropping in without an appointment.'

'He *is* your son-in-law,' said Woody with a grin.

Oakes shot him a dirty look. 'Yeah, and don't I know it. Well, you can tell him to wait.'

*

Forty-five minutes later, after polishing off the sandwiches and a round of Jamaican beer, Sir Harry Oakes and Woody Bascomb sat expectantly as Jenkins escorted a tall, thin man, wearing a navy blazer and gray flannels, into the study. He had an interesting if not handsome face, with an aquiline nose, small, lively eyes, and dark, oiled hair, neatly parted and combed back. Not a face, Oakes had once remarked with more wit than usual, to inspire trust when playing cards. 'The Count de Marigny,' announced the butler as the visitor strode confidently across the polished floor. Sir Harry winced at the word 'Count', though it was infinitely preferable to the French 'Compte'.

''Allo, Zir Harry,' said de Marigny breezily as he walked up.

Seated with a sour expression, Oakes merely said, 'Afternoon, de Marigny. What brings you here?'

De Marigny turned to Bascomb, who awkwardly rose from his chair. 'How do you do?' said de Marigny, extending his hand.

'Oh, yeah,' said Oakes. 'This is Woody Bascomb. Friend of mine from Miami.'

'Alfred de Marigny,' said the count, giving Woody's large hand a shake. 'A pleasure.'

'Pleased to meet you,' said Woody.

Ignoring Oakes's question, de Marigny said, 'Lovely time of the year to visit Nassau. Have you been out on the water?' He glanced at Woody's sunburned arms and face.

'Listen, de Marigny,' said Sir Harry impatiently, 'what do you want? Can't you see I'm busy?'

'Oh,' said de Marigny with a smile, 'Merely to drop by and say 'allo, and tell you that Nancy, that sweet girl, is doing well—'

'Great,' said Sir Harry.

'And to share some information I thought you might find useful.'

'Oh, really?' said Sir Harry, arching his eyebrows.

'There's a wealthy young American in town,' continued de Marigny. 'A well-known playboy from Texas. Flew in last week on his own plane.'

'I see,' said Sir Harry with a quick look at Woody. 'So what?'

'He's looking into a hotel venture. With a casino. According to my sources, he's got the backing of the Jew Sassoon.' De Marigny paused and smiled expectantly. 'I doubt the chaps on Bay Street would approve such a thing. I thought you might want to know.'

'Well, thanks,' said Sir Harry, thinking the word 'chaps' sounded ludicrous in de Marigny's French accent.

'That's all,' said de Marigny, as though expecting to be invited to draw up a chair and light a cigar. In the awkward silence, he added, 'Nancy and I were hoping to have you for dinner soon. And little Sidney.'

'Sure,' said Oakes. 'You bet. Tell her to call. Goodbye, de Marigny. Thanks for the dope.'

'*Adieu*,' said de Marigny with a Gallic hand gesture. He bowed toward Woody, turned, and walked briskly from the room.

As soon as he was out of earshot, Woody grinned and said, 'Well, Harry, like I always said, you were way ahead of the old boy. He's got nothing on you.'

Oakes nodded. 'Except,' he said, 'for that bit about Sassoon. I'll have to look into that.'

In the week he'd spent on the island, Tom Hamilton had done his best to convey the general impression of an idle young man sitting out the war at an out-of-the-way resort and speculating in real estate. He'd frequented the few decent nightspots, principally the Prince George Hotel, a fixture of the island's upper class Britons, and the bar at the British Colonial and its older rival, the Royal Victoria. He'd also managed to see a well-connected Nassau solicitor about purchasing the Hog Island tract and the necessary approvals to develop a hotel. And he'd finally succeeded in arranging to see Evelyn Shawcross again, receiving a cream-coloured envelope at the front desk of his hotel with an invitation to 'dinner at Greycliff' in her distinctive cursive. But most of all he'd enjoyed the company of the Sassoons at their lovely beach-front home. Hamilton was fit and tan after a week of morning swims in the turquoise water off Cable Beach, accompanied by

Marnie in a shockingly revealing two-piece swimsuit. Though attracted by her looks and voluptuous figure, Hamilton would never have considered a liaison, however casual, nor was there any question of Marnie's fidelity to Sir Philip. After their swims they would take lunch by the pool, joined by Sir Philip in his cane-back wheelchair, under the rustling fronds of the coconut palms. And bit-by-bit Hamilton had gradually extracted the story of Sir Philip and Lady Sassoon.

The large Sassoon fortune, Hamilton discovered, had been made centuries earlier in the mercantile trade on the Malay Peninsula, provisioning the East India Company for return voyages to England. It was only in the 1920s that Sir Philip had relocated from Singapore to London, where he was knighted for his service to King and country in helping to supply the home front during the Great War. In London he put his considerable wealth to good use assembling the finest thoroughbred stable in England and, though snubbed by society for his name and religion, he was widely admired by the better men in business and government for his acumen, tact, and considerable charm. While on holiday in America in the summer of '28, he contracted what was then known as IP – infantile paralysis – swimming in the cold waters of Long Island Sound. A virile sportsman in the prime of life, the bout with polio left him crippled, unable to walk. And so in 1935, weary of the cold and damp of London, the invalided Sir Philip moved again, to the gentle, tropical climate of the Bahamas. There he built Eves on Cable Beach, and there he met Mary Ann Crenshaw – 'Marnie' – a beautiful young blonde from Tennessee, who signed on as Sir Philip's personal nurse. A life-long bachelor, Sir Philip was highly vulnerable to Marnie's supple beauty and unaffected Southern charm. He proposed marriage within a year. For her part, Marnie had quickly come to regard Sir Philip as a far finer man than any she had known, was flattered by his genteel courtesy, and saw in the marriage the opportunity for a life beyond anything she had ever imagined. And so, despite the difference in age and back-grounds and Sir Philip's disability, the marriage flourished, rewarding them both with deep happiness founded on mutual respect and dependency.

In the sudden peril facing Britain after the fall of France in 1940, Sir Stewart Menzies, the head of MI6 – the British Secret Service – had contacted Sir Philip, a longtime acquaintance, to advise him of the government's plan to name the Duke of Windsor as Governor of the Bahamas, and of Menzies' deep suspicions regarding the former king's desire for a negotiated peace with Germany. Notwithstanding his age and infirmity, Sir Philip had unhesitatingly agreed to act as a discreet agent to shadow the new governor and apprise London of any questionable behaviour on the part of the Windsors. Despite his best efforts, Sir Philip had been unable to penetrate the intimate circle surrounding the glamorous duke and duchess, owing largely to the anti-Semitism that was rampant among the Nassau social elite and well-to-do British evacuees to the colony, a prejudice strongly shared by the duke.

'And, so, Mr Hamilton,' said Sir Philip, who politely refused to use the familiar *Tom*, 'you're on for dinner at Greycliff with Mrs Shawcross?' They were seated on the terrace in the late afternoon shadows.

'Eight o'clock sharp,' said Hamilton. 'With bells on.'

'Perhaps His Highness will be joining you,' suggested Marnie, who was wearing a coral cover-up over her swimsuit that complemented her tanned shoulders.

'Who?' said Hamilton. 'Oh, the duke, you mean. I doubt it.'

'You shall have to meet him,' said Sir Philip. 'And the former Mrs Simpson, of course. Her comings and goings are the source of endless fascination for the local populace.'

'Tell me about Evelyn,' said Hamilton to Sir Philip. 'What do you know about her background?'

'Her father's a rich industrialist from the Midlands,' said Sir Philip. 'Or was, at any rate, before the Depression. Married to a cousin of Halifax. Part of the inner circle surrounding the King before his abdication. And so Evelyn comes from that rarified atmosphere—'

'Boy, does she,' interjected Marnie.

'As for her marriage,' Sir Philip continued, 'her husband is something of a cipher. Good family, moderately wealthy, but a member of the circle of dissolute young men at Oxford who were notorious for their admiration of the Fascists.'

'This was the mid-30s?' asked Hamilton. Sir Philip nodded. 'Well,' said Hamilton, 'if Oxford was anything like Yale in those days, the place was probably crawling with red-lovers. So you could excuse somebody who veered off to the right wing and admired the way Mussolini cleaned up Italy.'

'True,' said Sir Philip.

'But I'd bet that any pro-Nazi sentiments evaporated after Dunkirk and the blitz.'

'Presumably,' agreed Sir Philip. 'In any case, it raised a question with MI5. Though not enough to keep Shawcross out of the army. Well, Mr Hamilton,' concluded Sir Philip, 'good luck on your dinner with Evelyn.'

Though he might have walked, Hamilton chose to take a jitney up the hill to Government House and around the corner, where the driver stopped in front of an imposing residence. In the pleasantly cool night air he could make out the sounds of a piano. With a glance at his watch, he squared his shoulders and walked up to the front door, where a small brass plaque with the inscription 'Greycliff' gleamed in the porch light. Hamilton rang the bell, and within a few moments a servant swung open the door.

'Come in, sir,' he said with a smile. 'Miz Shawcross is right up the stairs.'

Hamilton could hear the piano clearly now, played very well. He glanced from the hall up a wide staircase, thanking the servant as he started up the stairs. The large house had a lived-in, cosy feeling, handsomely appointed like a grill at one of the better clubs in London. Evelyn Shawcross was seated at a full concert grand piano with a satin-black finish on the far side of a spacious living room. Hamilton paused at the top of the stairs as she finished the difficult piece, her face still with concentration. Only when the final chords faded away did she look up, making eye contact with Hamilton with a shy smile.

'Bravo,' he said with a brief clap of his hands. 'That was wonderful.' He walked across the room to greet her as she rose from the bench. She reached out to take his hands, a warm, pleasurable sensation, which, with her deep blue eyes and the fragrance of her perfume, evoked a surge of excitement.

'Welcome to Greycliff,' she said, releasing his hands.

'Thanks for inviting me. You look lovely.' 'Lovely' was clearly not adequate to describe the overall impression of her dark-brown hair, worn stylishly back, the delicate beauty of her face, and her bare shoulders above the black dress that accentuated an hourglass figure.

'Thank you,' she said with a modest smile. 'I see you've been in the sun.' Hamilton had chosen a navy-blue blazer and white pinpoint shirt that nicely offset his tanned face and hands. 'Let's have a drink,' she suggested, 'while we wait for the others.' She led him out to an open-air porch, with wood floors painted dull grey, fans suspended from a high, beaded ceiling, and comfortably upholstered furniture. Evelyn placed a hand on the railing and took a deep breath of the cool night air. 'Mmm,' she said. 'Smell the plumeria.' Hamilton walked over and inhaled the sweet bouquet drifting up from the garden. She turned and spoke to the servant. 'I'll have a planter's punch, Samuel. And Mr Hamilton would like a...?'

'Scotch on the rocks.'

'Yes, ma'am,' said the servant with a slight nod before disappearing into the living room.

'This is such a lovely home,' said Hamilton. God, he chided himself, couldn't he think of another word for lovely?

'The loveliest in Nassau,' Evelyn agreed. 'Let's sit.' She walked over to the sofa and sat down, Hamilton taking the armchair next to her.

He smiled at her and said, 'Do you live alone here?'

'For now. Mummy and Daddy are coming for Christmas, and hopefully they'll stay for the winter. They always have in the past, but with the war ...'

'You mentioned your husband is in Africa with the army?'

'Yes, the Eighth Army.'

'That was some victory over Rommel I saw in the papers the other day. This British General Montgomery must be quite good.'

'Yes, well, Dirk's not involved in the desert fighting. He's a staff officer, in Cairo.'

'I see.' Hamilton casually crossed his legs, thinking about Evelyn's husband's unusual name. The servant returned, stooping over to serve their drinks. 'It must be lonely here,' said Hamilton, 'with your husband so far away.'

'Lonely? I'd say boring, at least at times. But I have friends here. It's not a bad life.'

'Compared to Nazi bombs raining down on you.' He sipped his drink.

'Well, that's all stopped. But still, Daddy thought it best ...' She paused and seemed to be listening to the faint sound of voices from the floor below. Placing her drink on a table, she rose from the sofa and said, 'The other guests have arrived.' He stood up and looked at her expectantly. 'Alfred de Marigny,' she added, 'and his wife Nancy.' Hamilton nodded, quickly trying to assemble the bits of information he'd heard about the young daughter of Sir Harry Oakes and her much older husband.

De Marigny, wearing a poplin suit with a blue shirt and yellow silk tie, appeared at the landing arm-in-arm with a young woman, a girl really, with auburn hair and a rather plain face. Hamilton tried not to stare at what seemed an absurd mismatch: the much older, dashing Frenchman with his neatly combed hair and foppish attire and the awkward girl who looked as if she'd just arrived on holiday from boarding-school. He followed Evelyn into the living room, where she said, 'Tom, let me introduce the Count and Countess de Marigny. This is Tom Hamilton, from Texas.'

Reaching out to shake de Marigny's hand, Hamilton said, 'Good evening.' Turning to de Marigny's young wife, he said, 'And you must be ...'

'Nancy,' she replied.

'Hello, Nancy,' said Hamilton with a smile. Addressing Evelyn, he said, 'I wasn't expecting to meet another member of the French nobility.'

De Marigny gave Hamilton a puzzled look, but Nancy said, 'Freddie's not really French. Are you, Freddie? But he *is* a count.'

'Tom met Georges de Videlou the other night,' explained Evelyn. 'We're having drinks on the porch.'

After the newly arrived guests' drink order had been taken, Hamilton retrieved his Scotch and approached de Marigny. 'Where are you from, Alfred,' he asked, 'if not from France?'

'Mauritius,' said Nancy, pronouncing it like 'delicious.' 'It's an island,' she added.

'Yes,' said Hamilton, 'in the Indian Ocean. A long way from Nassau.'

'I think you're going to discover, Mr Hamilton,' said de Marigny in a superior tone, 'that most of the people you're likely to meet here, apart from the Bahamians, naturally, have come from a distant place. Such as Texas.'

'I had forgotten,' said Hamilton, 'if I ever knew, that Mauritius was a French possession. So how does that work? Is it still French, or do the Boche have a claim on it?'

'We have our empire, sir,' said de Marigny, 'our colonies in Africa and the Far East. The terms of our peace with Germany have nothing to do with that.'

'I see,' said Hamilton. The servant returned with drinks for the de Marignys.

After taking a sip, de Marigny said, 'Tell me, Mr Hamilton—'

'Tom.'

'Yes, Tom. What brings you to the Bahamas?'

'He's exploring the possibility of building a hotel,' said Evelyn.

'A hotel?' said de Marigny. '*Incroyable!*'

'I'm looking at some land on Hog Island, right across the channel from town. For after the war, naturally.'

'Hog Island? Oh ho,' said de Marigny with a sort of laugh. 'You will have to deal with Monsieur Ericsson.'

The white-jacketed servant who'd answered the door appeared tentatively, cleared his throat and said, 'Miz Shawcross? Dinner is served.'

Evelyn led the way to the small but elegant dining-room, with dark-green wallpaper above the wainscoting, a round mahogany table and matching sideboard that gleamed in the soft light of faux candle sconces. Hamilton was shown to a chair facing the sideboard, above which was a large oil portrait, by Sargent, of a beautiful woman with dark, flowing tresses who bore a striking resemblance to Evelyn. 'Who is she?' asked Hamilton, glancing up at the portrait.

'My grandmother,' said Evelyn. 'Lady Rebecca Soames. Grandfather built Greycliff for her.' The servants appeared with the first course, a lobster bisque, which prompted de Marigny to launch into a rambling account of his experiences spear-fishing for the small Bahamian lobsters near Green Turtle Cay. The soup was followed by roast beef, accompanied by new potatoes, haricots, and a carafe of French claret. The conversation drifted from the weather – beyond the hurricane season but hoping to avoid the Christmas rains – to the latest social gossip, and finally, by the time dessert and coffee were served, to the news of the war. Nancy de Marigny remained silent throughout, smiling when she thought it appropriate at her husband's observations or attempts at humour. Hamilton listened with poorly feigned interest, wondering why the arrogant French peacock and his child-wife had been invited, and wishing he'd had more time alone with his hostess.

'I think the Russians are *finis*,' declared de Marigny, holding his demitasse aloft. 'The Germans have them encircled at Stalingrad. It's simply a matter of time.' His wife looked at him admiringly.

'I don't know,' said Hamilton. 'The Germans still have the Russian winter to contend with. I wouldn't count the Red Army out.'

'May I ask you a personal question?' said de Marigny, giving Hamilton a serious look. 'Why is it you have chosen not to, ah, join the military? Not that it is of any concern to me.'

Hamilton could feel Evelyn's eyes on him, though he continued to look across the table at de Marigny. 'It's a fair question,' he said. 'Flat feet, according to the army doctor at the draft board. But the truth is, I've got things to do and I'm in a hurry to do them. So I don't mind missing out on this war.'

'Well, frankly, Tom,' said de Marigny, 'I admire your sentiments. I think you Americans and the British would be far better off reaching an accommodation with the Germans, as we French did. You would still have the Japanese to deal with, of course.'

Hamilton glanced at Evelyn, who sat with her hands in her lap, listening with evident interest.

'Daddy says the British should keep fighting the Nazis even if it means moving the government to Canada,' said Nancy unexpectedly.

'Hah,' said de Marigny dismissively. 'What does the old fool know about anything? He's just worried about his gold.'

'I understand this fellow Ericsson's all for peace with Germany,' said Hamilton pleasantly. 'Let the Nazis and the Soviets go at each other's throats, while we in the West stay out of it.' He briefly made eye contact with Evelyn, whose impassive expression revealed nothing.

'I don't know the gentleman personally,' said de Marigny, 'but I certainly share his point of view. You could secure an honourable peace, as we did.'

'I hope Daddy doesn't hear you talking this way,' Nancy stage-whispered to her husband.

'The dinner, as always,' said de Marigny with a glare at his wife, 'was fabulous, Madame Shawcross. But we must be getting home. Come along, Nancy.' Abruptly he rose from the table.

'Well, OK. 'Bye,' said Nancy petulantly.

Hamilton and Evelyn walked the de Marignys to the top of the stairs and wished them goodnight. 'An interesting pair,' commented Hamilton, once they were down the stairs and out the front door.

'Very,' said Evelyn. 'I expect there's going to be nothing but trouble between Alfred and Sir Harry. May I interest you in a nightcap?'

Hamilton smiled. 'I'd love nothing better.' Once their drinks were served, he joined her by the railing overlooking the garden. He turned to look at her in the silvery moonlight that caught the facets of a sapphire pendant at her neck. A cool breeze stirred the trees, mingling the exotic fragrances of the blossoming shrubs with Evelyn's subtle perfume. 'Mmm,' said Hamilton, taking a sip of his drink and fighting the impulse to put his arm around her. 'It's heavenly here.'

She turned toward him and, looking up into his eyes, said, 'It's only an illusion. Despite what you said about not caring about the war, and despite what de Marigny said about peace, there's not going to be any peace.'

Hamilton stared into her eyes, surprised by her intensity. 'No,' he agreed. 'Not any time soon.'

'Will you stay for awhile?' she asked softly. 'Here, in Nassau?'

He nodded. 'For a while.'

'What I said earlier wasn't true, Tom. It *is* lonely here, and so many of the people are ... well, you've seen for yourself. Will you call me again?'

'Yes, and you can show me more of Greycliff.' He leaned over and kissed her lightly on the cheek. 'And now,' he said, 'I'd better be going.'

CHAPTER FOUR

In COLONIAL NASSAU, the term Bay Street denoted power and influence, in reference to the complex of nineteenth-century public buildings – the House of Assembly, Colonial Secretariat, Council Chamber, and Courthouse – erected by the British on the street of that name opposite Rawson Square. And the clique of Nassau merchants who wielded the power and dispensed the influence in the chambers and cloakrooms of these public buildings was universally referred to as 'Bay Street Boys'. Tom Hamilton hurried along the shady side of Bay Street in the oppressive morning heat, his jacket slung over his shoulder, on his way to an appointment with his solicitor. By the time he arrived at a drab building opposite the Courthouse a damp stain had formed on his shirt and his brow glistened. With a glance at his watch, he started up the stairs, aware that he was late. At the end of the second-floor corridor, Dobbs & Iverson, Solicitors was neatly stenciled on a frosted-glass door. Shrugging on his jacket, Hamilton turned the knob and let himself in.

Looking up from her cheap novel, the middle-aged receptionist gave Hamilton a prim smile and said, 'I'll let Mr Dobbs know you're here.'

Harold R. Dobbs fitted what Hamilton imagined was the stereotype of the Nassau solicitor: British born and bred, a graduate of a red-brick university in Yorkshire with a degree in law who had emigrated to the Bahamas for the prospect of steady employment and the tropical climate, striving to obtain the quickest results for his clients with the least expenditure of time and effort, relying if possible on his contacts within the Bay Street regime.

'Good morning, Hamilton,' said Dobbs as he traipsed after his secretary into the small reception area, where his client was inspecting a framed map of the township of Nassau above a thread-bare sofa. In shirtsleeves with his collar open, Dobbs was wearing old-fashioned metal armbands around his thick biceps, and his large, round face was slightly flushed in the stifling heat. 'Let's step into the conference room,' he suggested, 'where there's a breath of air.' Despite the wide-open windows, there was just a breath of air in the adjoining, cramped room. Dobbs smiled at Hamilton, who, with his expensive American clothes and polished manners, seemed an excellent prospect for a fat fee. 'This is the abstract,' said Dobbs, placing a thick, blue-bound folder on the ink-stained table. He drew back a chair and motioned to Hamilton to sit next to him. 'The chain of title on the particular parcel,' he explained, 'back to the original grant from the Crown in 1763.'

Hamilton thumbed through the sheaf of legal-sized sheets, stopping to study a document at the back of the folder. 'What is New Providence Land Co., Ltd.?' he asked.

'Ah,' said Dobbs. 'The present holder of the title. A share company organized in June of '39, immediately prior to the conveyance of this parcel. You see, Hamilton, this forty-two-acre tract was carved out, as it were, of a much larger section of land on Hog Island.'

'And who owns New Providence Land? Who are the share-holders?'

'The identity of the share owners is not a matter of public record. But the registered agent is a solicitor on the third floor of this building. And' – he paused to pat his brow with a handkerchief – 'I happen to have obtained, confidentially of course, the names of the owners.'

Hamilton nodded. 'OK,' he said. 'Who are they?'

'As you might imagine, this particular tract, lying directly opposite the centre of town, could conceivably have value some day, if a bridge should be built across the channel.'

'Obviously. Why do you suppose I—'

'Oh, yes, of course. At any rate, several of the more influential

Bay Street gentlemen therefore decided to purchase the tract, as a rank speculation.'

'I see,' said Hamilton. 'You know these men?'

'Yes.' Dobbs smiled. 'I've spoken to several of them, and, at the right price, considering the disastrous effect the war's having, they would be willing sellers.'

'Good. Were you able to get me permission to take a look around?'

'Yes.' Dobbs handed him an envelope. 'A simple letter of authorization. And this,' he said, reaching into his briefcase, 'is a memorandum summarizing my conclusions with regard to the common law and civil ordinances. At present, of course, gambling is prohibited in the Colony.' He handed Hamilton the typewritten document.

'Fine,' said Hamilton. 'That's all I need for now.' He removed an envelope from his jacket and said, 'Here's a cheque for the first instalment of your fee.'

Hamilton hurried back to the British Colonial and placed a call to Sir Philip. Then, after double-checking the clip and action of the Beretta, he changed into his polo shirt, dungarees and canvas shoes, put the letter he'd obtained from Dobbs in his pocket, grabbed his hat and went down. Thirty minutes later, Hamilton was standing in the bright sunshine on Prince George's Wharf as Carter motored up in the gleaming Chris Craft. Hamilton clambered down an iron ladder and vaulted onto the deck. 'Afternoon, Mr Tom,' said Carter. 'Ready to go?'

'It's just Tom,' said Hamilton with a smile. 'No mister. And yes, I'm ready.'

'OK, Tom,' said Carter as he glanced over his shoulder and backed out of the slip. Cruising below planing speed, they chugged around the end of the wharf and crossed the narrow channel separating Hog Island from Nassau. Hamilton studied the shoreline. 'It shouldn't be much of a problem to build a bridge,' he commented. 'How deep is the channel?'

'Oh, not more than forty feet,' said Carter. 'But deep enough for deep-draught shipping.' Carter steered the boat alongside a tumble-down pier. Switching off the engine as Hamilton fastened a line to the pier, Carter said, 'I brought along some rubber boots, Tom. We'll need 'em.' After both men pulled on their boots and climbed onto the pier, Hamilton took a rolled-up document from his jacket and spread it on the weathered boards.

'OK,' he said, 'here we are,' tapping a finger on the survey. 'If we walk about three hundred yards north-east, we should reach the boundary. There's supposed to be a surveyor's stake.'

Carter, standing above Hamilton with his hands on his hips, frowned and said, 'There ain't much to see on this side of the island. Just marshland. What is it, exactly, that you're looking for?'

Hamilton squinted up into the sun and smiled. '*We're* not looking for anything, Carter, but hopefully, someone's looking for *us*.'

They started across the open ground, picking their way around the larger brambles and thorny shrubs. Compared to the interior of the island, it was more of a bog or slough, with standing water and mud that sucked at their boots. It was slow going with the sun at its zenith and, by the time they found the surveyor's stake, both men's faces were streaming. Further inland, the vegetation was denser, with low trees and brush that limited visibility to a few yards. 'Should've brought a machete,' muttered Hamilton as he struggled to free himself from thorns. Carter abruptly dropped to one knee and placed a finger to his lips. Hamilton detected both movement and indistinct colour and then caught a glimpse of a horse and heard men's muffled voices. Motioning to Carter, Hamilton said loudly: 'This must be the property line. Let's head back to the boat.'

A man riding a tall chestnut mare suddenly appeared, trotting up within several yards of them. Two others followed on foot, one with a German shepherd straining on a leash. They were wearing the same khaki uniform with military caps Hamilton had observed in the guard tower. The man on horseback carried a carbine, and the others had revolvers holstered on webbed belts. Reining in the horse, the man motioned to Hamilton with his carbine and barked,

'Hands over your heads!' The other two raced up, barely able to restrain the dog, who pawed the air, baring his teeth.

Hamilton and Carter stood motionless with their hands up. After a moment, Hamilton said calmly, 'You're trespassing.'

'What?' demanded the man. 'What did you say?'

Hamilton debated whether the accent was Swedish or German. The close-cropped hair under his cap was light blond. 'I said, you're trespassing,' repeated Hamilton. 'And put down that goddamn rifle.' He studied the insignia on the man's collar.

'You are the one who's trespassing,' said the rider with a sneer. 'You and your friend can be shot for this, you know. Tie them up,' he said to his confederates.

'*Was haben sie gesagt?*' said Hamilton in his best German. Carter gave him a curious look.

The mounted guard glared. 'Who are you?' he asked in heavily accented English, slinging the carbine on his shoulder and keeping a tight rein on his horse.

'I'm Tom Hamilton, and you're trespassing on property that belongs to the New Providence Land Company. Here ...' He reached into his pocket for the letter and handed it to the rider.

Quickly scanning it, the guard uttered an incomprehensible expletive and stuffed the letter into his shirt pocket. 'Tie them up,' he repeated to the others. As one of the men took a step toward them, the dog lunged at Carter with a vicious bark, causing the nervous horse to rear up. In the momentary confusion, Hamilton seized his opportunity, grabbing the Beretta from his waistband and taking aim at the nearest guard.

'OK,' said Hamilton, shifting his aim to the man struggling to control his horse. 'That's better.' Carter dropped his hands to his sides, where he patted the knife concealed in his pocket. The men slowly retreated, pulling the dog with them, while the rider tightened the reins, backing the jittery mare. 'Now,' said Hamilton, lowering the pistol, 'go back and tell Mr Ericsson I'm planning to buy this property. And I'll be over here to take a look around whenever I feel like it.'

'All right,' said the rider with a smile. '*Sehr gut*. I will convey your message. But next time ... I would be more careful.' With a jerk of the reins, he rode into the thicket.

'Are you all right?' Hamilton asked Carter.

After expelling a long sigh, Carter grinned and said, 'You were mighty handy with that pistol. I always was scared of big dogs.'

'Let's get the hell out of here.'

Following a hot shower, Hamilton dressed in a sports shirt and slacks and headed down to hail a jitney for Cable Beach. By the time Henry served him his ice-cold martini on the terrace, he was feeling utterly relaxed. Marnie sat next to Sir Philip with her hand on his arm.

'Well, Tom,' she said, 'to hear Carter tell the story, that was a close call with those guards.'

'You're sure they're Germans?' asked Sir Philip.

'Well, they were speaking German.'

Sir Philip motioned to Henry, standing in the shadows. 'A drink, darling?' he asked.

'I'll have a Bellini,' said Marnie. Hamilton gave her a curious look. 'You should try one. From that bar in Venice, made with fresh peach.'

'Harry's,' said Sir Philip. 'At any rate, Mr Hamilton, you got your message across.'

'What I don't understand,' said Hamilton, 'is why the Royal Navy doesn't pay a friendly call on our Swedish friend? Cruise right up into this Hurricane Hole of his and see what's up?'

'Ah,' said Sir Philip, 'perhaps I failed to explain. Ericsson is on very close terms with the duke and duchess. The duke admires the man greatly. The royal couple have been guests on Ericsson's yacht, the *Northern Lights*, an exceptionally large and luxurious vessel, including a well-publicized cruise to Miami. Under the circumstances, the local naval commander – an admirer of the duke – wouldn't dare do anything that might offend Ericsson.'

'Ericsson,' said Marnie, 'and old Sir Harry Oakes, despite being such a boor, are the only folk on the island who measure up to the duke's standards.'

'Well, then,' said Hamilton, 'I suppose I'll have to get to the bottom of this by myself. And, if you can spare him, with the help of your man Carter.'

'He's at your service,' said Sir Philip. 'Tell me, Mr Hamilton, how you're getting along with Mrs Shawcross?'

'I had a pleasant evening at Greycliff,' said Hamilton as he reached for his martini. 'It would have been perfect if it hadn't been for de Marigny and his child-bride.'

'That poor, silly girl,' said Marnie.

'I don't know why Evelyn invited them,' said Hamilton. 'It was obvious she can't stand them, unless it was to smoke me out.'

'I beg your pardon?' said Sir Philip.

'Use de Marigny to question what I'm doing here. Why I'm not off fighting in the war.'

'I see,' said Sir Philip. 'Did the tactic succeed?'

'I suppose. He asked me about it, and I gave him the usual answer. De Marigny seemed not to mind, since he thinks we should make a deal with Hitler, like the Vichy.'

'What about Evelyn? What are her views?'

'I'm not sure. She listened carefully to de Marigny, but didn't comment, except to tell me later that she thinks peace with the Germans is – what did she call it? An illusion.'

'What else were you able to learn about her?' asked Sir Philip.

'Oh, that's she's a gifted pianist, and lonely here all by herself, though she doesn't seem to feel much for her husband, who's a staff officer in Cairo. She mentioned that her parents are coming out for Christmas. She wants to see me again.'

'Oh, Lord,' said Marnie. 'You better watch out.' Hamilton responded with a smile.

'Her parents are traveling to Washington, according to my sources,' said Sir Philip, 'where they'll be the guests of the ambassador, Lord Halifax. Thence to Nassau, I assume. Before the war, they wintered here, at Greycliff.'

'So she said,' said Hamilton.

'See Evelyn again,' said Sir Philip. 'Get close to her, and see what you can glean about the attitude of the duke and Halifax as regards the war. And as regards your Swedish friend, Ericsson.'

'All right,' said Hamilton. 'I will. And Marnie – don't worry about me.'

Days passed without any luck in Hamilton's attempts to contact Evelyn Shawcross; languid days in the torpid rhythm of wartime Nassau, swims with Marnie on Cable Beach followed by lunches on the terrace with Sir Philip, and another meeting with the solicitor Dobbs, keeping up appearances as an indolent young man pursuing his Hog Island real estate speculation. He cabled his contact in Washington: BUSINESS PROSPECTS DEVELOPING MORE SLOWLY THAN ANTICIPATED STOP. Samuel, the Greycliff servant who answered the telephone, reported simply that 'Miz Shawcross' was 'away', expected to return in several days. It was thus a pleasant surprise when Evelyn answered Hamilton's morning telephone call. 'Tom,' she said, 'I was hoping you'd call. I've been out of town for the past several days. You must come for lunch and a swim.'

Hamilton elected to walk up from the hotel, pausing after several blocks to take in the panoramic view of the town and waterfront. After weeks of warm sunshine, thunderstorms had rumbled across the island in the pre-dawn darkness, leaving behind a high layer of thin clouds and a fresh northerly breeze with a distinct chill. He wondered whether he'd have any use for his bathing suit as he strolled past the fortifications surrounding Government House, the black cannons of which were sited on the approaches to the harbour. Turning the corner, he walked the final block, arriving at Greycliff's dark green front door precisely at half past noon.

Evelyn's servant answered the bell and led Hamilton through a passageway outside to a flagstone path through the garden, filled with plumeria, hibiscus, and tangled wisteria to an old green gate beneath a trellis blanketed with jasmine. Opening the gate, he observed a patio and rectangular pool, at least 25 metres in length, the colour of deep azure, enclosed by pale-pink walls overflowing with bougainvillea. The surrounding palms and ficus trees were so tall that the entire enclosure was shaded. As his eyes adjusted to the shadows, Hamilton could see Evelyn at the far end of the pool, resting her slender arms on the smooth limestone rim as she lazily stirred the water with her outstretched toes, sending ripples across the mirror-still surface.

'Hello,' he called out cheerfully. 'It's no wonder you don't get much of a tan. But you must be freezing.'

'It's marvellous,' she said as he walked up. 'We keep it heated in the fall and winter. The changing rooms are over there.' She pointed to a cabana at the end of the pool.

After a few minutes Hamilton emerged from the dressing room, tossed his towel over the back of a chaise, and dived into the pool, swiftly swimming its length with long strokes and a powerful kick and gliding smoothly out of the water like a seal onto a rock. 'My,' said Evelyn, 'where did you learn to swim like *that*?'

Hamilton smiled as he drew up his knees and ran his hands through his wet hair. 'The Australian crawl, you mean?' he said. 'Tex Robertson taught it at the University of Texas, so I tried it out at Yale.'

'You swam for Yale?'

'The freestyle and medley.'

She gazed up at him with her chin resting on one arm as she lazily floated in the warm water, admiring his wide-shouldered swimmer's build.

'This pool,' he said. 'I've never seen anything quite like it.'

'It's made entirely of mosaics,' she explained. 'Tiles of varying shades of blue. Creates quite an effect.'

'I should say so. And this setting is spectacular.'

'I thought you'd like it,' she said with a smile. 'Samuel says you've been quite persistent about calling.'

Hamilton looked into her eyes, thinking they seemed a deeper shade of blue against the backdrop of glittering tiles. 'True,' he said. 'I gathered you were away.'

Evelyn stood up in the waist deep water and gracefully vaulted out of the pool. 'Yes,' she said as she sat down next to him. 'I've been on a nice cruise about the islands.'

'Sailing?' he asked.

'No, a motor-yacht. Quite a large one actually. We cruised around Eleuthera and then up to the Abacos and back.'

'No worries about German U-boats?'

'Don't be silly. Why should the Germans bother with a pleasure craft? I should imagine they're hunting more valuable prey.'

Hamilton nodded and said, 'Whose yacht was this, though it's none of my business?'

'It belongs to a friend,' she said after a moment's hesitation. 'Nils Ericsson. You mentioned him the other night at dinner, if I recall correctly.'

'The Swedish industrialist?' said Hamilton. 'I've heard of him, of course. The one with the fabulous villa on Hog Island?'

'Yes. He and his wife are quite charming. He made his fortune in appliances....'

'The toaster king,' said Hamilton. And with armaments, he thought to himself.

'Yes.' She gave him a quirky smile. 'At any rate, he owns a fantastic yacht, the *Northern Lights*, and was kind enough to invite me on a lovely cruise. You must meet him, Tom.'

'I'd like to.' He wondered whether Evelyn was merely beguiled by Ericsson's apparent charm and luxurious lifestyle, or whether she shared the man's well-known fascist sympathies. Standing up, he leaned down to help her to her feet. For a moment they stood holding hands and gazing into each other's eyes.

'Let's change,' she suggested, 'and then have lunch by the pool.'

'An excellent idea.' He walked with her to the cabana, stealing a glance at her rounded breasts and slender waist accentuated by the clinging fabric of her swimsuit.

'Boys on the right,' she said with a soft laugh. 'Oh, Tom,' she added, stopping to look at him. 'Do me a favour, would you? Go up to the house and tell Samuel we'll be ready for lunch in fifteen minutes. And then be a dear and bring down the cold drinks I asked him to have ready.'

'At your service, ma'am,' said Hamilton, reaching for his towel from the chaise and draping it over his shoulders. As soon as he had disappeared through the gate, Evelyn hurried into the changing-room where Hamilton's clothes were folded over a chair. She felt in the back pocket of his slacks for his wallet; lifted it out and quickly studied its contents: a driver's licence, wad of bills, several business cards, and a folded slip of paper with the pencilled word 'Washington' and a phone number. Her heart pounding, she hurried from the dressing-room, went to her purse and copied down the number, and then quickly replaced it in his wallet, leaving his clothes as she'd found them. A few minutes later she was safely in her own dressing-room, hooking her bra as she studied her reflection in the mirror. When she emerged, wearing a low-cut, sleeveless cotton blouse and pale yellow pants, Hamilton was seated at the table by the pool, looking relaxed and refreshed in a plaid shirt and slacks with his damp hair neatly parted and combed. He smiled and reached for a frosted pitcher, pouring each of them a bubbly orange and pink concoction.

'Mimosa?' said Hamilton as he handed her a glass. 'I couldn't help but notice that Samuel fixed them with a bottle of Dom Perignon.'

'Oh, Daddy put up cases and cases of the stuff before the war. And now that you can't get it.... Well, why not?'

'Why not,' agreed Hamilton, taking a sip. He put down his glass and looked across the table at her, struck again by her delicate beauty. 'Your parents are coming for Christmas?'

'Yes. They're travelling to America first, on the Pan Am Clipper to Washington. Did I mention that Lord Halifax is my mother's cousin?'

'I don't believe so.'

'He invited my parents to visit the embassy.' She lifted her glass and took a sip. 'Do you dislike Halifax?' she asked.

'Why should I?'

'Well, most Americans are so taken with Churchill, and Halifax, of course, was Churchill's rival. They can't abide one another.'

'I see,' he said with a nod. 'I'll try to keep an open mind.' The gate swung open and Samuel appeared, bearing a tray with a porcelain bowl, plates, linen and silverware. 'My, my,' said Hamilton as Samuel lowered the tray to the table. 'What have we here?'

'Fresh lobster salad,' said Samuel with a smile. 'With diced conch, Bahamian style.'

After several servings of the delicious seafood and the last of the mimosas, Hamilton sat back with a sigh of contentment. 'You've been too kind, Evelyn,' he said. 'It's my turn to treat you.' She leaned across the table toward him and gave him a dreamy look.

'I expect you'll be leaving soon,' she said, as she lightly placed her hand on his.

He stared into her eyes, his heart pounding at the sensation of her touch. 'Actually,' he said, 'I'm planning to stay for … well, longer than I'd planned.' Impulsively, she rose from her chair and took a step toward him. Hamilton stood up, hesitated, and then opened his arms to her. For a moment she stared up at him, moulding herself to his body, and then kissed him; a slow, lingering kiss. At last he pulled away and said, 'You know, I could fall for you if I'm not careful.' She kissed him lightly again. 'I can't let that happen,' he said, as much to himself as to her.

'You seem the type of man,' she said softly, 'who's had a lot of women.'

'This is different.'

She gave him a curious, inquisitive look and then, with a light squeeze of his hands, said, 'Well, Tom, I should send you off before we get any deeper into trouble. But I'm going to hold you to your word.'

'Yes,' he said, strangely relieved. 'I'll call.'

*

Later, in his room, Hamilton felt almost light-headed, with a strange feeling, like butterflies, in his stomach. She was right, he reminded himself, as he studied his reflection in the mirror. He had been involved with plenty of other women. But none of them married. And *none* of them like Evelyn Shawcross, married or virginal. He swore under his breath. It was obvious that Evelyn might prove very useful in finding out more about the mysterious Nils Ericsson and, as Sir Philip suspected, that she was part of the inner circle surrounding the Duke of Windsor. He'd have to be very, very careful. With a quick glance at his watch, he reached for his wallet, extracted a slip of paper, and went to the telephone.

CHAPTER FIVE

'I NEED A stateside line,' said Hamilton impatiently. After a brief delay, he said, 'A toll call, to Washington, D.C. Capitol four, six-eight-four-seven.'

'Hello,' answered a woman after a few rings. 'How may I direct your call?'

'It's Tom, Betty,' said Hamilton. 'I need to speak to the boss.'

'Just a minute.'

'Hello, Hamilton,' said a man in gruff voice. 'Are you planning to retire down there?'

'It's taking longer than I expected.'

'Well, you need to finish up and get back here.'

'What's the rush? I'm still trying to put my, ah, deal together.'

'We've discovered that your man is involved in some interesting activities in South America. I'd like to send you down to look into it.'

Hamilton's heart sank. 'Listen, Bill, I think I'm on to something. I may be able to confirm our worst suspicions.'

'OK, but hurry it up. And be sure to bring home some nice snapshots.'

'Sure,' said Hamilton. 'Goodbye, Bill.' He walked out on the balcony and stared at the dark, heaving sea with patches of pale turquoise where the sun broke through the clouds. Colonel William J. Donovan, the Director of the Office of Strategic Services, was one of the smartest and toughest men Hamilton had ever met. The most highly decorated American officer in the First World War and afterward a prominent Wall Street lawyer, Donovan had been recruited by Franklin Roosevelt to oversee the creation of the OSS in 1942, the first US agency dedicated to espionage on foreign soil. Leaning against the railing in the cool breeze, Hamilton's mind drifted back to Evelyn, floating in the water, her pale skin and blue eyes against the glittering mosaic tiles of the pool. Not only beautiful and intelligent, but sophisticated in a way that none of the girls he'd known from Smith or Vassar had been. She obviously didn't care much for her faraway husband, nor did she seem to have much interest in the faraway war. Thinking back to the conversation over lunch, he felt a sudden pang of remorse. He had lied so effortlessly; lied about everything, even feigning surprise at her mention of the family connection to Halifax, while she unsuspectingly welcomed him into her home. God, this was such a dirty business. Maybe he should level with her and enlist her help in finding out what Ericsson was really up to. No, that would not only jeopardize his mission, it would also endanger her safety. Well, he would be leaving soon, and God knows if he'd ever be back. One thing was certain: he intended to see her again.

Like many older and very wealthy men, Nils Ericsson had grown fussy about his personal appearance and very particular about small, odd things such as his cufflinks and studs and the precise knotting of his tie. At the moment he was searching in a Florentine leather case for a missing silver and mother-of-pearl stud. 'Aha. There it is,' he said aloud, as he examined the article on the dresser. After inserting the stud, he carefully parted and combed his silver hair, once blond, observing himself in the mirror with his chin thrust forward, satisfied with the sheen imparted by his hair tonic and the pink glow of his cheeks. With a final tug on his bow tie, he slipped on his dinner jacket and walked from the room. The butler stood with a tray under his arm, wearing gloves and a white jacket trimmed in gold like a steward on an ocean liner.

'Good evening, sir,' said the butler with a bow. With the exception of the kitchen staff, all of the servants at Shangri-La had accompanied Ericsson from Sweden, and it pleased him to hear only his native tongue spoken in the large colonial villa.

Ericsson walked to the French doors that opened out on a screened-in gallery facing the sea. 'I'm expecting Major Krebs,' he said, as he unfastened the latch and opened the doors. 'Show him up as soon as he arrives.' Within minutes, the butler reappeared, followed by a short, compact man who looked uncomfortable in a borrowed tuxedo. Ericsson, standing at the French doors, turned to him with a smile and said, '*Guten abend*, Major.'

'Good evening,' repeated Krebs in German as he strode across the room and vigorously shook Ericsson's hand.

'Thank you, Johann,' said Ericsson in Swedish. 'That will be all.' Once the butler was gone, Ericsson, reverting to German, said, 'How was your voyage?'

'Well,' said Krebs, 'as a soldier, I'm not very fond of life at sea. Especially on an old merchant tub, or pretending to be a sardine in a U-boat.' He flashed a brief smile at his witticism.

'You came by way of Martinique?' asked Ericsson. Krebs nodded, reverting to his grimly serious demeanour. Ericsson motioned to the armchairs that faced the gallery. 'Let's sit, shall we? You must tell me the latest news of the war.'

Sitting next to his host, Krebs said, 'Well, according to my sources in Berlin, the situation on the Russian front is quite serious. Sixth Army is locked in a desperate struggle for Stalingrad. But Manstein has launched an offensive across the Don, and the Führer is confident a decisive victory is almost within our grasp.'

'Excellent,' said Ericsson. 'And now, Major, tell me about the submarine offensive.'

'Operations in the Caribbean,' said the German officer, 'are suspended. We don't want to arouse suspicions at this critical moment.' Ericsson nodded. 'But we have U-boats in the Gulf of Mexico,' Krebs continued, 'intercepting shipments of fuel. British stockpiles are perilously low.'

'And so,' said Ericsson, 'once Stalingrad has been taken, the time will be ripe for our ... our little surprise.'

'Precisely,' agreed Krebs. 'Those favouring peace in Great Britain will see that the time has come to take action, and with the prospect of no fuel for their ships and tanks—'

'And the turn of events in Nassau,' added Ericsson.

'We shall see,' concluded Krebs. 'But it is absolutely essential that the facilities here are ready before we act.'

'The submarine pens.'

'Of course. And how, may I ask, is construction progressing?'

Ericsson crossed his legs, dangling one patent-leather pump, and extracted a cigarette from the case in his breast pocket. 'Very well, I would say. The men are working in twelve-hour shifts. We've poured some twenty tons of concrete, and I've got sufficient Portland cement on hand to complete the job.' Taking a gold-plated lighter from his pocket, he lit his cigarette and exhaled a cloud of smoke.

'And the canal?'

'Progressing satisfactorily, with the exception of a minor nuisance. I've employed virtually every able-bodied man, and I see no reason why we shouldn't be ready in six weeks.'

'A minor nuisance?'

'A small strip of land on the Nassau side of the island,' explained Ericsson, 'is owned by local investors. An American arrived out of the blue and is negotiating to buy it.'

'Well, you mustn't let that happen. Who is this American?'

'A Texan, with oil money. Rather aggressive. With the backing of the wealthy Jew, Sassoon. But I'm checking to see if there's more than meets the eye.'

'An oilman from Texas,' said Krebs derisively, 'backed by an old, crippled Jew. I should think the men we've supplied you with should be able to manage him quite easily.'

Ericsson nodded, thinking how the American had turned back three of his best men. 'Of course,' he said. 'You needn't worry.' He puffed on his cigarette and said, 'Tell me, Krebs, have you finalized your plans?'

Leaning forward, the major, speaking in a low, conspiratorial tone, said, 'We have two infantry companies, crack troops, training on Martinique, under my command. When the order is given, we'll arrive by merchant ship, come ashore in rubber boats at night. Your men will lead us across the island to Oakes Field, which we'll assault at dawn. Meanwhile, a destroyer, the *Breslau*, will take up position overnight and will simultaneously begin shelling the port. As a diversion, the men I've assigned to you here will stage an attack on the army barracks in Nassau.'

'Do you worry about the Spitfires at Oakes Field?' asked Ericsson.

'With the exception of one or two instructors, all of the pilots are in training, with no combat experience. My men will secure the airfield in a matter of minutes and put down any resistance. Our destroyer will knock out the British patrol boat, steam into the harbour and begin shelling the army barracks. With Oakes Field secure, one party will proceed to Government House and place the duke under house arrest, while I lead the rest of my men to demand the surrender of the British garrison. Meanwhile, a squadron of six U-boats will proceed into their new base. If the attack begins at dawn, I'll be enjoying a cup of tea with the duke by eight o'clock.'

'What a grand surprise for the British,' said Ericsson with a grin. They'll wake up to discover a German submarine base and fully operational airfield lying astride the Straits of Florida. And with the Duke of Windsor under house arrest, possibly broadcasting an appeal for peace. Peace,' repeated Ericsson in a serious tone, 'among the civilized white races.'

'You're making progress with the duke?' asked Krebs.

'We're getting along quite well. He has let it be known, both privately and publicly, that he favours a negotiated settlement with your government.' Ericsson stubbed out his cigarette. 'It's time for dinner,' he announced. 'Follow me.'

Hamilton had invited the solicitor Dobbs to meet him for a drink at George's Tavern, a favourite of the legal establishment located around the corner from the sailors' dives on Bay Street. As he entered the dimly lit bar, Hamilton noticed a small, pitiful Christmas tree in the corner, fashioned from a native pine and decorated with tinsel and shiny red ornaments, while the 'The White Cliffs of Dover' played on a radio somewhere in the back. Choosing a booth by the half-curtained window, he considered the general seediness of the place; the stained carpets, split-open cushions on the barstools, and pall of cigarette smoke. A middle-aged waitress with sagging upper arms slowly walked over and, with an expression of infinite boredom, asked him what he'd like to drink. Thinking decent whisky might take his mind off the squalor, he ordered a Scotch. Moments after she returned with his drink, the bell over the entrance jingled, and Harold Dobbs appeared in the doorway. Pausing to clap a fat hand on the shoulder of a fellow solicitor, he quickly scanned the establishment and walked over to the booth.

'There you are, Hamilton,' said Dobbs in a voice loud enough for the table of men at the back to overhear, 'having a bit of Christmas cheer, I see.'

Hamilton gave Dobbs a tight-lipped smile and said, 'Have a seat.' Dobbs squeezed into the booth and made a funny face at the waitress with a gesture she apparently comprehended, as she appeared in a moment with a frosted mug of beer.

Lifting his glass, Hamilton said, 'Cheers.'

Dobbs hoisted his mug and took a swallow, leaving a ribbon of foam above his lip. 'Well, Mr Hamilton,' he said, 'I've ascertained some rather interesting information.'

Hamilton noticed out of the corner of his eye that a man at the bar was paying close attention, as were several others at a nearby table. 'Good,' said Hamilton. 'Were you able to contact the owners and let them know what I'm prepared to offer?'

'I spoke to Jennings.' Dobbs paused to listen to the throaty exhaust of an approaching motorcycle and rose from his seat to watch as a gleaming black sedan shot past, Union Jacks fluttering on the fenders. 'Blimey,' exclaimed Dobbs. 'It's the guv'nor!' Hamilton noticed that several other patrons also rose to catch a glimpse of the duke's Rolls Royce. After clearing his throat and taking another slosh of beer, Dobbs continued, 'Mason Jennings, who owns the haberdashery. Decent chap, with a good head for business. Jennings is the key man.'

Hamilton sipped his drink and said, 'What did Jennings have to say?'

'I advised him that you were prepared to offer five thousand dollars.'

'And?' Hamilton took another sip.

'Well, here's the interesting bit. Jennings says, why that's a very good offer, especially with the effect the war's having. Bloody disaster for the merchants on Bay Street,' said Dobbs with a thoughtful look.

Hamilton nodded and said, 'Yes, I'm sure, but what did he *say?*'

'It's a good price,' resumed Dobbs, '*but*, says Jennings, it won't clear the mortgage. Mortgage? I said. What mortgage? I've searched the title, and I assure you there's no mortgage of record on *that* piece of property.' Hamilton could feel eyes all around boring in on them.

'Go on,' said Hamilton in a low voice.

'Well, says Jennings, we'd be prepared to sell your client this parcel *subject* to the mortgage, plus a small cash consideration.'

'OK,' said Hamilton, 'and what's the balance on this unrecorded mortgage?'

'Well, Jennings reached into his desk and produced the document, a mortgage securing payment of a note for *twenty thousand pounds*. Why, that's over a hundred thousand dollars!'

'I can do the math,' said Hamilton irritably. 'Hold on a minute, Harold. That's ridiculous. Nobody in his right mind would pay a hundred thousand bucks for that piece of swampland, with no access from Nassau. Or loan a hundred thousand with that property as collateral.'

'Quite right,' agreed Dobbs.

'Surely they don't think I'd pay a dime for it, subject to that mortgage?'

'Well,' said Dobbs, giving his chin a contemplative rub, 'I honestly don't know. Jennings made a point of drawing my attention to the name of the mortgage holder, Lake Shore Mining, Ltd. Jennings seemed to place some emphasis on the name.'

'I see,' said Hamilton, increasingly exasperated. 'Let me think this over.' He reached for his wallet and counted out several bills. 'That should cover it,' he said as he slid from the booth. 'Merry Christmas, Harold. I'll be in touch.'

The more Hamilton thought about it as he walked along Bay Street the more bizarre Dobbs's story seemed. A group of local merchants, so-called Bay Street Boys who evidently ran things in the Colony, mortgaged a piece of swampland for more than ten times what it was worth? Some sort of game was obviously being played, but what? In any case, his plan to buy the property for a song was out the window. And with all the lawyers and courthouse scouts in that bar, it wouldn't be long before word was all over town. Glancing at his watch, he realized he'd have just enough time to change before dinner with the Sassoons. Perhaps Sir Philip could unravel the mystery.

The clerk at the front desk called out to him as he hurried past. Hamilton walked over and accepted a cream-coloured envelope, addressed to *Mr Thomas R. Hamilton* in blue-black ink. Hmm, he thought, as he stuffed it in his coat pocket and started for the lifts. Half an hour later, he strode through the lobby to the portico where he hailed a jitney. Another band of rain showers had passed from the mainland, streaking the sky fiery orange as the taxi turned into the drive at Eves. Hamilton listened to the rain dripping from the palm fronds as he strolled the wet flagstones to the front door where Annie was waiting.

'Evenin',' she said with a smile. 'Sir Philip's in his study.'

Hamilton considered Sir Philip's fondness for his book-lined study, which he was able to reach by a lift. As he passed through the living room, Marnie emerged from the hallway. 'Hello, Tom,' she said with a smile. 'Don't you look handsome.'

'And you look terrific, as usual,' he replied, letting his eyes fall from her brown eyes to her low-cut black cocktail dress, where a brilliant yellow diamond was suspended on a gold chain.

She leaned over, placed a hand on his arm and kissed him lightly. 'Tell me,' she said quietly, 'you're not falling for that Englishwoman?'

'My God, she's married. Besides, it's none of your business....'

'I knew it.' She shook her head, giving her blonde curls a bounce. 'I could tell that first night you were here.'

'Now, Marnie,' said Hamilton reproachfully.

'Listen to me, Tom,' she said, gazing into his grey eyes. 'Use her. Do whatever you have to do to get what you're after. But don't fall for her.'

'Don't worry about me. I can look after myself.'

'Maybe,' she said sceptically. 'But I've known women like Evelyn, and I don't want you to get hurt.'

'OK,' he said with a smile. 'Let's go upstairs.'

Sir Philip was in his favourite armchair with his pipe and a volume of Kipling's barracks verse. 'Come in, darling,' he said, closing his book. 'Hello, Tom.'

Hamilton sat beside Marnie on the sofa and said, 'Any news from London?'

'Yes, and most of it quite depressing. Shipping losses to these packs of U-boats have been dreadful. And with the success they've had sinking tankers coming out of the Gulf, our oil supplies are in real jeopardy. Now, Tom, how have you been getting along?'

'Getting along just fine with Milady Shawcross,' said Marnie tartly.

'Well, I did manage to see her again,' said Hamilton. 'And I'm sure I have her confidence. But, frankly, I think she's just a bored and lonely woman who doesn't have much interest in the war.'

'The most dangerous variety,' said Marnie under her breath.

'Perhaps you can gain some notion, through Mrs Shawcross, of the duke's views,' suggested Sir Philip.

'It looks like I'm going to be meeting the old boy.' He reached into his pocket for an envelope. 'An invitation,' he said, removing it from the envelope, 'to dinner and dancing at Government House, on Saturday, the 18th. From His Royal Highness, the Duke of Windsor, and the Duchess—'

'Her Royal Lowness,' interjected Marnie.

'Black tie, naturally,' said Hamilton. 'I'm escorting Mrs Shawcross.'

'Shocking,' said Marnie. 'I'm sure she cleared it with Wallis, who's bound to sympathize with the plight of a married woman.'

Sir Philip smiled. 'Well, Tom, that's excellent. The duke and duchess's Christmas ball is the talk of the town.'

'I'll have to hurry,' said Hamilton. 'OSS is pulling me out of here.'

'Why?' said Sir Philip. A disappointed look crossed Marnie's face.

'Donovan wants to send me to South America. It seems that Ericsson has been active in Peru. We need to find out what he's up to.'

'But what about your scheme to buy the land on Hog Island?' asked Sir Philip.

'That's the damnedest thing,' said Hamilton. 'When my solicitor approached the owners, he discovered there's a mortgage on the property for twenty thousand pounds.'

'Good heavens,' said Sir Philip. He paused to knock out his pipe on the heel of his hand.

'The leader of the group,' said Hamilton, 'some shop owner in town, had the nerve to offer me the property *subject* to the mortgage, plus some cash. What do you suppose is going on? I can't figure it out.'

'Did your solicitor learn the identity of the holder of the mortgage?'

'Some outfit called Lake Shore Mining, Ltd.'

'Well, then,' said Sir Philip. 'That explains it.'

'Explains it?' said Hamilton. 'Explains what?'

'It's Oakes,' said Sir Philip. 'Up to one of his usual games.' When Hamilton responded with a perplexed look, Sir Philip explained. 'Lake Shore Mining is one of Oakes's holding companies. The name refers to his gold strike in Canada. These local men are obviously his front men.'

Hamilton exchanged a glance with Marnie, who seemed unsurprised by her husband's astuteness. 'But why twenty thousand pounds?' asked Hamilton. 'No one would pay a fraction of that amount—'

'Precisely,' said Sir Philip. 'Oakes wants to make sure no one else acquires the property. Nor does he want it known that he's the owner. So he arranges for these local men to hold the title, while he takes an unrecorded mortgage. Thus, anyone wanting the property – including yourself – eventually has to come to terms with Oakes. Rather ingenious.'

'Very,' said Hamilton dejectedly.

'Well, cheer up,' said Sir Philip with a smile. 'You still have the Christmas ball to look forward to.'

'True,' said Hamilton. 'And before leaving Nassau, I intend to get a close-up look at Hurricane Hole.'

CHAPTER SIX

THE PROSPECT OF meeting the Duke of Windsor and the woman whose charms were such that he'd surrendered the crown for them gave Tom Hamilton an adolescent thrill. Or perhaps, he considered, as he studied his reflection in the mirror while he worked on his bow tie, his mood of expectancy was due more to the thought of another evening with Evelyn Shawcross. Satisfied with his tie, he put on his dinner jacket and slipped the car keys in his pocket.

Sir Philip's Bentley convertible was parked in the hotel drive. As Hamilton walked out of the lobby, the Bahamian doorman was slowly circling the vehicle, gazing admiringly at its dark-red leather upholstery and sensuous curves. 'Nice automobile,' he said as he opened the driver's door.

Slipping the doorman a note, Hamilton said, 'I'm just borrowing it for a date.' He turned the key, pleased by the deep, throaty rumble of the V-12 engine and swung out into the cool December evening. Government House stood alone at the top of the hill in a blaze of celebratory lights, from the chandelier above the fanlight on the portico to the lamps burning in the windows along the upper floors. Turning at the corner, Hamilton pulled up to a stop in front of Greycliff, leaving the engine running as he walked up to the front door. No sooner had he rung the bell, Evelyn appeared with a smile, wearing the same blue chiffon dress she'd worn to the Sassoons' dinner party, with a blue moiré stole over her bare shoulders.

'Evening, madam,' said Hamilton as he took her arm. 'All ready for the ball?'

With a glance the Bentley, she said, 'My, I feel a bit like Cinderella.'

'Swell, isn't it?' said Hamilton, as they started down the walk. 'I thought we'd make a grand entrance.' Compared with the lacklustre black sedans and jitney cabs in the queue at Government House, the Bentley convertible seemed grand indeed as Hamilton turned into the sweeping drive. As they queued up, Hamilton looked over at Evelyn and said, 'I'd better get a few things straight. How does one address the duke?'

Evelyn smiled. 'Despite the fact that he's *only* a duke,' she explained, 'he was the king, and therefore you should say, "your royal highness," with a bow.'

'And the duchess?'

'Simply "your grace", or "Duchess". I'm told the duke wasn't very happy about that, thinking she was entitled to a curtsy and "your highness", but the authorities in London were very firm.'

'I see.' Hamilton drove under the chandelier on the portico.

'Welcome, ma'am,' said the elaborately liveried doorman as he opened the door for Evelyn.

Hamilton took Evelyn by the arm and led her up a red carpet into the marble foyer, which was crowded with men and women in formal attire, buzzing with excitement at the prospect of meeting the duke and duchess. The staircase was festooned with garlands of holly, tied in red ribbons, and a string quartet in the corner played 'Greensleeves'. Evelyn nodded politely to the couple standing nearest them, who glanced at Hamilton with a curious but disapproving expression.

When their turn came at the top of the stairs, Evelyn handed a card to a tall British sergeant in a dress Cameron kilt, who announced, 'Mrs Evelyn Shawcross, and Mr Thomas Hamilton.'

Taking Evelyn by the arm, Hamilton walked up to the handsome former king, who, like his guests, was attired in evening dress, and the attractive woman at his side, bowed and said, 'Good evening, your royal highness.' Turning to the duchess, he smiled and added, 'Your grace.'

The duke shook Hamilton's hand stiffly and then leaned over to kiss Evelyn on the cheek. 'Merry Christmas, darling,' he said with a smile.

'Your highness,' replied Evelyn with a graceful bow.

'Evelyn, you look terrific,' said the duchess, taking her by the hand. 'I love your hair.' Turning toward Hamilton, she said, 'I'm so glad you were able to come.'

'Why, thanks,' said Hamilton. 'It was nice of you to include me.' He looked briefly at the duchess, who was wearing a lavender décolletage evening gown with an exceptional sapphire and diamond necklace around her swan-like neck. Feeling a gentle tug on his arm as the next couple in line was announced, Hamilton walked with Evelyn across the fine old parquet toward the centre of the elegant ballroom, where a group of men and women were clustered beneath a crystal chandelier. Scanning the room, he located the bar and said, 'I could use a drink. What can I get you?'

'Oh,' said Evelyn, 'champagne, if it's decent.'

By the time Hamilton returned, Evelyn was deep in conversation with a tall, distinguished-looking man. 'There you are,' said Hamilton, handing Evelyn her glass.

'Tom,' she said, 'meet Alastair Mackintosh, an old friend.'

'Good evening,' said Mackintosh, as he shook hands.

'Tom's a real estate speculator,' said Evelyn, 'and an oilman.'

'Oh, really?' said Mackintosh, giving Hamilton an appraising look. 'With the war, I shouldn't think there would be much worth speculating *on* in Nassau.'

'You'd be surprised,' said Hamilton.

An elderly woman, slightly stooped and wearing a black silk gown, walked up and placed a gloved hand on Evelyn's arm. 'Evelyn, my dear,' she said in a Southern accent that surprised Hamilton, 'you look gorgeous. And who's this handsome man you've brought with you?'

'Tom Hamilton,' said Evelyn, 'who's visiting from Texas. Tom, this is Mrs Bessie Merryman.'

'Evening, Mrs Merryman,' said Hamilton with a polite nod.

'Just call me Aunt Bessie,' she said. 'Everybody else does.'

'Bessie is the duchess's aunt,' explained Evelyn. With Evelyn's grace and beauty, and her ties to their royal host, Hamilton sensed they were attracting a crowd. He turned as Georges de Videlou strode up and, with one hand on the back of Evelyn's gown, lightly kissed her cheek.

'Madame Shawcross,' he said theatrically. '*Bon soir.*'

Moments later they were joined by the de Marignys. At 6' 5", the debonair Frenchman towered over his young wife and stood holding her hand as if escorting a schoolgirl across a busy road. ''Allo, Tom,' said Alfred cheerfully, clapping Hamilton on the shoulder.

Hamilton noticed that Aunt Bessie seemed to recoil at the arrival of the two Frenchmen. 'It's nice to see you again, Nancy,' he said to the young Mrs de Marigny, who responded with a blush and awkward smile.

'Tom,' said Evelyn, 'there's someone I want you to meet.'

'Excuse us,' said Hamilton. He followed Evelyn across the room where several middle-aged couples were gathered around an imposing, broad-shouldered man with a round, pink face and carefully parted silver hair, speaking in heavily accented English.

'And you see,' he was saying, 'there is truly a benefit to your interests here in Nassau from the economic development of the Out Islands— Oh, it's Mrs Shawcross,' he said with a wide smile as Evelyn walked up to him. He took her by the hands and kissed her on both cheeks.

'Nils,' said Evelyn, 'Let me introduce Tom Hamilton, from the United States.' Hamilton stepped forward and shook hands, surprised by the older man's powerful grip.

For a moment Ericsson caught Hamilton in the intense gaze of his pale-blue eyes and then said, 'Ah … Mr Hamilton. I've been looking forward to making your acquaintance.'

'Likewise.' Hamilton adopted a casual pose with one hand in his pocket as he took a sip of his drink. 'Maybe we can find time to meet.'

'I should like that,' said Ericsson. 'You know these other guests?'

After Evelyn politely introduced Tom to the local Nassau couples, who struck him as rather coarse in their manners and their poorly concealed interest, especially the wives, in the fact that he was escorting the beautiful, aristocratic, and married Mrs Shawcross, he gently insisted that they move on to the bar. Once they were out of earshot, Hamilton said, 'Tell me about Ericsson. Is it true what they say about him?'

'What do they say about him?' asked Evelyn.

'That he's a friend of Göring, for instance. That he thinks it was a mistake for England to take on Hitler.'

'I don't know,' said Evelyn in an off-hand way. 'What difference does it make? We're in the war, aren't we? Why should it matter what a wealthy man from Sweden, which *is* neutral, after all, thinks about it? He's quite charming and doing a great deal of good for the poor Bahamians...'

'OK,' said Hamilton, holding up a conciliatory hand. 'Sorry I asked. Now, who is that,' he asked, motioning with his glass, 'talking with the duke and duchess?'

'Sir Harry Oakes. Would you care to meet him?'

It would have been highly presumptuous for anyone other than Evelyn Shawcross to interrupt a private conversation between the former king and the wealthiest man in the empire. The duke, dispelling any doubts about his feelings, greeted her warmly with a welcoming smile and kiss. 'Please, go on,' he instructed Oakes as Hamilton stood somewhat awkwardly at Evelyn's side.

'Well, Governor,' said Oakes, 'I think you might want to beef up security around here. A lot of dough's been spent out there at Oakes Field, and if I was you, I'd be goddamn worried the Germans might pull something. Oh,' he said, noticing Hamilton.

'Sorry to interrupt,' said Evelyn, 'Let me introduce Tom Hamilton. Sir Harry Oakes.'

'Hamilton,' said Oakes with a frown. 'I knew your old man.'

'Really?' said Hamilton, as he stepped forward to shake hands.

'Yep. Helluva wildcatter from Oklahoma. My kind of man.'

After giving Hamilton a puzzled look, the duke said, 'Well, Sir Harry, I take your point. I shall have to speak to our chief of security. But I must say' – he gave Oakes a look of royal condescension – 'I rather doubt the Germans would have any interest in our charming little island.'

'Sorry, darling,' said the duchess, who was clinging to her husband's arm, 'but it's time we served our guests their supper. You must lead the way.'

After following Evelyn to the dining-room, Hamilton discovered that they were seated at the table of honour, with Evelyn next to the duke and Hamilton beside Mrs Ericsson. As he stood with his hands on the back of his chair, he observed the elaborate table decorations made of holly and white roses around bright red candles. Once all the ladies were in their places, the duke took his seat, and on cue the men sat down, Ericsson next to the duchess, and Evelyn's friend Alastair Mackintosh was paired with an attractive middle-aged woman. Hamilton noticed that Sir Harry Oakes was seated with the duchess's Aunt Bessie at the next table, whereas his daughter Nancy and Alfred de Marigny had been banished to a table on the far side of the room. Dinner was served, wild duck in addition to the usual roast beef. Though the surrounding tables were soon buzzing with conversation, the duke's table remained awkwardly silent as his guests waited upon his grace to lead the way. As it happened, he was more concerned with the tenderness of his duck and the bouquet of his wine, and it fell upon the duchess to comment first on the delightful weather and then the dreadful scarcity of fashionable clothes, with Paris shut off from the world. The duke in due course called on Mackintosh to repeat a clever story he'd told in the duck blind, which led to a general discussion of the quality of the game on the table, the excellence of the wine and, at last, to a long and tedious discussion of the crayfish cannery Ericsson was operating on Grand Bahama.

Through it all Hamilton occasionally made eye contact with Evelyn, who appeared to be relishing her private conversation with the duke. More than anything, he was struck by the duchess's charm; though not pretty, she carried herself in a confident, handsome way, with intelligent eyes, and dark hair parted in the centre and brushed back in a way that complemented her prominent cheekbones. In addition to the remarkable necklace, he was fascinated by the jewel-encrusted flamingo brooch pinned to the shoulder of her lavender gown. Because he'd been straining to hear Evelyn's conversation with Ericsson, he was somewhat startled when the duchess looked directly at him and asked, 'What brought you to Nassau, Mr Hamilton?'

'Well,' he began, noticing that all three men at the table were staring at him, 'I came out to investigate a business venture—'

'A speculation in real estate,' interjected Mackintosh, 'according to Evelyn.'

'That's right,' said Hamilton. 'Possibly buying some property opposite town, on Hog Island, for development after the war.'

'What sort of development?' asked Ericsson.

'Assuming I can convince the authorities to build a bridge, a first-class hotel with a casino.'

The mention of a casino aroused the duke's interest. 'Rather an intriguing idea,' he commented with a smile. 'An alternative to that wretchedly corrupt Havana.'

'That's right,' said Hamilton, 'a nice winter resort for the right sort of people, from Great Britain as well as the East Coast, where we're not likely to legalize gambling any time soon.'

'Unfortunately, Mr Hamilton,' said Ericsson in his heavy accent, 'I see several obstacles to this scheme. In the first place, this terrible war is continuing with no end in sight, and secondly, you may find it rather difficult to purchase this property.' He smiled unexpectedly.

'Yes,' said the duchess, 'it's well known that dear Nils owns virtually all of Hog Island.'

'That may be,' said Hamilton, who noticed that Evelyn was closely following every word. 'But perhaps, your highness,' he suggested, turning to the duke, 'there might still be a way to bring the war to an early conclusion, at least as far as Germany is concerned.' In the silence that followed, Hamilton held the duke in his gaze.

'I for one,' said the duke solemnly, 'regard it as a tragic mistake to sacrifice the lives of so many of our finest sons and the destruction of our greatest landmarks in what will likely prove to be a useless struggle with Germany, when the real threat to our civilization, nay, our way of life, comes from the Soviets.'

'Here, here,' said Ericsson, raising his glass.

'And so, to answer your question, Mr Hamilton,' continued the duke, 'yes, I believe we should rely on diplomacy, and not force of arms, to bring an end to the war. And then, perhaps,' he concluded, 'you might pursue this interesting idea of yours, providing Nils will co-operate.'

As dessert was being served, music drifted from the ballroom, a surprisingly good band, thought Hamilton, as he tapped his foot, capable of a good rendition of the latest swing tunes. The guests politely waited on the duke and duchess to finish their desserts and then followed them into the ballroom, admiringly standing back in a wide circle as the royal couple made a graceful turn around the parquet. As the duchess glided past in a flawless foxtrot, an audible gasp escaped several of the Nassau ladies, while others couldn't help but gape at her exquisite gown and jewels. The duke's Christmas ball was unquestionably the high point of the season, and the dance floor was soon overflowing with couples, turning and spinning to the up-tempo beat. Hamilton danced cheek-to-cheek with Evelyn, observing with a wry smile the antics of the local Bay Street Boys and their déclassé wives as they tried to outshine one another. He also noticed the rather appalling way Alfred de Marigny groped an attractive, middle-aged woman as they slowly danced past, while young Nancy was unhappily paired with de Videlou. The warmth of Evelyn's cheek, the fragrance of her perfume, the sensation of her body pressing close soon overwhelmed his awareness of everything around them. As the music died away, Hamilton stared into

Evelyn's eyes, reluctant to let go of her hand, and said, 'Let's get a breath of fresh air.' Evelyn, who clearly knew her way around the mansion, led him down a quiet corridor, passing through French doors onto a veranda overlooking the lawn and gardens. Without illumination, they stood in the shadows, enjoying the cool night air and silence, broken only by the chirr of crickets and an imperceptible calypso melody in the distance. Leaning against a column, Hamilton stared into the darkness. 'This is perfect,' he said, turning to face Evelyn. 'I'd about had my fill of that crowd.'

'Perhaps you're beginning to understand,' she said, 'what it's like for me here.'

He thought about saying, why not come with me back to the US? To New York, or Miami? In the next instant he realized how wrong it would be, and a wave of guilt passed over him.

'Tom,' she said with a concerned look, 'is something wrong?'

'It's just,' he said with a sigh, 'that I'm crazy about you, and I shouldn't be.'

Taking a half-step toward him, she clasped her arms around him and kissed him, lightly at first but then with a rising passion they both surrendered to.

'Evelyn,' he whispered when they broke at last, 'I—'

'Hush,' she said, as she stared urgently into his eyes, 'don't say it.' She kissed him again, and he held her tight, his hands wandering from her bare shoulders to the nape of her neck that elicited a murmur of delight. 'Let's go,' she said softly. 'Will you take me home?'

Pulling away slightly while he held her, he looked questioningly into her eyes. He was about to answer when suddenly he was aware of motion at the other end of the veranda. 'What is it?' she whispered. Hamilton stared into the darkness, able to make out the orange tip of a cigarette and the outline of someone in the shadows. He whispered, 'We've got company.' In the next instant, a set of French doors flew open, and another form appeared in the darkness.

'So there you are!' a man said angrily. He slammed the doors.

'Yes, here I am.' Hamilton recognized the voice of Alfred de Marigny, who added drunkenly, 'And what of it?'

'I saw you with your hands all over that woman,' said the other man. From his tone of voice Hamilton surmised that it was Sir Harry Oakes.

'We were dancing,' said de Marigny. 'This is a dance, is it not?'

'Well, Nancy saw it too, and the poor kid's all upset.'

'Oh, it's Nancy you're concerned about?' asked de Marigny sarcastically.

'You're goddamn right! I know your type, de Marigny. You're nothing but a sex fiend.'

'After what *you* did to poor Nancy, don't think you can lecture me—'

'What *I* did?'

'Murdering her baby,' said de Marigny in a louder voice. 'It broke her heart.'

'You sonofabitch,' said Oakes. 'I should bust your mouth.'

'Do you think I'm afraid of an old man? Hah. You make me laugh.'

'You sorry French bastard. What do you want? Money? I'll pay you money, but I want you out of here, do you hear me? Gone, for good!'

Hamilton, his arm around Evelyn's waist, could dimly see that Oakes had taken a step toward de Marigny and had menacingly raised his fist.

'I don't want your money, you old fool,' replied de Marigny. 'You can't pay enough money for what you've done to Nancy and me. Why don't you just leave us alone?'

'I'm not done with you, de Marigny,' said Oakes, advancing another step. 'Nobody crosses me and gets away with it,' he snarled, shoving de Marigny's shoulder. De Marigny suddenly stood up to his full height and pushed the much shorter Oakes backward, who lost his balance.

'Leave me alone!' shouted de Marigny. 'If you bother me again, I'll kill you!'

Evelyn clutched Hamilton, her face pressing against his shoulder. 'Oh, my God,' she whispered. A light came on in the hallway and other voices could be heard. The door opened and Nancy appeared in the pale yellow light, holding a hand to her mouth.

'Oh, Daddy!' she said. 'Freddie, is everything all right?'

'Yes, everything's all right,' said de Marigny sullenly. 'We're going,' he announced, taking her by the arm. Sir Harry watched with a malevolent expression as de Marigny led his daughter away. And then, as he straightened his jacket, he noticed Hamilton and Evelyn standing in the shadows. With an inscrutable look, he turned and quickly walked inside.

'How terrible,' said Evelyn. 'Tom, please, I want to go.'

'Don't worry,' he said, kissing her lightly on the forehead and giving her hand a squeeze. 'I'll have you back at Greycliff in no time.'

Standing under the porch light, Evelyn fished in her handbag for her key. 'There,' she said, taking it out. 'I was hoping not to wake Samuel.' Hamilton nodded, preferring that the servants knew as little as possible about his comings and goings.

'Let me,' he said. He turned the key and followed Evelyn into the darkened entrance hall. She reached for the switch and turned on the light and, with an encouraging smile, took his hand and started up the stairs.

Once they were alone, Evelyn turned on several lamps and said, 'There's ice and glasses in the bar,' she said. 'I'd love a nightcap.' After a few moments she joined him on the veranda.

'I hope Scotch is all right,' he said, handing her a glass.

'Yes,' she said, taking a sip. 'After that nasty encounter, I could use a whisky.'

'Awfully bad blood between those two,' said Hamilton.

'It's a shame the duchess felt compelled to invite de Marigny,' said Evelyn, 'but the aristocracy looks after its own, and he does have a title....'

Hamilton stared into the darkness beyond the railing and then drew close to Evelyn. 'There was something I didn't follow,' he said. 'The part about murdering her baby?'

'According to the gossip,' said Evelyn, 'Nancy was pregnant when they eloped. She was just seventeen, and de Marigny in his thirties and twice-married. Evidently,' Evelyn continued, 'her father spirited her away to a Miami hospital, where they aborted the pregnancy. Despite de Marigny's strenuous objection.'

'I didn't think that was legal,' said Hamilton.

'It isn't. But if you're Sir Harry Oakes ... In any case, the poor girl was disconsolate and has never forgiven her father. Oh, Tom, it's so awful. I thought de Marigny was going to hit him.'

'Let's not talk about it,' said Hamilton. Placing both arms around her, he leaned down to give her a slow kiss that both of them knew would quickly burn out of control. 'Evelyn,' he murmured, 'we shouldn't. Tell me to leave, please.'

'No, no,' she pleaded, fumbling with the studs of his shirt, 'don't leave me.'

Placing both hands gently around her face he kissed her again, surrendering to desire that quickly overwhelmed what was left of his inhibitions or virtuous intentions. She hastily tore open his shirt, running her hands over his back and shoulders while he traced the outline of her breasts beneath the sheer fabric of her gown. 'Mmm,' she said with a shiver. Taking him by the hand, she led him quickly, wordlessly, to her bed.

CHAPTER SEVEN

ROLLING OVER ON his side, Tom Hamilton shivered in the cool draught from the open window and pulled the warm quilt up around his chest. In the darkness, with eyes closed, he dreamily imagined he was back home, in his own bed, not the hotel room which, after more than six weeks, he'd grown weary of … No, he suddenly realized, his eyes snapping open. Where was he? First light glowed outside the shuttered windows, a glow too dim to illuminate the shadows. Clutching the bedcovers, he squinted into the darkness and reached over to pat the sheets next to him. Taking a deep breath, he detected a trace of her perfume, and it all came back to … bringing Evelyn home and then making love for what seemed like hours until they collapsed in contented exhaustion. The vivid memory was accompanied by a sharp jolt of guilt and remorse. If Evelyn were *my* wife, he considered unhappily … But where was Evelyn? Just enough light filtered into the room to make out what presumably was a closet door. Conscious of his nakedness, Hamilton hastily threw back the covers and hurried to the closet where he found a cotton robe on a hook. Switching on a lamp, he discovered his clothes neatly folded on a chair and his wallet, money-clip, and watch laid out on the dresser. Examining himself in the mirror, he was doing his best to straighten his hair when the door opened and Evelyn backed into her bedroom.

'Room service,' she said brightly, holding a tray with orange juice and coffee. 'Too bad,' she added. 'You found your robe. I was rather hoping to breakfast with a naked man.'

'You're up early,' said Hamilton sleepily, as he helped her with the tray.

'I usually am. But for some reason, I awoke this morning feeling *wonderfully* refreshed.'

Hamilton leaned over and kissed her on the cheek. 'You *are* wonderful,' he said. 'Mmm ... smell that coffee.'

'Let's enjoy it on the balcony. It's lovely looking out on the garden this time of day.'

In a sheer peignoir, with her dark hair brushed back and just a touch of make-up, Evelyn seemed even more beautiful than in her ball gown, nestled beside him on the sofa with one slender leg crossed over the other. 'In less than a week,' she said, putting her cup aside, 'it will be Christmas. Mother and Father will be here soon. Tom ... what about you?'

He stared into her eyes, thinking how much he hated the web of deceptions. And how much he wished he could stay, though he knew it meant becoming hopelessly entangled in an affair. 'Well,' he said, 'I've run into something of a brick wall with my plans to buy that property. And frankly, I've got business back home that needs looking after.'

'You're leaving.'

'Evelyn....'

'I knew it.'

'You don't understand. I've never felt this way about anyone before. I know it's wrong, and I was determined not to, but I swear I'm—'

'Don't say it,' she said with a forlorn look. 'If it's Dirk you're worried about, it's not just that we've been apart all this time. The truth is, there never was much ... well, in the way of feeling between us.'

'I've made a mess of things,' said Hamilton, rising from the sofa.

Evelyn stood up and placed her arms around him. 'You've been wonderful, and a gentleman. And you've been honest.' Hamilton gave her a rueful look. 'I just wish you would stay. I don't care how long it lasts ... days, weeks....'

Hamilton held her, running his hand through her hair. 'I know,' he murmured, 'but I can't.'

Pulling away, she looked intensely into his eyes. 'When are you leaving?'

'I'm not sure. A few days, I suppose. There's one more piece of business I need to take care of.' This time the lie was so feeble she must have seen through it. Whatever her thoughts, her expression revealed nothing.

'Tom,' she said softly, 'will you come back? Promise me?'

'I promise.' He kissed her lightly on the lips.

Hamilton felt slightly ridiculous as he pulled up at the British Colonial in Sir Philip's Bentley, wearing the same dinner jacket and rumpled shirt from the night before. Though he managed to make it through the lobby without any disapproving looks, an elderly woman in the elevator stared reprovingly at the smudge of red lipstick on his shirt collar. Grateful when the doors opened, he hurried to his room and went straight for the shower. What he needed, he decided, as he shaved before the fogged-up mirror, was a proper English breakfast.

Seated at a quiet table, Hamilton peered over his plate of poached eggs, crisp bacon, and toast at the two-day old Miami newspaper. 'More coffee, sir?' asked the waiter.

'Sure,' said Hamilton, sliding over his cup without taking his eyes from the paper. According to Red Army dispatches, the German Sixth Army was completely encircled at Stalingrad. It seemed incredible that Hitler had gambled so much and was actually in jeopardy of a major defeat at the hands of the Russians. Despite the heavy losses to U-boats in the Atlantic, the war news that filled the papers at last had something encouraging to report. Hamilton put aside the Miami paper and eagerly read an account of the duke's Christmas bash in the Nassau *Daily Tribune*, with a description of the duchess's ball gown and jewellery and the names of the fortunate few seated at the royal couple's table, including 'Mrs Evelyn Shawcross and companion.' After a final sip of coffee, Hamilton headed through the lobby out onto the hotel drive where the Bentley was parked. After folding down the top, Hamilton turned the key, shifted into gear and drove through town, smiling to himself as he sailed past Government House and onto the highway toward Cable Beach.

As he parked on the gravel drive, Hamilton could see Marnie wading out of the surf after her morning swim, lithe and deeply tanned with her wet hair on her shoulders. She waved as he climbed out and started up the flagstones. From the front hall he walked past Marnie's African grey parrot, which greeted him in a perfect Bahamian dialect, into the blue-tiled living room, where he found Sir Philip in his wheelchair, enjoying a cup of tea and the ocean view. 'Come in, Tom,' he said pleasantly. 'I'm keen to hear about your evening with the Windsors. Ah, darling, there you are.' Marnie, wearing a turban over her damp hair and a terrycloth robe, walked across the room and stopped in front of Hamilton.

'Let me look at you, Tom,' she said. 'All in one piece after an evening with the alluring Mrs Shawcross.' She gave him a knowing look, which Hamilton tried to ignore.

'Come now, darling,' protested Sir Philip, 'he was merely doing his duty. Now, Tom. Tell us all about the duke and the duchess.'

'I'll start with the duchess,' said Hamilton as he slumped on the sofa. 'I was expecting her to be cold and haughty, but she was charming. She's no beauty, but she's got a terrific figure and she's sharp as a tack. I can see how she was irresistible to the old boy.'

'Terrific figure,' said Marnie dismissively. 'With that flat chest, she ought to be wearing men's trousers.'

'It sounds as though you were in a position to observe them more than from a distance,' said Sir Philip.

'As it turned out,' said Hamilton, 'we were seated at their table. Along with Ericsson and his wife and a pleasant enough Scot, a friend of the duke's....'

'Alastair Mackintosh,' said Sir Philip. 'Decent chap. The Windsors are very fond of Mrs Shawcross, which accounts for your having ranked so high in the pecking order.'

'I should say so. Even old Harry Oakes didn't make the cut, or the duchess's Aunt Bessie.'

'A charming lady, from my brief acquaintance,' said Sir Philip.

'I'm impressed,' said Marnie, placing her hand on her husband's arm. 'Something every social climber in town would give his eye teeth for.'

'The duchess was a knockout in this lavender gown, and you should've seen her necklace.'

Marnie responded with an expression of mild curiosity, as she was the only woman in Nassau with jewellery to rival the duchess. 'Sapphires and diamonds,' explained Hamilton. 'God knows how many carats.'

'And what about HRH?' asked Sir Philip. 'Were you able to draw him out?'

'For most of the evening,' said Hamilton, 'he treated us to a discussion of the duck hunting in the Out Islands.'

'He's quite a sportsman,' said Sir Philip.

'But, finally,' said Hamilton, 'I got my chance. After I mentioned my plans for a hotel and casino, Ericsson said, in so many words, over my dead body. And, moreover, the war's not ending any time soon.'

'Fascinating,' said Sir Philip.

'So I turned to the duke and said, maybe there's a way to bring about an early end to the war. He picked right up on it. Rather sanctimoniously, he said the war with Germany was a big mistake, a 'useless struggle', or something like that, and that the Russians are the real enemy.'

'Never one to mince words,' observed Sir Philip.

'And then he finished,' said Hamilton, 'by saying we should try diplomacy, rather than fighting, to end the war with Germany.'

'Well, Tom,' said Sir Philip, 'congratulations. You've confirmed our worst suspicions. What, if anything, did Ericsson have to say about the duke's suggestion?'

'He raised a toast to it,' said Hamilton. 'If I'm right about Ericsson and what I think he's up to—'

'Yes,' said Sir Philip as he stared into the distance. 'You may very well be right about this U-boat base.'

'Well?' said Marnie, looking from her husband to Tom. 'What more can you do? I thought they were sending you back to Washington?'

'They are. I need to make one last reconnaissance trip to Hog Island.'

'Carter and the Chris Craft are at your disposal,' said Sir Philip. 'Just say the word.'

'I'll need a waterproof case for the camera,' said Hamilton. 'And a telephoto lens.'

'I'll see what I can do,' said Sir Philip. 'What do you have in mind?'

'I'll go ashore at night,' said Hamilton, 'and make my way to the construction site. The tricky part will be getting close enough to use the camera. In daylight, of course.'

'An awfully risky scheme,' said Sir Philip with a frown.

'Don't worry,' said Hamilton. 'I'll be fine.'

As dusk fell, Hamilton and Carter grasped the handles of a heavy wooden box and carried it the length of the pier. Hamilton knelt down and removed a pair of powerful binoculars, flashlight, coil of rope, and heavy wire-cutters, which he transferred to the Chris Craft. Lastly, he removed a waterproof case with his 35-mm Hasselblad camera. 'All right,' he said to Carter, 'that should do it.' When midnight had come and gone, Hamilton accepted a thermos of coffee from Sir Philip and walked down to the pier, where Carter blackened his face, neck, and hands with shoe polish. After a final check of his Beretta, Hamilton said, 'OK, let's shove off.' With the sliver of moon low in the sky, the boat was barely visible in the black water. Carter turned the ignition and after a few lethargic revolutions, the powerful engine roared to life. Hamilton took his place in the cockpit as Carter lowered the throttle and turned out to sea. Without running lights, it was almost impossible to distinguish the black water from the night sky, causing Hamilton a disturbing sense of vertigo as the boat knifed into the void.

'Don't worry,' said Carter, sensing Hamilton's unease, 'after a while your eyes will adjust. Besides we've got a nice stretch of open water ahead of us.'

As predicted, Hamilton's eyes soon adjusted to the point he could discern not only the horizon but a low mass of land off the starboard bow and the twinkling lights of Nassau in the distance. As the speedboat planed the gentle seas at 40 knots, he unfolded a rudimentary map in the dim light of the dashboard. 'The coral reef is here,' said Hamilton, pointing to the map. 'Four hundred yards offshore.'

Carter nodded and put the boat into a gentle turn. 'From here on in,' he said, 'we'll take it slow and easy.' He throttled back, and the bow settled into the oncoming waves. By the time they reached the reef, the moon had set and the night was utterly black and still. 'It's a good thing you know where you're going,' said Hamilton as the boat bobbed in the water. 'I can't see a damn thing.'

'Good,' said Carter, as he backed the boat into position. 'That means those guards can't see either.' Positioning the boat on the leeward side of the reef, he said, 'Now,' and Hamilton heaved a heavy anchor from the bow, where it caught and held on the coral. 'All right,' said Carter as he switched off the engine. 'That should hold us.' Hamilton dragged out an inflated rubber boat from the cabin below the bow. Slipping the compass into his pocket, he slung the camera case over his shoulder and loaded the other gear into the inflatable. 'OK,' he said. 'Let's go.' They lowered the boat and slithered over the side, kneeling in the tiny craft as it rose and fell. Carter pointed toward shore and they began to stroke, making as little sound as possible. After five minutes, a pale strip of beach was visible in the starlight, and the boom of the breakers filled the air. Crouching low, they caught a roller, spun sideways and, after a harrowing split second, glided smoothly into the wash. They leapt out and hauled the rubber boat onto the narrow beach. 'So far so good,' whispered Hamilton as he glanced at his watch. 'We've got at least a couple of hours.' Carter slung the binoculars and coil of rope over his shoulder and then helped Hamilton drag the boat under the low branches of a sea-grape. Hamilton crouched on one knee and trained the flashlight on their makeshift map. 'Hurricane Hole should be about a half-mile as the crow flies.' He opened the compass, rotating its radium-coated face. 'This is true north,' he whispered, signalling with one hand. 'If we stay on a bearing of three hundred degrees, we should get close enough to find it.' Closing the compass, he adjusted the strap of the camera case and moved out with Carter close behind him. The dark night was filled with the constant chirr of insects and croaking bullfrogs as the men fought their way through the dense thicket of catclaw, sawgrass, and palmetto. After ten minutes, Hamilton stopped and re-checked the compass. 'We're probably off course,' he whispered. 'Let's try this way.' He started off again, crouching and brushing aside the low hanging branches, peering into the blackness. After another few minutes he halted abruptly. Turning to Carter, he pointed to silvery loops of concertina wire strung along the top of an eight-foot barbed wire fence.

'You figure it's electrified?' whispered Hamilton.

Carter lifted the wire-cutters and brushed the steel tip against a strand of wire. 'No spark,' he observed. He quickly severed four wires, twisted back the dangling strands, and motioned for Hamilton to crawl under. Once they were inside the fence, Hamilton rechecked his compass and said, 'This way.'

Fifteen minutes later, their shirts stained with sweat and faces and hands covered with scratches, the two men halted before a second, clearly electrified fence. Hamilton stared at the multiple strands of smooth wire strung over glass spools. 'We might as well cut it,' said Hamilton with a smile that revealed his white teeth against his blackened face. He quietly dropped to one knee and listened to the faint hum of current. A beam of intense white light suddenly flashed, travelling slowly along the fence line. 'Damn,' he said, ducking back into the brush as the light passed by. 'Searchlights.'

In the protective darkness, Carter scrambled over to the fence and quickly severed the bottom strand with a spark and pop. Gently pushing the live wire out of the way, he slid the gear through the fence and carefully crawled underneath. Within seconds Hamilton was through and standing beside him. He unscrewed the cap of his canteen and took a long swallow before handing it to Carter.

'Thanks,' said Carter as he ran his hand over his mouth. 'Are we getting close?'

Hamilton peered at his watch. 'We must have covered at least a half-mile,' he said. Both men dropped to one knee and stared into the darkness, listening for sounds over the incessant sound of insects and bullfrogs. 'Hear that?' whispered Hamilton.

Carter listened to a deep rumble and the faint sound of men's voices, muffled by the dense foliage. 'Backhoe, maybe,' he said softly, 'or heavy trucks.'

'Let's go,' said Hamilton, rising to his feet. He brushed aside a branch and started walking in a crouch. As they crept forward, the sounds grew increasingly distinct and were soon accompanied by flashes of light through gaps in the brush. 'Looks like a construction site,' said Hamilton as he peered into the distance. 'Working all night.' With Carter close behind, he kept moving until he reached the verge of a wide clearing, illuminated by powerful lights on towers. Dropping to his hands and knees, he motioned for the binoculars. As he ranged the lenses across the clearing, Hamilton quietly described the scene: 'Guard towers, spaced about a hundred yards apart, deuce-and-a-half trucks moving up and down a dirt road, and an overhead crane with a big steel bucket of concrete. Whole thing lit up like a Christmas tree. Hundreds of men, and those same uniformed guards, with rifles.' He handed the binoculars to Carter, who softly whistled as he studied the scene.

'See that big banyan tree,' asked Hamilton, 'on the other side of the clearing?' Carter nodded. 'It's much closer. We can climb up, catch a little sleep and wait till daylight.'

CHAPTER EIGHT

EDGED INTO THE crotch of the sturdy old banyan, Hamilton awoke at the first hint of dawn with the sensation of aching numbness in his limbs. As a light breeze stirred the leaves, he quietly reached for a branch overhead, hoisted himself up, and stretched out his tingling legs. He could just make out Carter's blue shirt and black face on the branch below him. Even in the dim light, Hamilton realized, their hiding place commanded a superb view of Nils Ericsson's mysterious Hurricane Hole. Leaning his back against the trunk, he raised the binoculars, found a gap in the foliage, and focused on the remarkable scene. A wide canal meandered through dense vegetation, disappearing into a massive concrete enclosure, the thick roof of which was a good thirty feet above the water. Inside the structure, Hamilton could make out men on scaffolding under electric lights, while other men in khaki stood outside directing the pouring of concrete from a crane. Swarming like ants, black labourers scrambled to ready wooden forms on the unfinished section of the roof, while others raked and smoothed the last pour under the watchful eyes of armed guards. A convoy of trucks was bringing up fresh supplies of planks, cement, aggregate, and rebar. As many as 500 men, Hamilton estimated, were toiling on the massive construction project.

Hamilton leaned down to hand the binoculars to Carter. 'Take a look,' he said. The rising sun struck the site at just the right angle to brightly illuminate every aspect of the work, reflecting flashes of sunlight from the trucks' windshields and polished steel of the guards' carbines. Hamilton checked his watch and reached for his camera. 'OK,' he said, 'time for some snapshots.' He carefully removed the large, German-made camera and screwed on the tele-photo lens. He peered through the view-finder and carefully calibrated the focus, amazed at the clarity of the images that filled the Zeiss lens, even the bored expression of a guard smoking a cigarette. Hamilton snapped the shutter, advanced the film, and then took a rapid-fire sequence, capturing the loading areas, stock-piles, the workmen on the scaffolding, and the armed guards. When the last exposure was gone, he quickly disassembled the camera and fitted it back in its waterproof case. 'OK,' he said. 'Let's get the hell out of here.'

With the camera over his shoulder, Hamilton began his careful descent with Carter climbing down below him. Back on solid ground, they stretched their aching legs and quickly surveyed their surroundings. 'Let's head straight into the brush,' said Hamilton, 'until we hit the fence line, rather than try to back-track.' Carter nodded and followed in a low crouch as Hamilton plunged into the dense thicket. Looking out for water moccasins as they slogged through shallow, stagnant pools, they made better time than in the darkness and reached the electrified fence in under ten minutes. Hamilton flipped open his compass as he swatted away swarms of mosquitoes. 'If we go to the left,' he said, 'it should take us in the direction we came from last night.'

Carter looked uneasily up and down the clearing. 'We better hurry,' he said. 'I wouldn't be surprised if they patrol this fence.'

Hamilton started off at a rapid pace. Unhindered by brush, they were moving quickly when suddenly they heard a shrill whistle, followed by men shouting. 'Jesus,' said Hamilton, as he instinctively ducked into the undergrowth. After two more blasts of the whistle, a siren began to blare. 'They must have found where we cut the wire,' Hamilton whispered to Carter, whose wide eyes betrayed his fear. Tossing away the binoculars, Carter motioned toward the fence and said, 'Let's crawl under.' They hurried to the fence, knelt down, and Carter quickly severed the two bottom strands. As Hamilton dropped to the ground, a shot rang out, the slug smacking into the fence post above his ear. A quick glance revealed a group of uniformed men, one on horseback, a hundred yards down the fence line. In the next instant, a second shot rang out, striking Carter in the thigh and knocking him sideways like a heavy kick.

Hamilton stared at the dark red stain spreading on Carter's trouser leg. Hearing hoofbeats and more shots that kicked up puffs of dust, he crouched behind a palmetto and grabbed the Beretta from his waistband. Taking careful aim, he fired two rapid shots at an approaching rider, striking him in the chest and hurling him backward. When the horse reared, Hamilton sprang up, seized the reins, and swung into the saddle, expertly turning the horse toward Carter, who was lying on his side clutching his thigh. 'Let's go,' shouted Hamilton, leaning down to take Carter's hand, hauling him to his feet and up onto the horse behind him. Hamilton spurred the animal down the fence line with Carter hanging on for dear life. Once they were safely out of sight, Hamilton glanced at Carter's leg, where the dark stain had spread to his shoe.

Hamilton reined in the horse with a reassuring pat. To his left he could see what appeared to be a trail he guessed led to the beach. He gave the horse a kick, sending him down the narrow trail at a canter. Before long a patch of turquoise appeared in the distance. 'Hang on,' yelled Hamilton over the hoofbeats and the blaring siren. 'We're almost there.' Moments later the trail disappeared into the sand dunes and sea-grape. Hamilton slowed the horse and took a quick look up and down the deserted beach. 'Damn,' he swore. 'Where did we leave the boat?'

'Look,' said Carter, pointing to the surf. 'The reef!'

Shielding his eyes, Hamilton gazed over the lines of rollers until he could distinguish waves breaking over the coral. With a slap of the reins, the horse broke into a trot on the soft sand as Hamilton scanned the vegetation bordering the beach. He brought the animal to an abrupt stop. 'There it is.' Quickly dismounting, he helped Carter down and then gave the horse a slap on the rump, sending him galloping away. He ripped off his shirt and tore it into strips, fashioning a tourniquet at Carter's groin and binding the wound. Hamilton dragged the rubber boat from the sea-grape and, with Carter hanging on to his shoulder, hauled it into the surf. After helping Carter to sit, he unslung the camera and then scrambled in and began to paddle. After cresting one breaker that filled the craft with seawater, he stroked steadily, conscious of the hot sun on his back.

Hamilton paused to look back. A group of men stood on the beach beside an open-air vehicle. 'Damn,' he muttered, paddling even harder. He lunged for the ladder at the stern of the Chris Craft, reached for the camera, and scrambled over the transom. As he leaned down to pull Carter on board he was relieved to see the men driving down the beach in the opposite direction.

'Thanks,' Carter managed to say, before he slumped on the seat and passed out. Checking his faint pulse, Hamilton was relieved when Carter opened eyes with a look of vague recognition.

'OK,' said Hamilton, 'just take it easy.' He sprang into the cockpit and reached under the dash for the key. Aware of the sound of another boat in the distance, he pumped the throttle and the powerful V-8 engine roared to life. With a glance at the anchor chain, he gunned the engine and threw the boat into reverse, lurching backward as the bolts holding the chain ripped free. Quickly shifting, Hamilton spun the wheel and jammed down the throttle. As the Chris Craft gained speed, planing across the glassy sea, he looked over his shoulder at a patrol boat rounding the eastern point of the island. Hamilton glanced at the speedometer, the needle trembling at 45 m.p.h., a speed the patrol boat could never match.

Exhausted and craving water, Hamilton stared at the weathered boards as the boat drifted alongside Sir Philip's pier, where a massive frigate bird gave him an indifferent stare from its perch on a piling. He shut down the engine and turned back to Carter, who was lying motionless in the stern, but breathing normally. After checking his makeshift bandage, Hamilton climbed up on the dock, fastened a line to the bow cleat and loped up to the house. Marnie, who'd watched their return from the living room window, appeared on the terrace and ran down to meet him.

'It's Carter,' said Hamilton, gasping for breath. 'He's been shot.'

'I'll get Henry,' said Marnie, starting back toward the house.

Finally, after helping the broad-shouldered Bahamian carry Carter into a waiting car, Hamilton wearily returned to the boat for his camera. As he jumped down from the pier, he imagined Colonel Donovan's surprise when he saw the detailed images. Lifting up the case, he watched in disbelief as a small stream of seawater poured out. 'What the hell,' he murmured, as he examined the case, discovering a bullet hole in the side. He popped open the clasps and removed the water-soaked Hasselblad. 'Ruined,' he said, fighting the impulse to heave the camera into the sea.

After washing the grime of Hog Island and shoe polish from his face and hands, Hamilton changed into fresh clothes and found Sir Philip on the sun-dappled terrace, staring serenely out at the sparkling sea. Once Hamilton had drawn up a chair, Henry appeared and placed a tray in front of him with a plate of scrambled eggs, fried grouper, and hash-browns.

'I've taken the liberty of ordering your breakfast,' said Sir Philip.

'Thanks,' said Hamilton with a sigh, 'though I'm not sure I've got much appetite.'

'You'll need the nourishment,' said Sir Philip. 'And then you can give me a full report.'

'I feel terrible about Carter,' said Hamilton. 'Maybe I was over-confident.'

'Don't be absurd,' said Sir Philip. 'It's a wonder you managed to get him back alive. Marnie examined the wound and assures me he'll be fine, with a transfusion and injection of antibacterials. The bullet missed the femur and the artery.'

'Thank God.' Hamilton sampled the eggs and fish and then, feeling ravenous, greedily attacked his plate. Putting aside his fork, he pushed back from the table and looked at Sir Philip. 'What Ericsson is building,' he said after a pause, 'is a first-class submarine base for the Jerries.'

'You're certain?'

'Absolutely. They've dredged a canal wide enough for the latest class U-boats, the big VII-Cs, into these massive concrete pens. The roof has to be ten feet thick, reinforced concrete. We watched them pouring a section.'

'Where do you suppose he's able to find the re-bar?'

'Not only re-bar,' said Hamilton between mouthfuls, 'but the aggregate, lumber, the whole shooting match. Obviously, he's using that ship of his to bring in all the supplies, probably from Mexico. Tampico or Veracruz would be my guess.'

'This large concrete structure ... there's no other explanation?'

'No. Given the size, the height over the water, the flat roof, like a bunker, easy to camouflage. If only I'd managed to get out the photographs.'

'Yes, a pity. But that camera may have spared you from a bullet in the back.' Hamilton nodded as he took another hearty bite. 'Well, Tom,' said Sir Philip, 'I agree that what you've described are submarine pens. How close are they to completion?'

'Weeks, with the number of labourers working on the project. A month at most.' The door from the living room opened, and Marnie appeared, looking worn out, with no make-up, in shorts and a wrinkled blouse.

'How is your patient?' asked Sir Philip as Hamilton drew up another chair.

'He was out by the time we got him to the hospital. But he came around when they got some plasma into him. The biggest risk now is infection, but frankly, the saltwater should have done a lot of good.'

'What did you tell them?' asked Hamilton. 'I mean, how did you explain...?'

'Another Bahamian with a gunshot wound?' said Marnie with a wry smile. 'The British doc at the hospital just shrugged.'

'The usual condescending attitude, I'm sorry to say,' commented Sir Philip.

'At least they admitted him,' said Marnie. 'Which is more than I can say for our hospitals back home.' She wearily ran her hands through her thick blonde hair. 'The wound should heal, but he's lost a lot of blood, and is totally exhausted.'

'Carter's a remarkable individual,' said Sir Philip. 'A Jamaican serving with the local police when I found him.' He took a briar pipe from his jacket and began filling it from a small leather pouch. 'Mr Hamilton has deduced, darling, that a U-boat base is under construction on Hog Island.' He struck a match and cupped it over the bowl of his pipe.

'Unfortunately,' said Hamilton with a grimace, 'the only proof I had was ruined.'

'The camera, you mean,' said Marnie.

Hamilton nodded.

'What do you suppose Washington will do about it?' asked Sir Philip.

'If this was American soil,' said Hamilton, 'we'd send in the navy and blow the place out of the water, and Ericsson with it. But without proof, without the photos, I'm not sure. Donovan will have to go through all the channels. If it's just my word, do you really suppose the duke will allow any action to be taken against Ericsson?'

'Besides,' said Sir Philip, drawing contentedly on his pipe, 'it would be a mistake to expose your cover.'

'I hadn't thought about that. At least they're not on to me, and don't have a clue that I'm on to them.'

'So what happens now?' asked Marnie. 'We just sit back and wait?'

'I don't know,' said Hamilton glumly. 'I'll do what I can to persuade OSS to take action.' Hamilton gave Sir Philip an admiring look. 'I ought to get going,' he said, rising from his chair. 'There's no way I can thank you, for everything.' He reached down to take Sir Philip's firm grip.

'You're leaving?' asked Marnie. She stood up and walked over to him.

Looking into her dark-brown eyes, Hamilton nodded and said, 'Yes, Marnie, I'm afraid so. A plane's coming for me this afternoon.'

'Tom,' she said, 'will you come back?'

'I don't know. I'm not sure where they'll send me. But some day I'm sure I'll be back.'

'Tom,' said Sir Philip after a moment, 'tell Donovan that under no circumstances should he place any confidence in the Duke of Windsor. If Ericsson is allowed to complete this project, and the Germans strike, our supply lines will be in great peril. Tell them to *act*, Tom, and the Duke of Windsor be damned.'

Dressed in a blue blazer and charcoal slacks, Hamilton stood under the portico in the cool December breeze waiting for his taxi. Glancing down Bay Street toward Rawson Square, he thought back to his first morning in Nassau, walking down to the wharf to meet Carter. Though he didn't consider himself sentimental, his mind was flooded with memories – lunches on the terrace at Eves, the Christmas Ball at Government House, and Greycliff ... Evelyn by the pool or on the upstairs porch ... A jitney with a fringed top rumbled up the drive, and Hamilton broke into a grin, recognizing the same man who'd driven him to town. As his bags were loaded, Hamilton leaned in and said, 'I need a ride to the airfield.'

'Time to go home, cap'n?' asked the driver with a smile.

'I'm afraid so. But I need to make a quick stop in town.'

'You're the boss. Hop in.'

The driver pulled over at the kerb in front of Greycliff. 'Leave the engine running,' said Hamilton as he climbed out. 'I'll just be a minute.' Glancing at the upstairs bedroom window, he wondered if this would be the last time he would see the gracious home. He hurried up the walk and rang the bell, and after a moment Samuel, wearing his usual white jacket and black tie, appeared.

'Afternoon, Mr Hamilton.'

'Is Mrs Shawcross...?'

'Yes, sir,' he said. 'I'll send for her.'

Hamilton waited in the front hall, examining a framed photograph on a table of Evelyn as a blonde-haired girl, holding the hands of her well-dressed parents. Conscious of someone behind him, he turned to see her standing on the landing, wearing a pale blue dress belted at the waist.

Their eyes met, and for a moment neither spoke. 'I wasn't sure I'd see you again,' she said finally. 'Before you left.'

'You didn't think I'd leave without saying goodbye?'

'Perhaps.' She walked the rest of the way down the stairs and took both his hands. 'You won't stay at least till tomorrow?'

'No … Actually, there's a taxi waiting outside.'

'Oh, God.' She threw her arms around him, burying her face on his chest. At last she looked up at him and said, 'It's something about the war. I know it is.'

'What do you mean?'

'Why you're leaving. Something you haven't told me, but I don't care.'

'Don't worry,' he said firmly, his arms encircling her slender waist. 'I'm just going home to look after some business.'

'Whatever it is, just don't get yourself killed.' She pulled away and brushed her tears.

'Evelyn, it's all my fault. I should never have—'

'Don't say it,' she interrupted. 'Merry Christmas, darling.'

He leaned over and lightly kissed her. 'Goodbye.' He turned and let himself out.

CHAPTER NINE

ANDS CLASPED BEHIND his field-grey tunic, Major
Wolfgang Krebs slowly paced the upstairs sitting room at
Shangri-La, heedless of the spectacular view of the sunset,
his face a mask of concentration. Apart from the tap of his
infantryman's boots on the plank floor, the only sound was the whir
of the ceiling fans. Halting abruptly, Krebs withdrew a watch from
his pocket and checked the time. 'I say,' he asked the servant in the
corner of the room, 'you're certain Herr Ericsson knows I'm here?'

'*Ja, gewiss,*' replied the servant without averting his steady gaze,
'quite certain.'

'Hmph,' snorted Krebs, resuming his pacing.

Fifteen minutes later, Nils Ericsson appeared in the doorway,
immaculate in a dinner jacket with a starched shirtfront and
mother-of-pearl studs, his silver hair glistening with oil and his
round face suffused with a rosy glow. 'Ah, Krebs, there you are,' he
said in German.

Krebs halted and assumed a martial stance, with his hands at his
sides and the heels of his boots together. '*Guten abend,*' he said with
a nod.

'Sorry to be late,' said Ericsson as he strode across the room and
gave Krebs a firm handshake. 'I was on the telephone with my agent
in Tampico. Johann,' he said, turning to the servant, 'bring my
drink. Major? What will it be?'

'You have schnapps?' enquired Krebs.

'Of course.' Once the servant was gone, Ericsson motioned to his guest to sit on the sofa while he chose an over-stuffed armchair. 'Now, Major,' he said, 'tell me what you hear of the situation in Stalingrad. I know only what I read in the American newspapers.'

The young German officer stiffened and a slight blush appeared on the fair skin of his neck. 'The situation is dire,' he replied. 'The Sixth Army is completely encircled. The Führer insists there will be no surrender, but I don't imagine our troops can hold out much longer.'

'So it's true,' said Ericsson with disgust. 'What a disaster.'

Krebs nodded. 'The word within the army is that the Russians fight like devils. You kill two, and a third appears. And the winter conditions ... *Mein Gott im Himmel.*' The servant appeared with a tray and served each of them a tumbler of clear liquid, chilled vodka for the host and schnapps for his guest.

'*Skaal*,' said Ericsson, reaching out to clink glasses. 'Well,' he said, after taking a sip, 'after this set-back on the Eastern Front, it would place great pressure on the German Army if the Americans and British open a second front in the West.'

'Yes,' agreed Krebs, 'as in the last war. Something the Führer vowed would never happen.'

'It would be impossible for the Allies to stage an invasion of France without bringing virtually all of the equipment and supplies, to say nothing of the men, across the Atlantic.' He swirled his glass and took another sip. 'And therefore,' he concluded, 'the attacks on their Atlantic convoys offer the best protection against a second front.'

'I quite agree,' said Krebs, leaning forward to rest his arms on his knees. 'Which is why the operation here has such obvious importance. With our own U-boat base in the Caribbean, we can prevent fuel from the refineries on the Gulf Coast and Trinidad from ever reaching Great Britain.'

'Which brings us to the status of Hurricane Hole.'

Joined by the chief of his khaki-clad security force, Ericsson led Major Krebs to the rear of the villa where they boarded an open-air staff car for the short drive along the channel from the sea to the massive U-boat pens. Exiting the vehicle on a concrete apron, Ericsson and Krebs followed the security chief inside the brightly illuminated structure.

'As you can see,' explained the chief, 'we have berths for five boats.' Looking up, he said, 'The roof has a thickness of ten feet, built with reinforced concrete. We shall cover it with a blanket of soil, completely camouflaged from detection by enemy aircraft. We have loading cranes for torpedoes, underground fuel tanks, and refrigerated meat lockers.'

'When will it be ready?' asked Krebs, as his boots echoed in the empty space.

'The building is essentially complete,' replied Ericsson. 'But more time is needed for the barracks for the crews and a dining-hall. And to complete the canal across the island. In another six to eight weeks, we should be ready for the Kriegsmarine. When,' he added with a smile, 'your men will swing into action.'

'Very well,' said Krebs grimly, 'we shall be ready.'

Later in the evening, following dinner in Shangri-La's elegant dining room, Ericsson sat alone with Krebs, enjoying a snifter of French cognac. Krebs withdrew a cigar from his breast pocket, bit off the tip and allowed a servant to light it. 'I've been meaning to ask,' he said, expelling a cloud of smoke, 'if you've experienced any security breaches?' He swirled his cognac.

A dark look briefly clouded Ericsson's face. 'Well, Major, I intended to bring that up. We had one incident.'

Krebs gave him curious look and took another pull on his cigar.

'Last week,' Ericcson continued, 'just before Christmas, my men found a break in the security fence and discovered two intruders. During the attempted capture, one of my men was killed, and unfortunately the intruders managed to escape.'

'Did they observe what you're building here?'

'No doubt they did. We recovered a pair of binoculars, wire-cutters, and a small rubber boat. All in all, a very professional operation.'

'British commandos, in all likelihood,' said Krebs. 'Did your men get a look at them?'

Ericsson smiled unexpectedly. 'The security detail reported them as local Bahamians but one of our patrol boats sighted a speedboat in the vicinity at about the same time, and the driver of the boat was as white as you or I.'

'Interesting,' said Krebs as he puffed on his cigar. 'Perhaps they blackened their faces, a common tactic.'

'Perhaps,' said Ericsson. 'My hunch is that the man in the boat was Hamilton.'

'Hamilton? Ah, yes. The oilman from Texas.'

'Correct. I met the man, actually, at the duke's Christmas ball.'

Krebs stared impassively and took a sip of cognac. 'What is it,' he asked, 'that makes you think he was involved?'

'Because,' Ericsson replied, as he removed a cigarette from the case in his pocket, 'of an arrangement I have with an Englishwoman. She's keeping an eye on Hamilton and supplied me with some quite useful information.' He paused for a servant to light his cigarette. 'A telephone number,' he said after inhaling the smoke, 'taken from his wallet with the notation "Washington." '

'Were you able to trace the number?'

'Yes, with the help of the Spanish Embassy. To an inconspicuous office building on K Street – are you familiar with Washington? No? Nor I. A man sent round to investigate was unable to gain admittance. Very tight security.'

'What do you make of it?' asked Krebs as he reached for the decanter.

'Some sort of intelligence operation. Presumably, Hamilton's control is located there. So this business of developing a hotel on Hog Island is rubbish, just a cover.'

'Well,' said Krebs with a concerned look, 'what have you done about it?'

'Hamilton's gone,' replied Ericsson, expelling a cloud of smoke from his nostrils. 'He left the very next day, by private plane.'

'So,' said Krebs, 'the Americans may be aware of our plans.'

'It's possible, but by no means certain. But don't lose sight of who's in charge in the Bahamas. If need be, I can convince the duke that Hamilton's story is just some cock and bull tale. And besides, if he ever shows his face again in Nassau, he's a dead man.'

'All the same,' said Krebs, 'we'd better move quickly. And what about this woman? Are you certain of her loyalty?'

'Mrs Shawcross?' Ericsson smiled and drew deeply on his cigarette. 'Such a beauty. I have complete confidence in her, but not because of any sympathy to our cause.'

'No? What then?'

'Because if she betrays us in even the smallest way, it will mean the certain death of her husband.' Krebs shot his host a puzzled look. 'You see, Major,' Ericsson continued, 'Evelyn Shawcross's husband is a staff officer in Cairo. And he's one of your finest agents, supplying Rommel with useful information about the British Eighth Army. He was a student leader of the British Fascists before the war, but kept a low profile and managed to slip into the army. And so,' said Ericsson with a chuckle, 'our bargain with Mrs Shawcross is quite simple: co-operate with us in Nassau ... or else your husband will be exposed to the British ... and summarily shot.'

Hamilton shivered in the icy wind as he mounted the steps to a large brick building in one of the shabbier neighbourhoods of central Washington. Almost a week had passed since he'd left Nassau in the twin-engine Cessna, bound for Miami where he'd boarded a train; spending three miserable days in stuffy railway compartments overflowing with young soldiers on leave; catching a few hours' sleep on the hard benches of the stations on his way north. Wearily pulling open the heavy door as another gust showered him with freezing rain, Hamilton entered the dimly lit lobby. A rather plain young receptionist put her cheap paperback aside and looked at him over her tortoiseshell frames. As Hamilton took off his hat and topcoat, her expression brightened at the sight of the tall, handsome man with the incongruously suntanned face.

'May I help you?' she said with a smile.

Hamilton glanced around the drab lobby, noting the absence of anything suggesting the nature of the office; no flag, portrait of FDR, or even an appeal to buy war bonds. Directly behind the receptionist were heavy oak doors, and he had the distinct feeling that somehow he was being watched. 'Good morning,' he said pleasantly. 'I'm Tom Hamilton. You can call Betty and tell her I'm here to see the boss.'

After a brief interval, a tall, severe looking woman in horn-rims appeared through the doors behind the receptionist. Without a word, Hamilton walked around the desk, where she stood holding the door open. Closing it behind them, the woman stopped and gave Hamilton an appraising look. 'Well, Tom,' she said, 'you're looking awfully tan and fit. Have you had a nice holiday?'

'Sure,' he said to Colonel Donovan's executive secretary, 'except for the people shooting at me.' They took the lift to the fourth floor and proceeded to a suite where plush carpets, walnut furniture and framed English fox hunting prints had more the look of a law firm than the office of the chief of the secret intelligence service of the United States. Hamilton waited with his coat over his arm as Betty opened the door and said, 'Colonel ... I have Mr Hamilton.'

'Send him in.'

She stood aside and let Hamilton enter the spacious corner office. William J. Donovan – known as 'Big Bill' or 'Wild Bill' for his large size and somewhat erratic temperament – rose from his chair and reached across his wide, cluttered desk. 'Hello, Tom,' he said, with a firm handshake. 'Have a seat.'

Hamilton tossed his coat over the back of a leather upholstered armchair and settled in the one next to it.

Donovan smoothed the waistcoat of his suit and slumped in his chair. 'Well,' he said, fixing Hamilton in his piercing blue eyes, 'what are we up against in the Bahamas?'

Hamilton cleared his throat and said, 'A German U-boat base.'

'What?' said Donovan. 'A U-boat base?'

'Nils Ericsson is building it for the Germans on an uninhabited island across from Nassau.'

'You can't be serious.'

'I've seen it with my own eyes. The word in Nassau is that Ericsson's building a marina for his yachts strong enough to withstand a direct hit from a hurricane. They call it Hurricane Hole. I was able to penetrate the security and reconnoitre the site. An enormous construction project, using Bahamian labour, with German armed guards.'

'German?' Donovan eyed Hamilton sceptically, pressed the intercom and said, 'Betty, would you bring me another cup?' Turning back to Hamilton, he said, 'OK, Germans guarding this construction project at … what did you call it?'

'Hurricane Hole. Anyway, Colonel, when I was able to get close enough for a good look, it turned out he's building submarine pens, with reinforced concrete thick enough to take a direct hit from a five hundred-pound bomb. They've dredged a deep channel from the sea. He has as many as five hundred men working in round-the-clock shifts. And they ought to be finished in about a month.'

'Hamilton,' said Donovan, running a hand over his wide forehead, 'I'm finding all this a bit difficult to swallow. How could Ericsson build something on such a vast scale without the British getting wind of it? And where would he get the materials?'

'The security's tight. Armed guards at the site – and they *are* krauts – and patrol boats with machine-guns to keep anyone curious away. And Ericsson has this motor-yacht that's plenty big enough to bring in the necessary supplies, probably from Mexico.' Hamilton paused as Donovan's secretary entered, placed a cup of coffee on his desk and wordlessly walked out. 'But more importantly,' Hamilton continued, leaning forward, 'the governor has made it clear it's hands off as far as Ericsson is concerned.'

'The governor,' repeated Donovan, blowing lightly across the surface of his cup. 'Oh, you mean the duke….'

'That's right, the Duke of Windsor. The two are close. So Ericsson can get away with murder, literally, right under the noses of the British.'

Donovan took a sip of coffee and gazed at Hamilton. 'It doesn't add up,' he said. 'We've spent all this money to build the Brits an airbase down there, with a full squadron of Spitfires. And they've got an army garrison. What's the use of this sub base, if in fact, that's what it is?'

'The garrison is nothing more than a company of Highlanders whose main function is to show up with their kilts and bagpipes for ceremonial occasions. As for the RAF base, Sir Philip tells me they're using it to train green pilots. Hardly a man with any combat experience.'

'Are you suggesting the Germans might actually attack Nassau?'

'Absolutely,' said Hamilton. 'And look at what they'd get? Not only bomb-proof pens for their Caribbean U-boats but a fully equipped airfield.'

Donovan frowned and rubbed his chin.

'But that's not all,' added Hamilton.

Narrowing his eyes, Donovan said, 'How do you mean?'

'If the Germans take Nassau, which I think they could do rather easily, think what else they'd be getting. *The Duke of Windsor*. Just imagine the propaganda possibilities if they had the former king under house arrest, conveniently situated to broadcast appeals to his countrymen to come to their senses and negotiate an end to this tragic war with Germany.'

'Jesus, Hamilton,' muttered Donovan. 'I don't like the sound of this. What does Sassoon think?'

'He's convinced the duke is all for a negotiated peace, but that he'll take his cue from Halifax, here in Washington. But if the Germans seize Nassau, and are holding the duke and duchess, think about the public reaction in England. It could be the perfect catalyst for Halifax and the other doves to push for a deal. Sir Philip maintains that after the slaughter of the last war, that bunch doesn't have the stomach for an invasion of France.'

Donovan took a deep breath and slowly exhaled. 'The key to all this, Hamilton,' he said, 'is the construction of this so-called Hurricane Hole. The rest is pure conjecture. Intriguing, but still conjecture. But you've actually seen the construction site. What about proof? Have you got recon photos?'

Hamilton ran his hand through the patch of grey hair at his temple. 'I *did* have photographs that proved beyond any doubt what Ericsson's building. But we were jumped by his guards and in the mêlée, a rifle round pierced the camera case, so when our boat was swamped, the case filled with seawater and the photos were—'

'Ruined.' Donovan shook his head. 'With only your word to go on, the duke is certain to reject the story. There's no way we could persuade the Brits to take action. Not now, at any rate. It's too damned hypothetical.'

Hamilton nodded glumly.

'Well,' said Donovan, 'I'd planned to send you to Peru—'

'But, sir—'

'I'll think about it, Hamilton,' said Donovan, raising a hand.

'I've got to get back to Nassau, sir.'

Donovan studied Hamilton's earnest expression. 'Is there some reason,' he asked, 'you're in such a hurry to go back, apart from stopping this German invasion?'

'Sir? I'm afraid I'm not following you.'

'A woman, for instance?' Donovan steepled his fingertips at his chin.

Hamilton smiled, beginning to appreciate why Donovan was regarded as such a shrewd lawyer. 'To answer your question,' he replied, 'she – an Englishwoman I met – is one of the best things going for us. She's very close to the duke and duchess, and also to Ericsson.'

'Well, be careful – assuming I decide to send you back. I know your reputation with the ladies. Take the next week finding out everything you can from R & A about Ericsson's operations in Mexico and South America. And then I'll decide.' Donovan shook his large head. 'If you're right, Tom ... God help us.'

CHAPTER TEN

HE DISTINCTIVE *pop* of a tennis ball on a tightly strung racquet floated across the lawn at Westbourne, Sir Harry Oakes's rambling estate on Cable Beach. A lanky young man wearing a snap-brim fedora slightly back on his head, his sleeves rolled up in the late morning heat, paused along the path to listen to the sounds of the match. He smiled inwardly at Sir Harry's regular tennis game with the pro he'd brought down from Fort Lauderdale, an older fellow who took care almost never to hit to Sir Harry's backhand and did a fair job of acting that he was just unable to get to the drop shots Oakes was fond of placing at the net. The young man continued along the path, listening to the *pop*, and Sir Harry's gasps and grunts.

'Whew!' exclaimed Oakes. 'You almost had me. What's that make it? Forty-fifteen?'

'Right,' answered the pro, whose white-clad form was visible through the dark-green screen enclosing the clay court. 'Set point, Mr Oakes.'

The visitor walked unobtrusively up to the gate and watched through a gap in the screen as Oakes served the ball ineffectually to his opponent, who easily returned it to Oakes's forehand. Evidently tiring of the contest, the pro drilled Sir Harry's return into the net, smiled and said, 'Good match, Mr Oakes. Remember your foot-work. Keep moving.'

Oakes looked patronizingly at the pro and took a handkerchief from his pocket to pat his brow as he walked toward the gate. As Oakes approached, the young man lifted the clasp and swung open the gate. 'Nice work, Harry,' he said with a grin. 'You beat the old boy damn near every time.' Oakes responded with a malevolent glare that melted into a bemused expression.

'You know me, Charley,' he said, with his racquet over his shoulder. 'I like to win. Hot out here,' he added as he squinted at the sun. 'What do you say we get a beer, and you can fill me in.'

Oakes repaired with his visitor to the quiet library in the east wing of the mansion, a room filled with leather-bound volumes he'd never bothered to open, let alone read, that created the ambience desired by the adopted English baronet. Oakes rang for Jenkins, the English butler, who shortly appeared in the arched doorway. 'Bring us a couple of Red Stripes,' commanded Oakes, 'ice cold the way I like 'em.'

'Yes, sir,' said the butler with a deferential bow.

'Now,' said Oakes, when the butler disappeared, 'how was your trip? Any luck with the boys from Miami?'

Charley Katz, a deceptively pleasant-looking man in his early 30s, served as the unofficial director of Oakes's security operation. Lowering himself into a comfortable armchair, he said, 'Well, Harry,' adopting a casual tone that no one else would dare use, 'Havana is pretty swell after being stuck on this crummy little island.'

'What about Lansky?' asked Oakes. 'Were you able to make contact?'

'Meyer Lansky,' said Katz. 'That's quite an operation he's running in Havana. He's got it all, the girls, the nightclubs, big-time casinos. Anyhow, I had a drink with one of his bosses.'

'Good,' said Oakes, walking over to an antique desk and distract-edly picking up a bronze paperweight. 'Did you broach the subject of the Hog Island project?'

'Broach the subject,' said Katz with a little laugh. 'Yeah, you might say so.' Oakes looked at him expectantly. 'I mentioned to him, real casual like, that a certain so-and-so was thinking of building a hotel in Nassau after the war, a first class operation, for the tourists from Miami and back East. And opening a casino next door.'

Oakes put down the paperweight and gave Katz a cold stare. 'Well ... what did he say?'

With a tap on the door, Jenkins appeared, holding a tray with two bottles of Jamaican beer and frosted glasses. 'Here you are, sir,' he said, lowering the glasses onto the desk. 'Shall I pour?' Oakes nodded and Jenkins emptied the bottles with exaggerated concern. Oakes gave Jenkins a dismissive look and, with a tug on his starched shirtfront, the butler strode from the room.

Charley Katz walked over and reached for one of the glasses. 'Cheers,' he said, raising the glass to his lips. Oakes picked up his glass and took a sip. 'Now,' said Katz, 'what did he say?' He laughed again to himself. 'Let's just say he expressed a negative opinion, in somewhat colourful language.'

'Cut the crap, Charley,' said Oakes irritably. 'You can get on my nerves, you know that? Now what did this stooge say?'

'That nobody builds a goddamn fucking casino in the Bahamas. I believe that's the expression he used.'

Oakes snorted. 'He's got his nerve. This is a Crown Colony, after all. Just because that goddamn Jew Lansky can run things in Cuba doesn't mean he can tell *me* what I can and can't do in Nassau.'

'I wouldn't be so sure,' said Katz. He took a long pull on his beer, put down the glass and ran the back of his hand across his mouth. 'This wise guy is nobody's fool. He says, "Who sent you? Who's your boss? Sir Harry Oakes?" '

'Well,' said Oakes defensively, 'surely you didn't—'

'And he says, go back and tell Oakes that Meyer Lansky says, "If he knows what's good for him, stay out of the gambling rackets. Stay out of our goddamn back yard." Quote-unquote.'

Oakes turned to gaze out the window. 'I see,' he said quietly. 'Well,' he said after a moment, turning around to face Katz, 'we'll see about that. I know how to deal with these thugs. I may have to cut him in. Now what about Hamilton? Where does *he* stand?'

'I lost track of Hamilton,' said Katz. 'That plane he took out of here landed in Miami. Where he headed after that is anybody's guess. But he's been gone a couple of weeks, so maybe he decided the hell with it. Just give up on that piece of swampland.'

'Maybe,' said Oakes. 'But I wouldn't be so sure. He's got plenty of dough, and a damned good idea to put a hotel and casino right on that spot. So good, in fact, I intend to do it myself.'

'Well, just in case,' said Katz, sitting casually on the edge of the desk, 'I've got my boys at the airport keeping a lookout for him.'

'If he does come back,' said Oakes, as he paced in front of the bookshelves, 'he still has to deal with me. And what about the Shawcross woman?'

'Hamilton's lady friend? We're keeping a tail on her, like you wanted, though she hasn't been out much since her folks arrived in town.'

'You're sure that she and Hamilton were, ah ...'

'Oh, yeah,' said Katz with a grin. 'We're sure. He left that Bentley parked out in front all night.'

Oakes gave Katz a shrewd look. 'That information might prove very useful. I've got my suspicions about the lovely Mrs Shawcross. I'm especially interested in whether she's had any more contact with Ericsson. Are you checking that angle?'

'Well, Harry, we're trying. But you know it ain't easy—'

'What the hell am I paying you for? Watch her like a hawk. And I want to know the minute that boy Hamilton shows up on this island.'

'Excuse me, sir,' said Jenkins with an obsequious cough. 'Your lunch is served.'

The crunch of fresh snow under Hamilton's shoes and a deep cobalt sky never failed to evoke memories of his boyhood in Oklahoma, walking home from school with his sister, or hunting rabbits in the country on a bright winter day with his dad. Squaring his shoulders, he walked up to the entrance to Washington's venerable Metropolitan Club and opened the intricately carved door. After checking in his coat and hat, he approached the *maitre d'* and said, 'I'm meeting Colonel William Donovan....'

'This way,' said the *maitre d'* without hesitation. Hamilton followed the man through the high-ceilinged lobby where silver-haired men in dark suits or the uniforms of senior army and navy officers were buzzing with the conversation of wartime Washington. Beyond the library, he showed Hamilton to a private dining-room with a fire burning brightly in the corner fireplace. Seated alone, Donovan looked up from his newspaper and said, 'Hello, Hamilton. Have a seat.'

The *maitre d'* asked, 'Something to drink, gentlemen?'

'An Old Fashioned,' said Donovan. He looked every bit the Wall Street lawyer in a navy-blue three-piece suit and regimental tie.

'Beefeater martini, on the rocks,' said Hamilton. He glanced at the nautical brass clock on the mantel, the prints of racing sloops on the walls. 'Very nice,' he said.

Donovan nodded. 'Best food in town. But unless you've got one of these private rooms, there's no decent place to talk, with all the politicians and brass hats. Well, Hamilton … how have you been getting along with the boys in R and A?' In the scant six months OSS had been in existence, Donovan had recruited a large team of academics into the Research and Analysis Department, conducting global economic analysis on a hitherto unheard of scale.

'That stuff's way over my head,' said Hamilton. 'They've just completed a study of the entire German industrial requirement for ball-bearings. But they were helpful in digging into the different enterprises Ericsson has his hands in.'

A uniformed waiter entered the room and served their drinks. 'You gentlemen ready to order?' he asked.

'I'll have the lamb chops,' said Donovan, as Hamilton hurriedly scanned the small printed menu, 'with scalloped potatoes and mixed vegetables.'

'The fried chicken,' said Hamilton.

'*A votre santé*,' said Donovan, lifting his glass.

'Cheers,' replied Hamilton, swirling his martini.

'I understand Ericsson's been active in South America,' said Donovan when they were alone again. 'Particularly Peru.'

'He's back and forth to Lima,' said Hamilton, 'along with trips to Mexico, though we don't know much beyond that.'

'I'm still considering sending you down there,' said Donovan. Hamilton took a sip and looked expectantly across the table. Anticipating Hamilton's objection, Donovan said, 'Nassau's too risky. I've also spoken to Menzies in London and he shares Sir Philip's assessment of the Duke of Windsor.'

'But, sir,' protested Hamilton.

'The British can send in one of their own agents,' continued Donovan.

Hamilton stared absently into the fire, listening to the hiss and pop of the embers as images of Greycliff filled his mind. 'If I might make a suggestion, sir,' he said at length, looking back into Donovan's blue eyes. 'Before sending me off to South America, you might want to speak to Sir Philip. With so much at stake.'

Donovan took a swallow of his drink and said, 'I'll do that. But let's say Sassoon wants you back. You'll have to go undercover. How would you manage that?'

'I've given that some thought. I failed to mention that I actually made some headway buying that property on Hog Island. If I'm right, Ericsson needs it to complete his canal across the island, and Harry Oakes wants it for himself.'

Arching his eyebrows imperceptibly, Donovan said, 'Go on.'

'I could charter a fishing boat out of the Keys and slip back onto the island. And then I could use this solicitor I retained to keep the ball rolling with the land purchase. That ought to stir things up with Ericsson. With my own money, of course.'

'Of course.'

'In the meantime, it would allow me to get some hard evidence about Hurricane Hole, before it's too late.'

'I doubt you'll get another chance to take a close look,' said Donovan thoughtfully. 'But it might be worth a try. You'd have to be very careful. You never know who's keeping tabs on you.' He looked up as the waiter entered with a tray, which he gently lowered onto a stand. 'I'll give Sir Philip a call,' Donovan concluded.

*

After several days of equivocation, Donovan finally made up his mind. Sir Philip's response had been direct and unhesitating: Send Hamilton, without delay. A British SOE agent, assuming there was one to spare, would be utterly useless to him. And so with just enough time to pick up a handy new piece of hardware from the weapons desk and arrange a sizeable transfer of personal funds to an account at the Nassau branch of the Royal Bank of Canada, Hamilton hitched a ride on an army transport south to Tampa, caught the UP passenger train to Miami, rented a sedan and started driving south on Highway A1A. When he reached Key Largo, exhilarated by the tang of sea-salt and glimpses through the palmettos of the turquoise sea, the lurid orange sun was just slipping below the flat horizon. Seeing lights burning in a two-storey frame building, he turned into an oyster-shell parking lot with a faded sign advertising the Blue Marlin Inn. Walking inside, the screen door slamming behind him, it was apparent that the place was virtually empty. A heavy-set woman with a cigarette dangling from her lips lounged on a stool behind the counter, listening to the radio.

'Evening,' said Hamilton, letting his bag drop. 'I need a room for the night.'

'OK,' she said, expelling smoke from her nostrils. 'Ten bucks, in advance.' Her attention reverted to the radio as Hamilton counted out several bills. Scooping up the cash, she produced a brass key. 'Room six, second floor. The john's down the hall.'

'I don't suppose there's some place to get a bite to eat?' he asked. 'Or a drink?'

'There's a beer joint down the road toward the docks.'

'Thanks.' Hamilton reached for his bag and headed for the staircase.

At the nearby lounge he passed the word over a couple of beers among the other customers that he was interested in chartering a fishing boat and had ready cash to pay for it. Approached by three captains from the sport fishing fleet, he settled on terms to charter the largest of the vessels for a day of bill-fishing. After a night tossing on a thin mattress, Hamilton rose in the darkness, quickly dressed, and drove the short distance to a marina crowded with fishing boats. In the darkness, he could make out a light in the chartroom of a vessel moored halfway down the second row. After hefting the duffel bag out of the trunk, he placed the keys under the visor with a note to the rental agency and started for a boat with the name *Mary D* on the stern. The captain was standing at the transom dumping a large sack of ice into the hold. 'Hello,' Hamilton called out in the still morning air. He slung the duffel bag over the side of the 34-foot diesel cruiser and vaulted onto the deck. 'I forgot to ask,' he said as the captain eyed him, 'how much fuel you're carrying.'

'Fuel?' repeated the captain, taking off his cap and scratching his head. 'A hundred and fifty gallons. What of it?'

'Enough to get to Nassau?'

'What are you talking about?'

The first light of dawn faintly illuminated the captain's faded-blue work shirt. 'I need you to take me to Nassau,' said Hamilton in a matter-of-fact way. 'You can refuel for the trip back.'

'And you can shove it. We made a deal for a one-day fishing charter, period.'

Hamilton reached into his pocket for his wallet and withdrew a crisp fifty dollar bill. 'Here's an extra fifty bucks,' he said, holding up the bill. 'Take it or leave it.'

The captain rubbed the stubble on his chin, weighing the offer. 'Fifty bucks?' Hamilton nodded. 'What about the extra fuel?'

'I'll pay for it,' said Hamilton. He unzipped his jacket, revealing the Beretta.

Glancing uneasily from Hamilton's gun to the large duffel bag, the captain said, 'I don't want any trouble, mister.'

'Relax,' said Hamilton. 'Just take me to Nassau and everything will be fine.'

'Well ... OK.' Unexpectedly he thrust out his large, horny hand

and gave Hamilton a quick handshake. 'See to those lines,' said the captain, turning for the chartroom, 'and we'll shove off.'

Seated comfortably in the fighting chair with his shoes on the transom, Hamilton stared out at the long ribbon of wake that stretched to the horizon, enjoying the warm sun on his face and bare torso. With a glance at his watch, he jumped up, grabbed his shirt from the back of the chair and started up the ladder to the flying bridge. Making almost twenty knots, the *Mary D* rolled gently on the mounded seas, a motion that seemed wildly exaggerated on the platform high above the deck. When he reached the small bridge, the captain was keeping an eye on the compass and a steady hand on the helm.

'Another hour and we should be there,' he said.

Hamilton gazed out over the mottled blue sea. Flinching with the pitch of the bow, he glanced dizzily over the side as a school of bright yellow flying fish sailed gracefully over the waves.

'My kind of charter,' said the captain with a grin. 'No lines to bait, no fish to clean.'

'I think I'll go below,' said Hamilton. 'Let me know when you see land, and I'll show you where we're headed.'

Hamilton spread out a chart of the shoreline of New Providence Island on the chartroom table. He studied the chart, running a finger along a line from Prince Georges Wharf to Cable Beach and the approximate location of Sir Philip's pier. He glanced up at the sound of the captain on the ladder rungs. After checking his gauges and throttling down the engine, the captain smiled briefly at Hamilton. 'If you look out the starboard porthole,' he said, 'you can just make out the shoreline.' As Hamilton peered out across the calm seas, the captain reached into a locker and extracted a bottle of beer. 'Now just where are we going?' he asked as he popped off the cap.

'Cable Beach,' said Hamilton, 'on the north-west side of the island.' He tapped a finger on the chart. 'Friend of mine has a place there, with a hundred-foot pier.'

The captain spread his calloused hands on the table. The colour of the chart faded from medium blue to the palest aqua as Hamilton traced the location of the pier.

'How much does she draw?' asked Hamilton.

'Five feet.' The captain took a swig of beer.

'Then we'll be fine,' said Hamilton. They stepped out on deck. The pale-green island was directly ahead of the pitching bow. 'Think you can find it?' asked Hamilton.

Giving Hamilton a dismissive look, the captain grunted and said, 'Leave that to me, mister.'

Five minutes later, the captain throttled back the engine and turned toward the shore. Hamilton could clearly see the white structure of Eves beyond the breakers and could just distinguish the pilings at the end of the pier. Steering directly for the pilings, the captain said, 'Too rough to tie up. So get your gear and be ready as soon as I bring her alongside.'

'Right,' said Hamilton. 'Thanks for the ride.' He lugged the duffel bag over to the starboard railing as the pier loomed in water so clear he could see the colourful tropical fish darting around the pilings. At the last minute the captain idled the engine, expertly bringing the boat alongside. Within seconds the duffel bag was over the side, and Hamilton vaulted after it onto the weathered boards. He watched for a moment as the captain hit the throttle and noisily turned back out to sea. With a sigh of relief, Hamilton looked toward the house beyond the low seawall. With a slight smile, he raised his hand and waved to Marnie on the terrace, who hurried down to greet him.

CHAPTER ELEVEN

'LOOK AT YOU, Tom,' said Marnie, standing on the pier with her hands on her hips. 'So pale, except for that sunburned nose.' After weeks in bitterly cold Washington surrounded by East Coast girls in long woollen skirts and heavy overcoats, Hamilton couldn't resist a glance at Marnie's bare shoulders and deep cleavage revealed by her two-piece swimsuit.

'And you look wonderful,' he said as he looked in her eyes, 'with that golden tan.'

With an appreciative smile and a toss of her sun-bleached hair, Marnie started for the house and said, 'C'mon. You can leave your things for Henry. Philip's dying to hear all about Washington.'

By the time Hamilton emerged from a refreshing shower, Henry had laid his things out neatly at the foot of the bed in the guest suite. Well, Hamilton thought contentedly, it looked like Eves was going to be home for the foreseeable future. He dressed and found his way to the panelled den, and hearing voices, up the stairs to Sir Philip's study. 'Hello, Tom,' said Sir Philip, casually elegant in a linen jacket with a silk scarf knotted at his shirt collar. 'Have a seat.'

After a quick glance around the study, the shelves of which contained a complete, leather-bound set of Kipling and a collection of Chinese jade, Hamilton settled on the sofa with a view of the sea.

'Well ...' said Sir Philip expectantly. 'I gather from Colonel Donovan that he was rather reluctant to send you back.'

'I'm afraid he found my story about the Nazi sub base a bit far-fetched. Until I persuaded him to give you a call, he was planning to send me to South America.'

'He raised a good question about your cover. Though it's doubtful you were identified by Ericsson's men with your face blackened. Despite the risks, you're a damn sight more useful to me than one of our SOE agents, and we haven't much time.'

Hamilton leaned forward and asked, 'What's your assessment of the situation here? Any developments?'

'Ericsson continues to employ virtually every able-bodied Bahamian on his construction project, and the *Northern Lights* has made two more trips to the mainland.' Sir Philip reached into his pocket for his pipe and tobacco. 'Considering that a month has passed since your reconnaissance,' he continued as he filled the pipe and tamped the tobacco, 'I've no doubt the project is nearing completion.'

'Except for the canal,' interjected Hamilton.

'Precisely. Ericsson appears to be stymied by the local syndicate—'

'Fronting for Oakes.'

Striking a match over the bowl of the pipe, Sir Philip drew deeply. 'At any rate, Tom,' he said, 'now that you're *au courant*, what are we going to do with you?'

'An interesting question,' said Marnie in her Tennessee accent as she appeared at the top of the stairs. She gave Hamilton an amused look and said, 'I guess we'll have to keep you in hiding.' She walked over to her husband and kissed him on the cheek.

'I've been working on an idea,' said Hamilton. 'I'd like to know what you think.'

'Certainly,' said Sir Philip, drawing on his pipe, which filled the sunlit room with a pleasant aroma.

'You remember that lawyer I hired? Dobbs?' Sir Philip nodded with the pipe clenched in his teeth. 'Well, my instructions before leaving town were to tell the local syndicate to go to hell. I wouldn't pay them a dime for that property, saddled with such a large mortgage.'

'So I recall,' said Sir Philip.

'My take on Sir Harry Oakes,' continued Hamilton, 'is that he's the competitive type. If somebody else wants something, then, by God, he'll make damn sure they don't get it. Or at least try. And I'm sure he's aware Ericsson wants it too.'

'What do you have in mind?' asked Sir Philip, putting his pipe aside.

'Taking the syndicate up on their offer,' replied Hamilton with a grin. 'Instructing Dobbs to go back to them with a cashier's cheque for a thousand dollars and an earnest money contract.'

'OSS would advance such a sum?' asked Sir Philip sceptically.

'I'll use my own funds. It might not be a bad investment, even at such an inflated price.'

'I thought you were supposed to lie low, darlin',' said Marnie.

'I don't intend to let on that I'm in Nassau. As far as Dobbs is concerned, I'm in Texas.'

'And if the syndicate accepts your offer?' asked Sir Philip.

'I'll arrange a nice spread in the local paper. "Wealthy investor buys Hog Island property and announces plans for world-class hotel." '

'But what about Oakes?' protested Marnie, crossing her legs and dangling a sandal from a slender foot. 'I thought these local merchants were just straw men?'

'I'm betting greed will trump loyalty,' said Hamilton. 'I suspect these Bay Street gentlemen resent the way the great Sir Harry Oakes throws his weight around.'

'OK,' said Marnie with a fascinated expression, 'what happens next?'

'Once the news is out, the ball's in play,' replied Hamilton with a sparkle in his intelligent, grey eyes. 'Oakes will weigh in, trying to break the contract, and Ericsson will ... well, to be honest, I don't know what Ericsson will do. I'm hoping it will throw him off. stride.' Hamilton gave Sir Philip an expectant look.

'That's it?' said Sir Philip. 'The sum and substance of your plan?'

'Not entirely. I mean, I didn't have to come back to Nassau just to make an offer for that property.'

'True,' said Sir Philip.

'I've got to find a back channel to Ericsson.'

'How do you plan to do that?' asked Marnie.

'Through Evelyn. She's not only close to the duke and duchess,' said Hamilton earnestly, 'but also to Ericsson. And, frankly, I know I can trust her.'

Sir Philip frowned, tapping the bowl of the pipe in his palm. 'I don't know,' he said. 'I fear word that you're in Nassau could leak out. Ericsson's men are bound to be watching. Perhaps there's another explanation for your desire to see Mrs Shawcross?'

'Of course there is,' said Marnie, her dark eyes flashing. 'Lord, Tom, I warned you—'

'And I told you not to worry. Sure I want to see her again,' he said, looking at Sir Philip. 'And I believe she could be extremely helpful.'

'Well,' said Sir Philip in a resigned tone, 'use your discretion.'

'I'd like to send her a note,' said Hamilton. 'Maybe Carter could deliver it.'

Marnie stood up abruptly and walked to the window. 'Carter's doing fine,' she said, turning to face Hamilton. 'But let me deliver your note. I'd like to explain a thing or two to Evelyn.'

'An excellent idea,' said Sir Philip. 'Less likely to arouse suspicion.'

Hamilton nodded. 'All right,' he conceded. 'We've got a plan.'

The satin finish of the dining-room table at Shangri-La gleamed in the soft light of an antique silver candelabrum. Evelyn Shawcross sat across from Nils Ericsson, picking at her food and struggling to make small talk. When she'd received the hand-written dinner invitation, she naturally assumed the party would include the usual social circle surrounding the wealthy industrialist, perhaps the Duke and Duchess of Windsor and the duchess's Aunt Bessie. But she'd been alone with her host for over an hour.

'You're sure you won't have dessert?' asked Ericsson. 'The cook prepared an excellent strüdel.'

'Thank you, but no,' said Evelyn, erect in the high-backed chair, her hands folded in her lap.

'Coffee, perhaps?' said Ericsson. 'Or a liqueur?'

'A demitasse of coffee,' replied Evelyn.

Without taking his eyes from her, Ericsson depressed a buzzer under the carpet, summoning a young servant, who appeared almost instantly, wearing gloves and a starched white jacket. 'Bring the decanter of vintage cognac,' commanded Ericsson in Swedish, 'and a demitasse of coffee for Mrs Shawcross. Cream or sugar?' he asked Evelyn, reverting to English.

'No, thank you,' she said, her heart sinking with the realization that the intimate evening was not drawing to a close.

'Do you mind if I smoke?' asked Ericsson, reaching for a silver case from his dinner jacket as the door closed behind the servant.

'Of course not.'

Extracting a cigarette, he tapped it on the case and then lit it. 'I've been meaning to ask you, Evelyn,' he said, 'what's become of your American friend?'

So that's it, she thought, her heart beginning to pound. 'My American friend?'

'Yes, the gentleman who escorted you to the duke's Christmas ball.'

'Oh, yes,' said Evelyn, quickly feigning a smile. 'Tom Hamilton.'

'Yes. Mr Hamilton,' said Ericsson with exaggerated emphasis. The servant reappeared and served Evelyn a petite cup and saucer before placing a snifter and the decanter of cognac at Ericsson's elbow. 'What's become of Mr Hamilton?' asked Ericsson casually as he poured a glass.

'Why, he left before Christmas. I assumed you were kept informed of such things.'

'I am,' agreed Ericsson after taking a sip and running his tongue over his lips. 'But my question to you, Evelyn, is where has he gone? I presume he confided in you.' Taking a pull on his cigarette, he exhaled a cloud of smoke, which drifted across the flickering candles.

'Not really,' she said as nonchalantly as she was able. 'Merely that he was going home, to attend to business.'

'Surely you don't believe such a transparent falsehood?' said Ericsson with surprising vehemence. 'The man's obviously an espionage agent.' Leaning back in his chair, he swirled the glass and took a sip.

Evelyn's pale face betrayed no reaction to the assertion, though inwardly she despaired that it was true. 'I gather you invited me here,' she said coldly, 'for this intimate dinner party, thinking you could frighten me—'

'I'm merely seeking information,' said Ericsson with a menacing glare.

'But you were mistaken. The truth is, I have no idea whether he's a spy or where he was going when he left. I supplied you with what little information I had, and now it's your affair.'

'Perhaps,' said Ericsson with a shrug. 'But I should warn you: in case you should hear even a word from ... your lover; or even better, if you should see him ... you must tell me at once. Your husband is in a very – how should I put it? A very delicate position.' Evelyn trembled involuntarily, staring into Ericsson's pale-blue eyes.

'So long as you co-operate,' he continued in a conversational tone, 'your husband should be fine. But if you should fail to honour your commitments ... Well, I'm sure you understand.'

Breathing slowly, Evelyn raised the delicate cup to her lips and took a sip. Putting the coffee aside, she said, 'It's late and I should go.'

'The launch is at your disposal,' said Ericsson pleasantly.

Escorted by one of Ericsson's men to the sleek powerboat, Evelyn stood at the railing, staring forlornly at the lights of the British Colonial Hotel and Government House as the crew manoeuvred the boat alongside the public dock at Prince Georges Wharf. As the engine idled, troubling the black water at the stern, a crewman wordlessly took her by the elbow and steadied her for the step onto the dock. Clutching her stole over her bare shoulders, Evelyn hurried up the steps, where a jitney was waiting.

'Evenin,' ma'am,' said the driver as she opened the door and slid inside. 'Where to?'

'Greycliff,' she answered simply.

'Yes, ma'am,' he said and shifted into gear. Once the taxi was halfway up the block, a black sedan emerged from the shadows, following in the darkness without headlights. When the taxi stopped at Greycliff, the driver of the sedan pulled over in the shadows and watched as Evelyn paid the fare and hurried into the sanctuary of her home.

'Yes, I have the note,' said Marnie irritably as she stood beside the Bentley, tying her silk scarf under her chin. 'In my handbag.' She slid behind the wheel and leaned over to adjust her sunglasses in the rear-view mirror.

'OK,' said Tom, closing the door with a reassuring *chunk* and leaning against the side of the cream-coloured convertible. 'Remember what I said about seeing her alone, away from the servants. There's a porch upstairs—'

'Relax,' said Marnie, as she peered at him over her sunglasses. 'We'll have a nice little visit – assuming she's home – and I'll be back in a jiffy.' With a slight grimace, she turned the key, and placing her left arm on the seatback, backed out the gravel drive. With a smile and a wave, she shifted gear and hit the accelerator. Hamilton stood with his hands on his hips, watching as the powerful car disappeared down the drive. Fifteen minutes later, Marnie pulled over in front of the elegant Shawcross mansion, switched off the engine and untied her scarf, shaking out her thick blonde hair. Taking her handbag from the seat, she hurried up the flagstones to the door. After ringing the bell, she glanced up at the shuttered windows, struck by an unexpected pang of jealousy at the thought of Tom alone with Evelyn. After a few moments, a Bahamian servant answered the door, examining Marnie with a mildly curious expression.

'Hello,' she said with a smile. 'Is Mrs Shawcross in?'

'Yes, ma'am.'

'I'm Lady Sassoon. I have something for her.'

'Oh, yes, ma'am,' he said politely, holding open the door, painted the same shade of green as the shutters. 'I'll let the missus know you're here.'

As she walked inside, the servant started up the wide staircase. Placing her sunglasses in her handbag, Marnie briefly examined herself in a mirror before her gaze fell on a framed photograph of a beautiful young girl, wearing what Marnie would have called her best 'Sunday-school dress' and holding the hands of her rather severe looking parents.

'Hello, Marnie,' said Evelyn, standing on the stairs with her hand on the banister. Dressed in a blue satin robe and bedroom slippers, she looked uncharacteristically fragile.

'I hope I didn't disturb you,' said Marnie.

'No,' said Evelyn as she continued down the stairs. 'I've been up since dawn. I just haven't had the inspiration to dress. What a pleasant surprise.'

'You have a beautiful home,' Marnie said graciously. 'I apologize for dropping in.'

'Don't be ridiculous,' said Evelyn. 'It's lonely here, and I'm always happy to have company. Let's go into the sunroom and have tea … or a drink, if you'd prefer.' Without waiting for a response, she started down a passageway that led to an airy room overlooking the garden. 'How is Sir Philip?' she asked, as she entered the sun-filled room, placing her hands on an overstuffed armchair covered in bright chintz.

'Philip's fine. A bit bored, I'm afraid, and wishing he was closer to the action.'

'Would you care for tea? I'll call Samuel.' She reached for a small brass bell.

'No, thanks,' said Marnie as she sat on the sofa. 'I can only stay a minute.'

'All right,' said Evelyn as she put down the bell. She sat in the comfortable chair and gave Marnie an expectant look.

'I have something for you,' said Marnie, opening her handbag and removing a small envelope. Evelyn glanced briefly at the envelope and then gave Marnie another inquisitive look. 'Before we go any further,' said Marnie, tapping the envelope on her palm, 'we need to get a few things straight.'

'I see,' said Evelyn stiffly.

'I'm here because Tom asked me to come.'

'Tom?' said Evelyn softly. 'He's back …'

'Listen, Evelyn,' said Marnie, 'we're both married women, though I wouldn't know what it's like to be so far away from my husband, and for such a long time. But I don't want Tom getting hurt. And I don't mean just his feelings.'

Evelyn nodded, staring straight ahead, as though looking right through Marnie. 'Of course,' she murmured.

'You may think this sounds screwy,' Marnie continued, 'but he could be in real danger. Whatever happens between the two of you, just promise me you'll be careful and do as he says.'

Evelyn swallowed and took a deep breath, trying to calm her racing heart. 'I'm not sure I understand,' she said with some difficulty. 'But of course I'll be careful.'

'Just don't let on that you know he's back,' said Marnie. 'To anyone. OK?'

Evelyn nodded.

'There,' said Marnie with a sigh. 'I've said my piece.' Rising from the sofa, she reached out to hand Evelyn the envelope. 'It's a note from Tom,' she said. 'I don't know what it says – I'm just the delivery girl.'

Biting her lip as she examined the envelope, Evelyn looked up and said, 'Thank you,' in a barely audible voice.

'Bye,' said Marnie, with a look that suggested pity more than encouragement. 'I can see myself out.'

'Goodbye,' said Evelyn. She watched as Marnie walked quickly from the room, listening for the sound of the front door. When she was alone, Evelyn rose unsteadily and walked to the window. As she looked out over the garden, an image of Tom filled her mind, gracefully swimming the length of the long, blue-tiled pool. With a sigh of resignation, she tore open the envelope and read:

Dear Evelyn,
I'm writing this from Eves, Sir Philip's home on Cable Beach.
I'm anxious to see you, but it's very important that no one knows I'm here. I'll explain when I see you. Please call me and we can decide on a discreet place to meet. I can't wait to be with you.
  Tom

CHAPTER TWELVE

STIFLING A YAWN, Harold Dobbs hunched over his cluttered desk, staring with intense concentration at the morning newspaper. 'Damn,' he muttered, as he ran an ink-smudged finger down a column of small print, smiling inwardly when he found the scores of the English football matches faithfully reported in the Nassau *Daily Tribune*.

'Mr Dobbs ...'

He glanced up at his secretary. 'Yes?' he said. 'What is it?'

'A call, Mr Dobbs. From an overseas operator,' she added in a breathless tone.

'Blimey, an overseas call,' grumbled Dobbs, as he swivelled around in his creaking chair and lifted the receiver. 'Hello,' he said, leaning back and staring up at the ceiling. 'This is Dobbs.'

'Hold the line for Mr Thomas Hamilton,' said Marnie, delighted at the ease with which she'd passed herself off to Dobbs's dim-witted secretary as a mainland operator. After a brief delay, Hamilton came on the line:

'Dobbs? Is that you, Harold?'

'Why, hello, Mr Hamilton. Where are you calling from?'

'Where? Oh, here in my office. In Texas.'

'Why, the connection's so clear I could swear you were in Nassau. What can I do for you?'

'Listen, Harold, I've been mulling over that land deal, and while I don't like getting hi-jacked, I don't like losing, either.'

'Why, certainly not.'

'I've got another deal on the front burner, and I've got to choose. Either I do the Nassau deal, or I forget it.'

'Right-o,' said Dobbs, desperately searching for his pencil and pad amid the clutter.

'Here's what I want you to do,' instructed Hamilton. He paused for a moment and gave Marnie a wink. 'Draft a simple contract whereby this syndicate, the New Providence Land Company, sells the forty-two-acre parcel for a thousand dollars, subject to the unrecorded mortgage.'

'Price a thousand dollars,' said Dobbs as he scribbled notes, 'forty-two-acre parcel, subject to the mortgage ... I take it you're the purchaser?'

'Correct. Thomas R. Hamilton.'

'R,' repeated Dobbs.

'You can sign as my attorney-in-fact. Closing within thirty days. Then I want you to drop by the branch bank on Bay Street and see the manager.'

'The Royal Bank of Canada?'

'Right. I'll have a cashier's cheque waiting at the manager's office for the equivalent of a thousand dollars in pounds sterling.'

'The full purchase price?'

'Yes. When the contract's ready, swing by the bank and pick up the cheque. Got it?'

'Got it.'

'Then I want you to pay another call on your friend Jennings, the haberdasher. Present him with the contract and the cashier's cheque. And tell him he's got twelve hours.'

'Twelve hours?'

'That's right. Either they sign and take the money, or the deal's off. Take it or leave it.'

Dobbs paused. 'It's customary to afford the seller the opportunity to make a counter—'

'I don't give a damn,' said Hamilton. 'These men offered to sell me the property for five hundred bucks, subject to the mortgage, and now I'm offering to pay a thousand. I don't have time to dicker. I've got other fish to fry. Is that clear?'

'Yes,' said Dobbs quietly. 'Entirely clear.'

'When will you have something?' asked Hamilton.

'Well, if I start straight-away, perhaps by tomorrow—'

'I'm paying you, Harold. Do it today, and plan to pick up the cheque and call on your man Jennings first thing in the morning.'

'I'll get right on to it.'

'After you see Jennings, I want a report. Call me at the office. Taylor-4, 1-4-9-6.'

'Got it,' said Dobbs, jotting down the number.

'All right, Harold, let's see if we can bull the game,' said Hamilton. 'Make it clear there's no room to negotiate, no stalling for time.'

'Yes, well, Mr Hamilton, I'd best get started.' Hanging up, Dobbs spun around and called out, 'Miss Brooks! Come here, please, and bring your pad.'

Approximately ten miles away, Hamilton placed the receiver on the cradle in the panelled den at Eves with a satisfied smile. 'Now that that's done, I'm back to waiting. I wonder why she hasn't called?' he asked himself as much as Marnie.

Stroking her chin, Marnie said, 'She didn't look well. I was sure something was wrong but couldn't tell what. When I told her I had a note from you, she looked like she'd seen a ghost.'

'I don't get it,' said Hamilton. He absently glanced at a framed photograph of *Hard Ridden*, one of Sir Philip's four Epsom derby winners. The phone rang and he said, 'I'll get it', moving quickly toward the desk.

'No,' said Marnie. 'You're not thinking.' She picked up the phone and said, 'Sassoon residence.'

'It's Evelyn, Marnie. May I speak to Tom?'

'Just a moment.' Cupping her hand over the mouthpiece, Marnie said quietly, 'It's her. I'll leave you alone.'

Hamilton walked over and picked up the phone. 'Evelyn?' he said, as Marnie disappeared down the hall.

'Hello, Tom,' she said, trying her best to sound cheerful. 'Are you all right?'

'Yes, I'm fine.'

'I was worried about you. From what Marnie said—'

'I need to explain. In fact there's quite a lot I need to tell you. When can I see you?'

Seated at the desk in her living room, Evelyn massaged her forehead as she stared vacantly at the worn Persian rug. 'I don't know,' she said quietly, her attempt to sound cheerful having failed utterly. 'I just don't know.'

'Evelyn? Are you all right?'

'Tom, this is probably a terrible mistake. You're in some kind of trouble. You shouldn't have come back.'

'I *need* to explain. I should have explained it before, but well … I didn't. Is there some place we can talk privately?'

'You should leave, Tom,' she said wearily. Leave, she thought, closing her eyes. Before it's too late.

'I'm *not* leaving.' What had come over her? He had assumed, perhaps naively, that she would be anxious to see him. 'Listen, Evelyn,' he said, 'you made me promise to come back, and now that I'm here—'

'All right,' she said with a sigh. 'We can talk by the pool. No one will know.'

'But how…?'

'There's a gate at the back. Take a taxi to the street behind the house. A tall green gate.'

'When?'

Evelyn thought about her tattered robe and unwashed hair. 'Give me an hour,' she said. 'Take a taxi. You don't want to be recognized. Wear a hat or something.'

'Bye, Evelyn. I can't wait to see you.'

She hung up gently.

After rattling the ice in his glass and taking a sip of his drink, Sir Harry Oakes smiled and said, 'Your move.'

Seated across from Oakes at an elaborately inlaid card table, Sherwood 'Woody' Bascomb, his florid face in his hands, stared at the glass balls on the Chinese checkers board. 'Dammit, Harry,' he said at last. 'You got me.'

'Concede?'

'Yeah,' said Bascomb, interlocking his thick fingers and cracking his knuckles. 'I concede.' One of Bascomb's obligations as a house-guest was to humour his host's penchant for gin rummy, backgammon, and Chinese checkers, the latter being Oakes's favourite.

'OK,' said Oakes, 'rack 'em up and we'll play another game.'

'Ah-hem.' Jenkins, the English butler, coughed deferentially as he stood in the doorway. 'Excuse me, sir.'

'Yes?' said Oakes, looking up. 'What is it?'

'Mr Katz, sir.'

'Want me to clear out, Harry?' asked Bascomb.

'No, you can stay. Send him in,' Oakes instructed the butler. 'And while you're at it, I'll have another drink. Woody?'

'Sure,' said Bascomb.

Within minutes Jenkins returned to the study with Charley Katz. Wearing a shiny green double-breasted suit and a loud tie, Katz sauntered across the polished parquet, holding his fedora in one hand. 'Afternoon, Harry,' he said brightly, reaching out to shake his boss's hand, as Jenkins lowered a tray to the card table with the drinks.

'Charley,' said Oakes, 'you remember Mr Bascomb?'

'Sure, I remember. How ya doin', Woody?' He gave his hand a quick shake.

'Pull up a chair,' said Sir Harry. 'Need a drink?'

'Nah,' replied Katz. 'I'm on duty, remember?' he added with a chuckle.

'OK, Charley,' said Oakes in a businesslike tone, with a glance at Jenkins, who retired silently. 'I understand you've got something.'

'Correct,' said Katz. 'On the Shawcross dame.' He fished in his pocket for his cigarettes and eased one from the pack. 'She paid a call on her pal Ericsson the other night.' Taking a box of matches from his jacket, he lit the cigarette and waved the match in the air. 'Just the two of them.'

'How can you be sure of that?' asked Oakes.

'I followed her to the dock, where she gets on the boat all by herself. Nice boat, by the way. Off they go, and about two hours later, she's back. All by her lonesome, no other guests.'

'Then what?' asked Oakes.

'I followed her home. That's it.' Taking a deep pull and rounding his lips, Katz expelled a perfectly formed smoke ring that drifted up toward the ceiling.

'Sorry,' said Bascomb meekly. 'But I'm not sure I get it.'

'Ericsson's up to something on Hog Island,' explained Sir Harry. 'Something big. And this Englishwoman, named Shawcross, is mixed up in it. So we've been keeping an eye on her.'

'I see,' said Bascomb with a sombre expression.

'Do you have any idea what that Swedish bastard is building?' Oakes asked.

'No way to get close enough,' said Katz, balancing his hat on his knee. 'The place is crawling with guards and patrol boats. So I've been down to shantytown, to see what the locals will tell me.'

'Go on,' instructed Oakes.

'Most of 'em play dumb, too scared to talk. So I sprinkled a little cash around, and some booze, and managed to get a couple of these boys to say what they're working on. Pouring a lot of concrete for some kind of big building, like an airplane hangar. And digging this canal across the island.'

'I don't like it,' said Oakes with a frown. 'The guy's supposedly tied in with the Nazis,' he said to Bascomb. 'And what about Hamilton?' he asked, turning back to Katz. 'Any sign of him?'

'Nope,' said Katz. 'Not a trace.'

'Hamilton?' said Bascomb.

'Remember that fellow from Texas?' asked Oakes. 'Showed up last time you were here, with a lot of big talk about building a hotel and a casino?'

'Oh, yeah,' said Bascomb. 'I remember.'

'Well, I've made up my mind to move ahead with that project myself. When the war's over, gambling could make this place. Put in a first-class hotel and casino, and Nassau would be swarming with tourists.'

'Yeah,' agreed Bascomb, 'but what about the mob? You think Lansky would let anybody horn in on his territory?'

'This ain't Miami, Woody,' said Oakes. 'There's room enough for Havana *and* Nassau. Anyhow, I can deal with Meyer Lansky. Right, Charley?'

'Right,' said Katz doubtfully, stubbing out his cigarette.

'OK,' said Oakes, lifting his glass. 'Keep an eye on Mrs Shawcross, Charley. And keep a lookout for Hamilton. Meanwhile, I intend to pull the trigger on that tract of land, Woody. I'll call the note, and next thing you know, that property's mine.'

'Ah-hem.'

Sir Harry glanced up at Jenkins in the doorway. 'What is it?'

'The nanny wishes me to advise you that Master Sidney has disappeared.'

'Sidney? Where to?'

'She couldn't swear to it, sir, but believes she observed him leaving with the Count de Marigny.'

'What!' said Oakes, slamming his glass on the table and jumping up from his chair. 'Sorry, boys, but I've got to deal with this. Goddamn French sonofabitch,' he muttered under his breath.

Oakes's black Rolls Royce Phantom cruised slowly through an older section of Nassau inhabited by the more prosperous local merchants and transplanted Englishmen. Tapping a knuckle on the glass partition, he called to the chauffeur, 'See that yellow house, on the right?' The driver slowed and pulled over. 'I'll be right back,' said Oakes, as he climbed out. He adjusted his Homburg, straightened his jacket and strode up the walk to the modest two-storey house. As he lifted his hand to knock, he heard the sound of music. He gave the door a sharp rap, hoping that his daughter and not the despised de Marigny would answer. There was no response. Dammit, he thought, turn off that phonograph. He knocked again, even louder. After a few moments, he knocked a third time, and finally heard the thump of feet on the stairs followed by a man's irritated cry: 'All right, I'm coming!'

Throwing open the door, Alfred de Marigny gaped at Oakes. 'What?' exclaimed de Marigny, his shirt unbuttoned to his waist. 'Sir Harry?'

Glaring past de Marigny into the hall, Oakes could hear the music, a popular dance tune, much louder now. 'Where is he?' he demanded.

De Marigny took a step backward, gesturing to Oakes to come in. 'What?' he said. 'Where is who?'

'You know who,' said Oakes. 'Sidney!' he bellowed.

'Oh, little Sidney,' said de Marigny, fumbling with the buttons of his shirt.

Glancing at de Marigny's bare feet, Oakes seemed to notice his appearance for the first time. 'Jesus,' he said. 'Do you always run around without any clothes on? Sid-ney!' he called out again.

Oakes looked up and saw Nancy on the stairs, clinging fearfully to the banister, wearing only a thin cotton shift. With her uncombed hair, she looked like a child on Christmas morning. 'Where's Sidney?' he demanded.

'Sidney?' said Nancy, her voice trembling. 'Why, he's—'

'You don't have any right to come barging in,' fumed de Marigny, 'banging on the door – boom, boom, boom!'

'You ...' said Oakes, his voice quivering. 'I told you I didn't want Sidney around here.'

'The boy's lonely,' said de Marigny dismissively. 'What's a lad of fourteen to do all by himself on that estate of yours? Besides, he misses his sister.'

'He does, Daddy,' said Nancy as she crept timidly down the stairs. 'With Mommy away, we've only got each other.'

'Look at you,' said Oakes, his eyes darting from de Marigny, on whose aquiline face a smirk had settled, to his young daughter, who was wearing little more than a nightgown. 'I get it,' he growled. 'You sonofabitch,' he added, glaring at de Marigny.

'Stop it, Daddy,' pleaded Nancy, running down the last few steps and tugging on her father's arm. 'Freddie's my husband.'

'Good God, child,' said Oakes, brushing her hands from his arm. 'You'll just wind up pregnant again.' There was a sudden halt in the music. As the three turned to look, a gangling youth appeared from the next room, hanging his head and dragging his feet.

'Come here, Sidney,' said Oakes. 'Didn't I tell you not to come to this house?'

'Yes, Papa,' said the boy, looking up mournfully.

'Don't listen to him,' said de Marigny, placing a hand on the boy's shoulder. 'You should come here whenever you please. It *is* your sister's home.'

'Oh, yeah?' said Sir Harry wrathfully. He reached over and grabbed the boy by the scruff of his thin neck. 'C'mon,' he said. 'I'm taking you home.' With Sidney in tow, he turned toward the door, only to find the tall figure of de Marigny blocking his path. 'Out of my way,' said Oakes in a voice loud enough to be heard by a woman strolling along the sidewalk.

'I should teach you a lesson,' said de Marigny, clenching his fists.

'Go to the car,' said Oakes, half shoving Sidney out the door as Nancy began wailing. The woman on the sidewalk was joined by another curious neighbour.

'Get out of my house,' yelled de Marigny, 'before I smash your ugly face!'

'Oh, yeah,' said Oakes, raising his fist. De Marigny grabbed Oakes by both shoulders and shoved him onto the path, where he just avoided falling, his Homburg dropping to the grass.

'Don't ever come back!' cried de Marigny. 'Do you hear me? Or I'll kill you!'

'You!' said Oakes, his breaths coming in ragged gasps. 'You're nothing but a sex maniac!'

'Get out!' said de Marigny as Nancy cowered in the doorway.

Looking older than his sixty-seven years, Oakes stooped down to retrieve his hat and then staggered toward the waiting automobile, where Sidney, with an expression of intense shame, stood beside the horrified onlookers.

CHAPTER THIRTEEN

As the jitney rolled into town, Hamilton pulled his hat low and slumped down on the seat. After days sequestered at Eves, he gazed with a mixture of pleasure and trepidation at the pastel hues of Nassau. When the fortifications of Government House came into view, he leaned forward and instructed the driver to turn on a side street where, halfway down the street, he could see a tall green gate. 'Over there,' he said, pointing to the gate amid a bamboo grove. Exiting the cab, Hamilton cast a furtive glance down the empty street and hurried to the gate, where he could see the blue water of the Greycliff pool through cracks in the painted boards. Turning the handle, he gave the gate a gentle shove.

The blue mosaics glittered beneath the still surface of the water, which mirrored the graceful overhanging boughs and bougainvillea spilling over the pale pink walls. The late afternoon sun suffused the pool and patio in an evanescent glow, like the light, Hamilton considered, in a Maxfield Parrish painting. He began walking toward the cabana at the end of the pool, inhaling the sweet bouquet of the garden, mingled with another, more exotic fragrance. He closed his eyes. *Pois de Senteur.* Evelyn's perfume.

'Hello, Tom....'

She was standing by the cabana in a simple pink dress, staring expectantly. Hamilton went to her and leaned down for a kiss, but she threw her arms around him and held him tight. 'Oh, Tom,' she murmured, 'Tom ...'

'Evelyn,' he said, pulling away and gently lifting her chin. As she raised her eyes to meet his, her lips began to tremble and tears welled. 'Hey, it's OK,' he said, as he brushed them away. 'There,' he said. 'That's better. Why don't we sit down?'

Taking his hand, Evelyn nodded and, with his arm encircling her waist, they walked slowly to a wrought-iron bench and sat beside the pool. 'It seems like a long time ago,' he began, 'when I came for a swim and lunch.'

'It seems forever.'

'I wish we could go back, and start over.'

'Do you? I'd rather leave things just as they were.'

'Evelyn,' said Tom, looking in her eyes, 'there are things I wish I'd told you.'

'Sometimes we're better off not knowing,' she said softly. There's so much, she considered grimly, that he would never, never, know. Hamilton gave her a questioning look. 'At any rate,' she said, 'I found your note rather mysterious.'

'Unfortunately,' he said, resting his arms on his knees, 'I can't let anyone know that I'm back in Nassau.'

Thank God, she thought. 'Why?' she asked. 'You must have done something bad.' The attempt at humour falling flat, she quickly added, 'Seriously, Tom, it sounds as though you've put yourself in danger. Why *did* you come back?'

'To see you, of course,' he answered without hesitation, which was more than half true. 'You made me promise.'

'Yes, I did.' She silently cursed her selfishness.

Hamilton stared into the shadows beyond the pool, trying to decide how to begin. 'To be honest,' he said at last, 'I was sent back. By the man I work for.'

'I thought you worked for yourself, with your oil wells and cattle ranches—'

'Don't rub it in. Though there's a fair amount of truth in that.'

'Then who do you work for?'

'A man named Donovan,' he said evenly. 'He runs the Office of Strategic Services.'

'You must be a spy.'

'Well ... not exactly. But I am in intelligence. You know, like your husband. The difference is, I work undercover.'

'So all that rot about staying out of the war....'

He hung his head and nodded. 'Yes,' he said, staring at the flag-stones. 'All that rot.'

'Well,' she said, 'I don't know why you should feel ashamed. Scarcely anyone in this quaint little outpost of British civilization, as you once put it, is who they seem to be. They're all pretending, aren't they? The duke would be the king, Wallis is a duchess, de Marigny's a count, Videlou's a marquis—'

'Oakes is a baronet,' said Hamilton with a smile.

'I don't know about Sir Philip,' said Evelyn.

'Oh, he's the real thing,' replied Hamilton.

'Yes, but what else is he?'

Hamilton gave her a rueful look 'Everyone's pretending,' he said, gazing into her blue eyes, 'everyone, that is, but you.' She stared back at him, her face a blank slate. 'But what I really want to know,' he continued after a moment, 'is who is Nils Ericsson, and what is he up to?'

'Oh, I should think you could read him like a book. It's trans-parent, if you ask me.'

'Is it? Wealthy industrialist from neutral Sweden, champion of world peace, comes to the Bahamas and embarks on economic development projects for the good of the populace?'

'Something like that. It sounds as though you've been reading his press dispatches. Is that what you've come to talk about? Nils Ericsson?'

'In a way, yes.' Hamilton stood up abruptly and began pacing beside the pool. 'Or, in reality,' he said thoughtfully, 'is the man a front for the Nazis? Building a base for their Caribbean U-boat fleet?'

'Surely, Tom,' said Evelyn, her heart pounding, 'you can't believe—'

He stopped and stared at her. 'I need your help, Evelyn. That's why I'm here.'

She took a deep breath, trying to seem relaxed. 'What help can I possibly be?'

'You know Ericsson,' he said calmly. 'And you're close to the duke and duchess.' In the gathering dusk, the pool and the wall beyond it dissolved into the shadows.

'What do they have to do with this?' asked Evelyn in a voice that betrayed her growing panic. 'God ... I could use a drink.'

'Is there some place we could talk without being seen?'

'Samuel's in his room listening to the radio. I'll tell him he's not needed, and then it should be safe to go inside.' She disappeared through the garden gate. Five minutes later she returned and led him up the path to the back of the house. As they entered and started up the stairs, he thought back to his first night at Greycliff, with Evelyn at the piano, a memory that triggered a powerful wave of longing and desire. Now the only sound was the *tick-tock* of the grandfather clock.

She walked out to the porch overlooking the garden. 'We're alone,' she said. 'I listened to Samuel whistling his way down the block, off for an evening of dominoes with a friend.' She switched on a lamp, walked to a trolley, and reached for a bottle. 'Scotch?' she asked.

Hamilton nodded.

'Oh, and you Yanks prefer ice,' she added. 'Sorry, but I'm afraid ...'

'I'll drink it neat.' She poured each of them a shot of whisky in glasses decorated with the official seal of the Colony.

'There you are, sir,' she said in a far more confident tone. 'Now, then,' she continued, moving to the railing, 'what were you about to say about the duke and duchess?'

'You'll think I'm crazy.' He stood next to her and leaned against the railing. 'Why don't I lay the whole thing out, the way I see it?' A gentle breeze stirred the treetops and somewhere down the street a dog was barking. After taking a sip, he said, 'Nobody gets close to this project Ericsson's building on Hog Island – the so-called Hurricane Hole. His guards and patrol boats see to that. And the Royal Navy won't go near the place.'

'Why?'

'The duke won't allow it. He's a great admirer of Ericsson, and so the work goes on, under incredibly tight security.'

'Why should the duke care? Why should it concern him what Nils is building...?'

'Because,' said Hamilton, 'he's building submarine pens – sheltered docks – for German U-boats.' He paused to study Evelyn's face, an expressionless mask in the shadows. 'And excavating a canal to tie into the port in Nassau.'

'Do you know this?' she asked at last. 'Or is it just conjecture?'

'I've seen it myself. And when everything's ready, the Germans will launch an attack, take the airfield first, in all likelihood, and then deal with the small British garrison.'

'You still haven't answered my question about the duke.'

Hamilton paused to take a swallow of Scotch. 'I imagine they'll place the duke under house arrest. Others, like Sir Philip, will be tossed in gaol. But the Duke is the real prize.'

'You *are* dreaming,' murmured Evelyn.

'The Germans will have their submarine base, where they can rest and refit after wreaking havoc on the Florida shipping lanes, and a fully equipped airfield thrown into the bargain. And they'll have the former king, whom they ought to be able to persuade to broadcast an appeal to his countrymen to come to their senses and sue for peace.'

Staring at him in the semi-darkness, Evelyn said, 'You should have been a writer, Tom. It's a wonderful story. But it's absurdly far-fetched.'

'There's not much time,' said Hamilton. 'I'm trying to throw a wrench into the project. But what I really need is your help with the duke.'

'What could I possibly do?'

'Persuade him to send in the Royal Navy to have a look around at Hurricane Hole.'

'He'll think I'm mad.'

'Go see Wallis, then. Explain that her husband's at great risk.

Evelyn,' said Hamilton, standing erect and staring into her eyes, 'if the duke allows himself to be used by the Nazis, he'll be ruined. A national disgrace. Banished from his own country.'

Each phrase struck her like a blow, exposing the terrible reality of her complicity in the plot, and the brutal consequences she'd never considered for the poor, well-intentioned Duke of Windsor. 'Oh my God,' she said, leaning back her head and placing the back of her hand on her forehead. Her glass slipped with the gesture, falling to the floor and shattering. 'Don't worry,' said Evelyn absently, 'I'll have someone clean it up.'

'But Evelyn ...'

Staring at him with wide-open eyes, she blurted, 'You should never have come here! You'll ruin us all. Can't you just go away, before it's too late? Of course you're risking your own life. But what about me?'

'I ... I never meant to put you in danger. I guess I didn't think.'

'No, you didn't,' she exclaimed, fighting back tears. 'Perhaps, if you'd just go back to the States, things might be all right. Perhaps I could warn the duke. Oh, God,' she muttered, turning away and slumping onto the sofa.

Walking over to her slowly, avoiding the broken glass, he gazed down and said softly, 'Evelyn. I'm sorry.' She gave him an anguished look. 'I knew it was wrong,' he continued, 'but I fell for you. I should never have dragged you into this. It was wrong to ... fall in love, and it was wrong to ask you to help me.'

'Don't even say it,' she whispered.

'I'd better go. I'll call a cab, if that's OK.' He reached down and placed a hand gently on her shoulder. 'Let's just pretend tonight never happened. As far as anyone else is concerned, you've not seen me again.' Staring up at him, her lips trembled and the tears came, wetting her cheeks. He bent down and kissed her lightly on the forehead. 'Goodnight,' he said and then turned and walked away.

Ten minutes later, a jitney pulled over at the back gate where Hamilton stood in the shadows. A solitary figure in the darkness at the corner watched as Hamilton climbed in and the taxi disappeared down the street.

The steady sea breeze rustled the palm fronds overshadowing the terrace where Hamilton sat alone, staring at the aquamarine sea. After declining Marnie's invitation to join her for a swim, he'd been left to his ruminations, while Sir Philip adhered to his routine, working in his study until lunchtime. Hamilton leaned back with the warm sun on his face, imagining the Chris Craft pulling up to the pier with Carter at the helm. After a quick run over to Nassau to pick up Evelyn, they would cruise northward to Green Turtle Cay, leaving Greycliff and the war far behind....

Opening the sliding glass door, Marnie walked outside. 'Tom,' she said, 'you have a phone call. It's your office.'

Peering over his shoulder, Hamilton yawned and said, 'I'll be right there.' He walked to the panelled den and reached for the phone. 'Hello? ... Oh, hi, Barbara ... Dobbs called? Let me get a pencil.' He jotted down a number. 'Anything else? ... No, that can wait. Bye.'

Marnie leaned against the doorjamb and said, 'I suppose you want me to place a call?'

'Yep. The same routine.' He stared briefly into her eyes, conscious that he'd been taking her for granted. 'I'm sorry,' he said. 'You don't have to do this, you know.'

'I know.' She squeezed his hand and kissed him lightly on the cheek. 'I'll tell you when I've had enough.' She walked over and reached for the phone and slip of paper. After dialling, she said, 'This is the long distance operator. I have a person-to-person call for Mr Harold Dobbs, from Mr Thomas Hamilton ... She's getting him,' she added, handing Hamilton the receiver.

Hamilton tapped the pencil on the desk and then said, 'Hello, Harold. It's Tom Hamilton. Yes, in my office. What do you have?'

The swivel chair creaking under the weight of his large form, Dobbs cleared his throat and said, 'Well, sir, I've just returned from a meeting with Mr Mason Jennings. I brought along the contract and the cheque I picked up at the bank, just as you instructed.'

'And what did Jennings say?'

'Once we were situated in his office, I explained that I was calling on behalf of a client to make a proposal as regards the property on Hog Island—'

'But what did he *say*?' said Hamilton testily.

'Well, he was taken aback when I stated that my client was prepared to pay the sum of a thousand dollars. "But what about the mortgage?" he says. "Look here," I said, directing his attention to the contract. "Paragraph two, I believe it is. The purchase shall be *subject to* the first lien mortgage in the amount of twenty thousand pounds". Without further ado, I reached for the cashier's cheque and handed it to him.'

'Get to the point, man. What did Jennings say?'

'Well, for a moment, he was speechless, staring at that cheque. Then, he says, "A thousand dollars – a tidy sum. I assure you," he says, "we shall give your proposal very serious consideration"'.'

'What about the deadline?'

'"Take note", I explained, "that the offer shall be null and void unless accepted by ten o'clock tonight. Twelve hours hence." "Why, that's impossible", he says. "Well, I'm sorry", I told him. "That's all there is to it. Sign within the time specified, or the deal's off".'

'OK,' said Hamilton. 'How did you leave things?'

'Well, Jennings kept eyeing that cheque. Said something about getting his partners together, and, if I heard him correctly, "serve the old sod right".'

'Fine,' said Hamilton. 'You know how to reach me. Call as soon as you hear anything.'

'Right-o, Hamilton. Good day.'

Hamilton hung up with a sigh. 'Well,' he said to Marnie, who was curled up on the sofa, 'There's nothing more I can do but wait.'

'Why don't you relax?' she asked.

'Relax? If there's one thing I'm sure of, the Germans are planning something, as soon as those submarine pens are ready. And that could be any day.'

She gave him a sympathetic look. 'But what about this plan of yours?'

'That will just buy time, if I'm lucky. I've got to get proof of what Ericsson is up to.'

'I gather your visit with Mrs Shawcross was unproductive,' commented Sir Philip, who had silently rolled into the room in his wheelchair.

'Yes,' said Hamilton with a frown.

Sir Philip propelled himself smoothly with his strong arms, pivoting beside the sofa where Marnie was lounging. 'May I get you something, darling?' she asked, making a motion to get up.

'Pray let Henry know,' he replied, 'that we're ready for lunch.' Once he was alone with Hamilton, Sir Philip asked, 'How much did you disclose to Evelyn?'

'I explained I'm working for the OSS as an undercover agent and my suspicions about Ericsson and the Nazi sub base.'

'Her reaction?'

'That the story was absurdly far-fetched, in her words.'

'She declined to offer any assistance?'

'Not exactly. When I told her the Germans might seize the island and place the duke under house arrest, she was visibly upset.'

'Understandably.'

'And pleaded with me to leave Nassau. She was obviously fright-ened of getting involved, and, if what I said was true, worried for her safety.' He shook his head. 'It wasn't fair to drag her into this.'

'Don't make the mistake of placing your feelings for the person,' counselled Sir Philip, 'ahead of the cause. Though I must say, I'm surprised by her reaction.' Hamilton gave him a questioning look. 'That she pleaded with you to leave,' said Sir Philip. 'It's almost as though ...' He paused and touched his fingertips to his chin.

Marnie reappeared, having changed into slacks and a white blouse that contrasted nicely with her deep tan. 'Lunch,' she said, 'will be ready shortly.'

'Tom was explaining the results of his visit with Mrs Shawcross,' said Sir Philip.

'A mistake,' commented Hamilton. 'I don't plan to see her again.'

'Oh, really?' said Marnie.

'She wants me to go back to the States,' said Hamilton, meeting her gaze.

'Hah,' said Marnie. 'I'll bet she does. Your problem is you don't understand women.'

After lunch, Hamilton lay down on the sofa for a nap while Sir Philip and Marnie retired to their adjoining bedrooms. Just as he had fallen lightly asleep, he was startled awake by the phone. He hurried to the desk and caught it on the third ring. 'Hello?' he said.

'Hello, Tom,' said Hamilton's secretary in Texas. 'Your man Dobbs called back and seemed quite excited. You need to call him right away.'

Glancing at his watch, Hamilton said, 'Thanks, Barbara. I've got the number.' He walked down the hall and tapped gently on Marnie's door. After a few moments, she opened it a crack, clutching her satin robe to her neck in a rare gesture of modesty. For a moment she searched his eyes. 'Tom,' she said softly, 'do you—?'

'Sorry to bother you,' he said quickly. 'It's just that I need you to place another call.'

'Oh,' she said, with a look of mild disappointment. 'Give me a minute.'

Hamilton waited in the den, where after several minutes Marnie joined him. 'OK,' she said without enthusiasm as she walked to the desk. 'I know the drill.' She glanced at the scrap of paper and dialled the number. After a moment, she handed Hamilton the phone.

'Harold?' said Hamilton. 'What's up?'

'Jennings called after lunch and asked me to meet him. And to get straight to the point, he signed the contract!'

'I'll be damned,' said Hamilton.

' "I've spoken to the others",' he says, "and though we probably ought to hold out, a bird in hand is worth two in the bush", as the saying goes. So we sat ourselves down and I took him through the document. "Blimey", he says, when we came to the bit about the

mortgage, "your client Mr Hamilton certainly has some large …"
Ha, ha, you get the idea.'

'Yes,' said Hamilton. 'I do.'

'Jennings went on to say something about high time somebody
stood up to the old coot, and that Sir Harry was now your problem.
I handed him the cheque, and Jennings grins from ear to ear. "A
thousand dollars. Who would've thought it?" Pretty swell work for
an afternoon, wouldn't you admit?'

'Yes, very swell. There's one more thing.'

'What might that be?' asked Dobbs nervously.

'I have a press release,' answered Hamilton. 'I'd like a nice spread
in the local paper.'

'A bit out of my line….'

'Don't worry. Does your gal take shorthand?'

'Well, yes …'

'Fine. I can dictate it to her. Then I want you to run it over to the
paper. You can leave it with the city editor.'

Ten minutes later, after making a few revisions to the brief but
sensational announcement, Hamilton hung up the phone with a
satisfied smile. He turned to Marnie and said, 'I guess that does it.
Let the fireworks begin.'

CHAPTER FOURTEEN

RAWING BACK THE gauzy netting, Sir Harry Oakes swung his pyjama-clad legs over the side of the bed and sat upright, rubbing his bloodshot eyes. Judging from the bright sunshine, it was well past eight o'clock and time to rise and shine. He reached for the buzzer on the bedside table to summon Jenkins and then rose and shuffled to the spacious bathroom, the black and white marble tiles cold to his feet. As he re-entered the sunny bedroom, tying the sash of his silk dressing-gown, the door swung open, admitting Jenkins with the morning newspapers, coffee, and a single yellow rose. Without a word, he waited for his employer to take his customary seat in an armchair.

'Shall I pour, sir?'

Oakes nodded, running a hand through his thinning hair. 'I'll be down for breakfast shortly. Tell the cook to grill me a chop with my eggs.'

'Certainly, sir,' said the butler as he poured a stream of piping hot coffee. With a stiff bow, he turned and let himself out.

Oakes lifted his cup and deliberately splashed some of its contents into the saucer, poured the spilt coffee back into the cup, repeated the ritual, and then blew across the surface of the cup. 'Saucered and blowed,' he mumbled contentedly before taking his first sip of the Jamaican Blue Mountain brew. 'Ahh,' he said, placing the cup and saucer on the tray and reaching for the Miami *Herald*. He absently scanned the headlines, filled with the usual war news, before turning to the stock quotations and commodity prices, muttering 'Humbug', as he checked the price of gold bullion.

Tossing the paper aside and taking another sip of coffee, he reached for the Nassau *Daily Tribune*. When he looked at the front page, Oakes started so violently that he almost dropped the cup in his lap, splashing hot coffee on his pyjamas and almost toppling over the bud vase. 'Christ!' he exclaimed as he gaped at the bold headline: AMERICAN BUYS HOG ISLAND TRACT and the smaller type beneath it: *Announces Plans for Hotel and Casino.* With a trembling hand, Oakes carefully read the article:

> American businessman Thomas R. Hamilton announced today the purchase of forty-two acres on Hog Island opposite the city docks from a syndicate of Bay Street merchants. Terms were not disclosed. In a prepared statement, Hamilton, a Texas oilman, stated that he intends to develop a premier resort hotel, which will necessitate construction of a bridge from Nassau. 'I am convinced,' stated Hamilton, 'that the economic future of the Bahamas lies with tourism as opposed to schemes such as crayfish canneries,' an apparent reference to the project undertaken by the Swedish industrialist Nils Ericsson on Grand Bahama Island. He also announced his intention of seeking a change in gambling laws to allow the operation of a casino. 'This project,' said Hamilton, 'will make Nassau the preferred destination over Miami Beach and Havana.' The statement ended with a flourish, asserting that, 'The hotel and casino will transform Hog Island into a virtual paradise island.'

'*Goddammit,*' snarled Oakes, flinging the paper aside. 'Paradise island, my foot,' he muttered. He rose stiffly and walked to the telephone. He dialled and then said, 'Peterson? This is the boss. Where's Katz? ... What? Well, find him!' He slammed down the receiver.

Seated in the small breakfast alcove, Oakes, with a forkful of scrambled eggs, looked up at a gentle tap on the door. 'What is it?' he said, to which a timid voice replied, 'It's Mr Katz, sir. He's here to see you.' After a moment Charley Katz entered the small room, looking uncharacteristically sheepish as he fingered the hatband of his fedora.

'Mornin', boss,' he said. 'What's the problem?'

'Sit down,' said Oakes. 'Now,' he said, fixing his gaze on Katz. 'Have you seen this morning's paper?'

'The local Nassau paper? Hell, I never look at that lousy fish wrapper.'

'Maybe it's time you did, Charley. You never know what you might learn.'

'Jeez, boss, what's the—?'

'There's a front-page article, says our friend Hamilton has bought that forty-two-acre tract. And what's more, it says he's planning a world-class hotel *and* a casino *and* he's gonna draw all the tourists away from Miami Beach and Havana.'

'Jesus,' said Katz. 'If Lansky hears about that ...'

'Exactly.' Oakes paused to sip his coffee. 'I thought you told me,' he said, 'that Hamilton hadn't shown his face on the island?'

'Listen, Harry, I've got men watching every plane that lands at Oakes Field and every boat from Miami, and I swear nobody's laid eyes on him.'

'Well, I want you to pay a call on this fellow who sold Hamilton the property. Jennings, or some such name. Has a shop on Bay Street.'

'Sure, I know the place. That's where I bought my hat—'

'Listen, Charley – you tell that sonofabitch that nobody double-crosses Harry Oakes and gets away with it. I wonder how much dough Hamilton put in their pockets? Tell him I'm gonna foreclose that mortgage. That should fix Hamilton. And then check with the newspaper. We need to find Hamilton.'

'I swear he ain't in Nassau.'

'Well if he is, one thing's for sure: sooner or later he'll show up at his lady friend's place. So keep a lookout on her.'

'Anything else?'

'No,' said Oakes with a frown. 'Report back as soon as you're done.'

There were days when Evelyn imagined she might never leave her bed, drifting in and out of the sanctuary of a dreamless sleep, awakening only long enough to stretch and rearrange the pillows before shutting out all thoughts of the war and Tom and Nils Ericsson and seeking only to sleep ... Drawing the soft down comforter around her neck, she curled in an embryonic ball in the warmth of the covers, savouring the cool freshness of the pillow, and slipped back into the nether world between sleeping and waking, dimly conscious of the faint light from the shuttered window while images of the English countryside floated across her mind. Her reverie was suddenly broken by the blare of a delivery truck's horn. With a sigh, Evelyn opened her eyes to consider the day. The mere thought of rising and dressing filled her with despair; despair – mixed with intense foreboding. Perhaps if she surrendered to her deep, carnal lassitude, curled up in the soft bedcovers, the dilemma would somehow work itself out. Cursing the temptation, she threw back the covers and swung her legs over the side of the bed. As she sat there, feeling the coolness of the hardwood floor on her bare feet, she suddenly felt sick of her indolence, craving the sensation of hot water pouring over her, the scent of lilac soap, and fresh, clean clothes after the long hours abed.

Having slept past noon, it was almost one when Evelyn emerged from her bedroom, appearing, at least outwardly, her old self again, with her dark hair stylishly curled, a touch of make-up, and an attractive pale-blue dress. She sent word for the cook to prepare her a light lunch and settled with a cup of tea at the rattan table on the porch. Warmed by a shaft of bright sunshine, she sorted through a neat bundle of letters until she found a wrinkled envelope with a colourful stamp and Cairo postmark, her husband's last letter, penned before Christmas. She withdrew the sheets of military stationery and reread the letter. Though the words reflected Dirk's usual wit and intellect, and he managed to fill several pages with amusing observations, the tone was flat and the content vacuous. Why even write, she wondered? Of course there were military censors, and besides, he wasn't about to hint at his clandestine activities. Though he ignored it, the Germans were faring badly in North Africa, having been driven by the British all the way back to Tunisia with appalling losses. What would Dirk do if the Germans lost the war? Go home to England as though his secret efforts to aid the enemy had never happened? She doubted it. He was an absolute ideologue, as rigid in his beliefs as the Bolsheviks both of them loathed. She was sure he would skulk away somewhere to some suitable Fascist haven, perhaps in South America. Well, he would have to go without her. She cared not a damn for the bloody Fascists, especially the Nazis, who struck her as ludicrously crude and savage. God, what fools she and Dirk had been at university before the war. With or without him, she was determined to go home to England and the life she'd known. The admission failed to evoke even the slightest twinge of regret. With a sigh, she folded the letter and placed it in the envelope.

Taking a final swallow of tepid tea, Evelyn looked up as Samuel approached the table, with a steaming bowl of soup and an assortment of sandwiches. 'Anything else, Miz Shawcross?' he asked.

'No, thank you.' She unfolded the linen napkin and removed her grandmother's cutlery, polished to a fine patina. Alone again with her thoughts, she blew gently over her steaming spoonful of bisque and stared into the leafy green distance, thinking back to the look on Tom's face as he explained his fear of an imminent German attack. If only there were a way to help him by warning the duke, without risking exposure of her husband. Tom had suggested that she say something to Wallis. So long as no one knew he'd returned to Nassau – or worse, she considered with a flutter in her chest, that he'd seen her – it might be possible.

Her thoughts were interrupted by the telephone. Samuel appeared after a moment and said, 'You have a call, ma'am. It's Mister Ericsson.'

Oh, God, she thought desperately. 'Tell him I'm ... No, Samuel,

I'll take the call.' Tossing her napkin on the table, she rose from her chair and hurried to the living room. Forcing herself to be calm, she picked up the phone and said, 'Hello?'

'Hello, Evelyn. I trust I'm not disturbing you.'

'No.'

'You're alone, then?'

'I'm always alone.'

'A pity. I thought you might be entertaining your friend Mr Hamilton.'

'What? Are you mad?'

'You disappoint me, Evelyn. I should have thought you would have called to tell me he's back, rather than having to read about it in the newspaper.'

'In the newspaper?' she said, fighting panic. 'I'm afraid I don't understand.'

'In this morning's newspaper, to be precise,' said Ericsson with a carefully modulated blend of sarcasm and hostility. 'You haven't seen the article?'

'Why, no. I've only just—'

'Hamilton's announced that he's proceeding with his hotel and casino project. He's merely trying to thwart my plans, and I won't stand for it! Why didn't you call me?'

'I swear I had no idea he was here.'

'Why should I believe you? Don't you value your husband's safety? Don't you know that with one telephone call—'

'Stop!' she pleaded. 'Of course I know. But an article in the local paper about this hotel venture doesn't mean he's actually in Nassau.' Taking a deep breath, she said, 'If you keep threatening to expose my husband, why should I even lift a finger to help you?'

'If Hamilton's here, my men will find him. As for you, I should be very, very careful. If he so much as telephones—'

'I understand,' she said calmly. 'You won't say anything about Dirk?'

'For the time being, no. You are both more useful to me alive than ... I'm sure you understand. Goodbye, Evelyn.'

'Goodbye.' She hung up with the words echoing in her head: more useful alive ... alive. Shivering with a sudden chill, she thought, No. Perhaps more useful dead.

Charley Katz was the sort who fancied himself a natty dresser, a man with style who could turn the heads of the nightclub girls. Strolling the counters at Mason Jennings on Bay Street, he examined the array of accessories laid out under the glass: pearl-inlaid and lapis studs and cufflinks, tortoiseshell combs, sandalwood shaving soap in a china mug next to an ivory-handled straight razor. He smiled at a nickel-plated flask, just the right size for his hip pocket, and a silver money-clip he imagined in his pants pocket, bulging with greenbacks.

'Is there something I might show you, sir?'

Katz looked up at the sales clerk in his shabby tweed jacket that reeked of tobacco. 'Nice merchandise,' said Katz with a smile. He fingered a brightly coloured tie hanging from a carousel on the counter. 'However ... I need to speak to the proprietor.'

'Excuse me?'

'You heard me. The *proprietor*. Jennings.'

'I'm sorry, sir, but Mr Jennings—'

'Here.' Katz reached into his pocket and handed the man a business card.

'Oh, I see,' said the clerk, studying the reference to Sir Harry Oakes. 'Just one moment.'

Within several minutes he returned and said, 'Mr Jennings wonders if you would see him in his office.'

'Sure,' said Katz. He followed the clerk up a badly lit staircase to a garret-like office. The balding storeowner was hunched over his desk, examining a pile of receipts under a green-shaded lamp.

'Morning, Mr Jennings,' said Katz as the clerk hurriedly departed. 'The name's Katz. Charley Katz.' Gazing down at Jennings, he ran his fingers over the grainy blond finish of the desk.

Making no motion to offer his hand to his visitor or invite him to sit, Jennings scowled and said, 'So Oakes sent you. I shoulda figured.'

'Yeah,' said Katz with a smile. He hiked up his trouser leg and placed a well-polished oxford on the chair. 'Sir Harry sent me.'

'So what does *he* want? I'm busy, you know.'

Katz leaned down and rested his elbow on his knee, letting his wide, garish tie dangle in front of him. 'Where's Hamilton?' he asked.

'Who? Oh, Hamilton.'

'Yeah, Hamilton.'

'Christ, I dunno. Listen, mister—'

'Whaddaya mean, you don't know? You made a deal with the sonofabitch, you took his dough, right? So where is he?' Taking his foot from the chair, Katz glared menacingly at Jennings, who seemed to shrink.

'Hey, listen,' said Jennings nervously. 'It's none of your business. Who says you can barge in here—'

'I says.' Stepping quickly around the desk, Katz grabbed Jennings by the shoulder and raised his fist. 'Now tell me where that sono-fabitch is,' he said, 'before I bust your chops.'

'I swear I don't know!' cried Jennings, raising an arm to ward off the blow. 'I never laid eyes on him! He ain't even in Nassau, so far as I know.'

Katz studied Jennings's face, pleased by his terrified reaction. 'OK,' he said casually, lowering his fist and releasing his grip. 'Let's get this straight. You never saw Hamilton. But you sold him the property—'

'I dealt with the lawyer,' interjected Jennings, his voice quaking. 'A man named Dobbs,' he added before Katz could ask. 'A solicitor here in town.'

'Who signed the papers?' asked Katz sceptically.

'Dobbs signed. He had a power of attorney.'

Katz blinked at him uncomprehendingly. 'What about the dough?'

'The dough?'

'The money! Where'd Dobbs get the money?'

'He had a cashier's cheque. From the Royal Bank of Canada....'

'How much?'

'What? Oh, I'm not sure I should—'

'How much?' growled Katz, raising his fist again.

'A thousand,' said Jennings timorously. 'Ah, the equivalent of a thousand dollars.'

'A grand?' said Katz. 'So he sends his lawyer over here with a, what did you call it?'

'A power of attorney.'

'And a cheque for a grand, and, *bingo*, you make a deal.'

'Yes,' admitted Jennings, 'that's about it.'

'So where do I find this Dobbs?'

'His office is by the courthouse. Harold Dobbs.'

'OK,' said Katz, slipping on his fedora and buttoning his suit jacket. 'Oh, by the way,' he added with a smile. 'Nice hat. I'm gonna pay Mr Dobbs a little visit. And meanwhile, keep your trap shut. Got it?'

'Got it,' said Jennings meekly. He slowly exhaled as Katz quickly left the office.

Sir Harry Oakes paced in his library, hands clasped behind his back, wearing the pin-striped Savile Row jacket in place of his usual rumpled cardigan. Charley Katz, lounging comfortably with legs crossed in an armchair, looked at him expectantly. 'Soo,' Oakes said at last, staring at a print on the panelled wall, 'Hamilton's not in Nassau.'

'Nope,' said Katz as he twirled his hat in his lap, 'he ain't.'

'You're certain the lawyer's telling the truth?'

'His story jived with Jennings,' replied Katz, 'as far as the ah, whaddaya call it, the—'

'Power of attorney?'

'Yeah, right. And the cashier's cheque.'

'A thousand dollars,' said Oakes, pausing to stare out the leaded glass window. 'Nothing but a goddam bribe.'

'Dobbs swore that each time Hamilton phoned, the call was from Texas. He even called in his gal, and she says, Oh, yessir, the calls were from an operator with a Southern accent.'

'What about the newspaper?'

'I checked that angle, too,' said Katz, reaching into his pocket for a cigarette and then thinking better of it. 'Dobbs gave 'em a press release, which he says Hamilton dictated over the phone.'

'Hamilton's smarter than I thought,' said Oakes, sitting on the edge of the desk and unbuttoning his jacket. 'Why show his face on the island? I figure he's on to something with Ericsson, and doesn't want to take any chances.'

'But what about the dame?'

'Who? Oh, Mrs Shawcross.' Oakes scratched his head. 'I figured he'd come back to see her, but you never can tell.'

'So what do we do?' asked Katz.

'The first thing I'm going to do is foreclose and see what kind of poker player Hamilton is. Meanwhile, keep a close watch on Mrs Shawcross, Charley. My gut tells me something's happening with Ericsson, and I don't like it.'

'OK,' said Katz, slipping on his hat. 'Anything else?'

'No,' said Oakes curtly.

CHAPTER FIFTEEN

WEARING A FADED pair of shorts, Hamilton clasped his hands around his knees, basking in the hot tropical sun on the pier as he watched a formation of brown pelicans sail low over the waves. He closed his eyes and listened to the cries of the gulls and the gentle surf, thinking about the news from home ... another classmate killed, shot down in the South Pacific. Everyone he knew was in the war, in the navy or marines in the Pacific or, like his brother Charles, an infantry officer in North Africa, while he was idling away his days in Nassau. Thinking about Evelyn. He tried to imagine that there was no war, nothing to stop him from driving into town and calling on her at Greycliff. No, he considered, if there were no war, she would be gone, home to England to be with her husband. Opening his eyes just as a pelican dove into the glassy sea, he decided he had to get her out of his mind. Having convinced Donovan to send him back, what more could he do? Maybe he'd bought some time, but he was one man against Ericsson's well-armed security force, and the rest of the Germans would probably be arriving soon enough. The British, meanwhile, adhered to their indolent colonial routines as if there were no war, keeping the natives in line, and doing little to protect the colony from the threat Hamilton believed was imminent.

'Mind if I join you?'

Shielding his eyes, Hamilton squinted up at the tall, muscular black man. 'Hello, Carter,' he said. 'Pull up a chair.'

Carter dropped lightly down on the weathered boards and gently massaged his thigh where a bright pink scar had healed over the bullet wound. 'Nice day to go fishin',' he said with a smile.

'Fishing?'

'I've been workin' on the boat. She's in tip-top shape. Good time of year for bonefish.'

Hamilton studied the man's handsome features, trying to penetrate his dark eyes. 'You're not here to talk about fishing,' he suggested.

'Maybe not.' Carter traced a circle with his finger on the boards. 'What are you planning to do, Tom?' he asked after a few moments. 'It's got me worried.'

'It's got me worried too.'

'There's got to be *something* we can do,' said Carter in a low voice. 'Those Germans take over this island, it would be a terrible thing for Sir Philip. And for my people, too.'

Hamilton nodded and said, 'Yes it would be.'

'We've got a fast boat,' said Carter, his eyes flashing, 'and I know where we could get our hands on a 30-calibre machine-gun and a box of grenades.'

'Wait a minute,' said Hamilton. 'I admire your courage, but all we'd manage to do is go down in a blaze of glory. Sure, we could shoot up the place, but there's no way we can head off a German attack.'

Carter hung his head. 'Then what are we gonna do?' he asked quietly.

'I'm working on it,' said Hamilton, regretting his tone the instant the words left his mouth.

'I think you ought to ask Sir Philip,' said Carter. 'No offence intended.'

'You're right,' said Hamilton. 'I'm out of ideas.' Scooping up his shirt, he jumped up and slipped on his leather sandals.

Sir Philip Sassoon was alone in his study with a book in his lap and pipe clenched in his teeth. He grasped the wheel of his chair and pivoted toward them as Hamilton and Carter appeared on the stairs. 'Come in, Tom,' said Sir Philip. 'I've been watching you. You remind me of a schoolboy, daydreaming the morning away.'

Hamilton frowned. 'Not exactly daydreaming,' he said, though it was more accurate than he cared to admit. 'But trying to think.'

'Sit down,' said Sir Philip. Hamilton dropped onto the sofa and Carter into the chair beside him. 'You've managed your real estate ploy rather nicely,' said Sir Philip, as he reached for a book of matches. 'With the coverage in the newspaper, I'm sure you've given Oakes and Ericsson something to think about.' He struck a match and cupped the flame over the bowl of his pipe. 'Knowing Ericsson, I'm certain he's had someone check his leads, which would cause him to conclude that you're in Texas. A clever manoeuvre.' Hamilton nodded with a tight-lipped smile. 'So what's your next move?' asked Sir Philip.

'No matter how hard I try,' said Hamilton, 'I can't seem to work out a solution. Hurricane Hole is virtually impregnable to a commando-type raid. Without photographic proof, there's no way the duke will send in the Royal Navy. And our government's not about to take unilateral action on British soil.'

'You might make another reconnaissance,' suggested Sir Philip.

'Too risky,' said Hamilton. 'And besides, we're out of time.'

'You've ruled out Evelyn as a go-between?' asked Carter.

Hamilton frowned. 'It wouldn't be fair. Anyway, I asked, and she … Well, she was upset and pleaded with me to leave Nassau.'

'At any rate,' said Sir Philip, 'unless you can change the duke's mind, which is highly unlikely, it appears you're powerless to stop Ericsson.'

'Unless,' interjected Carter, 'there's another way.' He gave Sir Philip an encouraging look.

Leaning back in his wheelchair, Sir Philip thoughtfully sucked on his pipe. 'Well …' he said after a moment, 'one thing you said, Tom, makes me wonder.' Hamilton's eyes widened. 'That the Americans would refrain from action on British soil.'

'I can't imagine that we'd—'

'No, you're quite right,' said Sir Philip. 'But the point is, what if Ericsson were *not* on British soil, or at least not within the jurisdiction of Nassau proper?'

Hamilton smiled. 'Why didn't I think of that?'

'If there were a way to lure him out of his hiding place, his Shangri-La,' said Sir Philip, 'you might be able to do a snatch-and-grab.'

'We'd have to set a trap,' said Hamilton excitedly. 'A suitable bait, something to draw him out.' Sir Philip nodded. Hamilton abruptly stood up and began to pace in front of the plate-glass window. 'If the Americans seize Ericsson,' he said, pausing to look at Sir Philip, 'and announce to the world they're interning him as a Nazi sympathizer and threat to Allied security, the British would *have* to take action, no matter how loudly the Duke of Windsor objects.'

'We can do it, Tom,' said Carter. 'We can grab him. If we can just get him to come out.'

'All right,' said Sir Philip, knocking out the unburnt tobacco on the heel of his hand. 'But you'd better move quickly. This press report of the land sale may spur the Germans to speed up their timetable. And one other thing,' said Sir Philip. He fixed Hamilton in his gaze. 'You may need Evelyn's help if this plan has any chance of success. She has access to Ericsson. And there's something about her reaction to seeing you that causes me to wonder ... You may discover that you have, shall we say, some leverage with her.'

Hamilton shook his head and started to speak.

'Put aside your feelings,' said Sir Philip gravely. 'And do what you have to do. We haven't much time.'

Like some tropical Versailles, Shangri-La shimmered in the noonday heat at the end of a long alleé of areca palms. Nils Ericsson smiled as he admired the creamy-white villa, with its graceful arches and red-tiled roof, through the shady bower of palm fronds. Wearing a Panama and a white linen suit, he strolled along the path, studying the rare flora he had meticulously collected for his island retreat: delicate irises and gaudy orchids, bright green casuarinas with their feathery foliage, and the massive kapok tree whose folded, smooth-skinned trunk reminded him of an elephant's haunch. The branches were alive with flashes of colour: chartreuse parakeets flitting from tree to tree, scarlet and blue macaws overhead, and the black and yellow toucan on its perch. Ericsson strolled to the limestone-rimmed reflecting pool, pausing to inspect the bright orange koi swirling beneath the lily pads.

Taking off his hat, he considered the stupendous implications of the bold plan he was on the verge of carrying out. With its new, bomb-proof sanctuary, Doenitz's U-boat fleet would be free to roam the Caribbean and attack every American and British tanker venturing out of the Gulf of Mexico. Their precious cargos of fuel were the vital life-blood sustaining the Allied war effort, without which the promise of a second front against Germany would be a mere fantasy. The British and Americans would be forced to come to their senses, seeing Churchill and Roosevelt as the fools they really were. What madness to embrace Stalin as an ally. No, with their ill-conceived war plans in a shambles, the British and Americans would turn to new leaders, men like Halifax, who would bring the senseless war with Germany to a rapid close. There would have to be concessions, of course – certain coveted overseas possessions, hegemony on the Continent – but the British would have their Empire and, he considered with a smile, his friend David, Duke of Windsor, would resume his rightful place on the throne, with his American queen at his side. Nodding to himself as he ambled along, he thought of the extraordinary opportunities peace would bring for an enterprising man like himself, positioned to exploit the vast mineral resources of Mexico and South America under the protective shield of the new *Pax Germanica*.

As he trudged up the steps to the loggia, Ericsson withdrew a thin, gold hunter watch from his ample waistcoat pocket and snapped open the cover. Either Krebs was uncharacteristically late, or no one had sent for him during his perambulations to announce his guest's arrival. The moment he stepped under the cooling shade, he observed the German officer standing by the windows. Moments later Krebs, distinctly uncomfortable in his wool, field-grey tunic, strode out on the loggia, halting with the heels of his boots touching and a quick nod of his head.

'*Guten tag, mein Herr*,' he said, reaching out to give Ericsson a firm handshake.

'Major Krebs,' said Ericsson with a smile. 'Let us sit here' – he motioned to the wicker furniture – 'where we can enjoy the view.' Once they were seated he noticed the perspiration wetting the fringe of pale-blond hair above Kreb's stiff collar. 'Rather warm today,' he remarked. 'Perhaps you would care for lemonade, or a beer?'

'*Danke*,' said Krebs, tugging at his collar. 'A beer would be excellent.'

'Johann,' said Ericsson to the servant standing in the shadows. 'Bring us two Becks and a plate of herring. And now, Major,' he said, dispensing with the pleasantries, 'when will you be ready to launch your attack?'

'My men are prepared,' replied Krebs, sitting ramrod-straight. 'Once we have established a firm date, I shall send for the transport.'

'And then?'

'Six hours to load, eight hours to sail from Martinique.'

'Were the maps adequate?'

'Excellent. We should have no difficulty.'

'Very well,' said Ericsson, 'let us choose a date.' A servant appeared with their drinks and a plate of pickled herring. Once the man had gone, Ericsson lifted a frosted mug and said, 'Skaal. Perhaps by this time next week, Nassau shall be ours.'

Krebs repeated the toast and joined his host in downing a large swallow. 'I'm afraid I don't understand,' he said, 'how we can proceed before the canal is ready?'

A dark look clouded Ericsson's stolid face. 'The canal will have to wait,' he said flatly. 'I would prefer it were otherwise, but we haven't any choice.' In response to Krebs's puzzled expression, he said, 'The newspaper reported that the American has purchased a parcel of land that lies directly in our path.'

'The American?'

'We're virtually certain the man's an intelligence agent. And now, with the publicity, we can't proceed with the excavation.'

'But our navy insisted on access to the port.'

'Yes, and they shall have it. It will only take a few weeks to complete the canal, and that can be done *after* you've seized the island. What matters is that the pens are ready for your boats. The time is ripe.' Lifting his mug, he took another long swallow, and then reached for a piece of herring. 'Excellent,' he said. 'From Norway.'

Krebs sampled a morsel. 'If this American agent is in Nassau,' he said, with a pensive look in his pale-blue eyes, 'how can you be sure he's not planning an action?'

'An action?' said Ericsson with a hearty laugh. 'One man? In any case, I'm certain he's nowhere near Nassau, but back in America, afraid to show his face.'

'But how, then, was he able—?'

'Through a local lawyer. We've checked it out thoroughly. And what's more, Mrs Shawcross is keeping an eye out for him.'

'I see. Her home is under surveillance?'

'Naturally. Someone was observed leaving by the back entrance last week, but it was dark and there was no reason to believe it was Hamilton.'

'Women like that,' said Krebs dismissively, 'are not terribly particular about the men they sleep with.'

'Perhaps you should meet her,' suggested Ericsson. 'After we've completed the operation, naturally.'

'Perhaps,' said Krebs, reaching for another piece of herring.

'Let's choose a date, then,' said Ericsson emphatically. 'The British are notorious for their beloved weekends. Should we say a week from Saturday?'

'Saturday,' said Krebs. 'Nine days hence. More than enough time to get ready.'

'Excellent,' said Ericsson. 'You have the Bofors guns I sent you?'

'Yes, the 77s. An excellent weapon. I can assure you that the island will be secure and your friend the duke under house arrest before breakfast.'

Lifting his mug, Ericsson concluded, 'Let's go indoors, then. Our lunch is waiting.'

Lying on a *chaise-longue* by the pool, Hamilton trailed his fingers across the surface of the water as he enjoyed the afternoon sun on his back. Marnie, lying beside him with the straps of her bathing suit untied, slowly flexed and unflexed the hamstring of a long, slender leg as she turned the page of the novel on the flagstones beneath her. 'Have you read du Maupassant?' she asked, without looking up.

'No. Mind if I ask something?' said Hamilton, rolling over on his side. Shading his eyes, he said, 'Did Sir Philip say anything about Evelyn? His suspicions?'

Marnie closed her book. 'What Philip shares with me,' she replied, 'is none of your business. Besides, I don't know what you're talking about.'

'Both times I mentioned Evelyn's reaction when I went to see her, Philip made this elliptical remark about his suspicions....'

'Elliptical?'

'Yes, elliptical,' said Hamilton with a trace of asperity. 'I thought he might have explained.'

'Well, what *was* her reaction?'

'That she wanted me to leave, pleaded with me to leave Nassau.'

'Hmm,' said Marnie. 'Did she think you'd been seen?'

'No. I made it clear no one knew I'd come back.'

'Well,' said Marnie slowly. 'From a woman's point of view, I'd have thought she would have begged you *not* to leave. I'm sure that's what Philip meant.'

'Then why would she want me to leave?'

'Maybe she knows something you don't. Something that makes her think you're not safe.'

'Or maybe,' said Hamilton, suddenly sitting up and clasping his arms around his knees, 'something that tells her my being here isn't safe for *her*.'

'What does that mean?' asked Marnie with a puzzled look.

'I don't know,' admitted Hamilton.

She sat up, reached back to tie the straps of her suit, and said, 'Why don't you ask *her*?'

Hamilton gave Marnie an affectionate smile and said, 'I think I'll do just that.'

CHAPTER SIXTEEN

EVELYN SAT ALONE in the formal dining room, wearing a yellow robe, staring vacantly at the portrait of her grandmother, unable to touch her breakfast or even look at the newspaper. Every sound – the grandfather clock, the quarrelsome jays outside the window – seemed strangely amplified. A tremor passed over her as she wondered whether she might be going mad. How long could she go on like this? With a sigh, she took a sip of strong, black coffee and lifted her fork with a slice of melon. She froze at the sound of the telephone. Holding her breath, she waited for Samuel to answer it, and then strained to make out his words. It had to be Ericsson … Calling to say they'd found Tom.

'Miz Shawcross …'

She cautiously looked at Samuel in the doorway. 'Yes,' she said softly. 'Who is it?'

'Mister Hamilton. Can you speak to him?'

'No. Tell him I'm not in.'

'Yes, ma'am.' With a slight bow, he turned toward the living room.

'No, wait,' said Evelyn. Samuel stopped and gave her a troubled look. 'Ask him,' she said in a calmer voice, 'where he is. Where he's calling from.'

'Yes, ma'am.'

After a moment, the servant returned. 'He's at the Sassoon place.'

'All right,' said Evelyn in a composed way, pushing back from the table.

Sitting at the writing-desk in the living room, Evelyn picked up the receiver and said, 'Hello? Tom?'

'Evelyn ... I was afraid you wouldn't talk to me.'

'I probably shouldn't. Don't you know it isn't safe?'

'No one knows I'm here.'

'What? After that story in the paper?'

'I can explain that.'

'Oh, Tom.'

'Everyone thinks I'm in Texas, even my own lawyer. Evelyn, I *need* to see you.'

After a brief silence, she said wearily, 'You told me yourself how dangerous it is to go out. Nils Ericsson is ... well, if he's who you say he is, he must be very ruthless.'

'I need your help, Evelyn.'

'My help?' Looking desperately around the empty room, she massaged her forehead and then said, 'No, I can't help you. Won't you please just leave me alone?'

Stunned, Hamilton considered giving up. No, he thought, she was his only chance. 'Listen to me,' he said calmly. 'Will you at least do that?'

'Yes,' she said, wiping a tear from the corner of her eye.

'Sure it's risky for me to see you. But it's even riskier if I do as you say and leave Nassau. Not just for me, but for you and Sir Philip and the whole damned Colony. You've got to believe me.'

'All right,' she with a tone of resignation. 'I believe you.'

'I swear, no one knows I'm here.' He sensed he was making headway. 'I can come to the gate at the back.'

They're watching, thought Evelyn, watching the house day and night. 'No,' she said. 'It's too risky.' She paused and bit her lip. 'You know the Royal Victoria?' she asked.

'The old hotel?'

'Yes. Could you arrange to pick me up there? After dark.'

'How would you get there?'

'Leave that to me. There's an entrance on a side street. Could someone pick me up there, say at nine this evening?'

'I'll send Sir Philip's man, Carter. Just make sure no one's watching.'

God, thought Evelyn, was this madness? 'Don't worry,' she said.

'Evelyn,' sighed Hamilton. 'I can't wait to see you.'

'Goodbye, Tom.' Afraid she'd change her mind, she hung up and summoned Samuel with a bell. When he entered the room, she said, 'You mustn't say a word about this to anyone.'

'No, ma'am.'

'No one must know Mr Hamilton called. Or even that he's in Nassau. Is that clear?'

'Yes, ma'am.'

'Can you drive, Samuel?' asked Evelyn, rising from the desk. 'Father's old car?'

'I s'pose so, but it's been a long time.' He gave her a questioning look.

Dressed in a long, dark coat, belted at her trim waist, with a black scarf wrapped around her hair, Evelyn descended the stairs shortly after 8.30, careful to leave the usual lights burning upstairs. Samuel was waiting in the kitchen, dressed in his white jacket. 'Take off that coat,' she instructed him, 'and put on a dark shirt. And then meet me in the garage. Once you're there, don't say a word.'

'If you say so, ma'am,' said Samuel, turning toward his room. Evelyn let herself out the back door and hurried to the garage where her father's 1936 Buick was parked. She was sure no one had driven it since her parents had left for London. She opened the back door and climbed in, closing the door as noiselessly as possible. Moments later Samuel appeared, almost invisible in a long-sleeved black shirt, peering nervously around until he saw Evelyn in the back seat. She rolled down the window and handed him the car keys. 'Open the garage doors,' she whispered, 'and then get in and drive out. Turn right and drive to the Royal Victoria Hotel.'

'Yes, ma'am.'

'Act relaxed, Samuel. Whistle a tune or something. And if anyone follows us, let me know, but don't turn around. Is that clear?'

'Yes, ma'am.' He slid open the heavy garage doors and whistled a cheerful tune as he climbed in the driver's seat and started the engine. After a few pumps of the accelerator, he started down the driveway. Evelyn slumped flat on the seat, her heart racing. Switching on headlamps, Samuel slowly swung into the street, adopting a casual pose, with his head back and arm resting on the open window. As he cruised down the street, a man behind the wheel of a car concealed in the shadows flipped up the brim of his hat and watched as the Buick slowly passed by. As its red tail-lights disappeared down the block, the observer lowered his hat and slumped back on the seat.

Lying on the cloth seat-covers, Evelyn listened to the rush of wind through the open window and the squeal of the tyres as Samuel made several turns. At last she could feel the car slowing down under the glare of a streetlamp. 'Did anyone follow us?' she asked softly.

'No, ma'am,' said Samuel. 'We're comin' up on the hotel.' He pulled over at the entrance.

'All right,' said Evelyn, casting a quick look through the rear window, satisfied the street was empty. 'I'm getting out here. Just kill some time before going home.'

The kindly old black man turned around in his seat and gave her a worried look. 'You be all right, Miz Shawcross?' he asked. 'You send for me?'

'I'll be fine,' she said, opening the door. 'And don't worry. I'll get a ride home. If anyone should telephone, tell them I've gone to bed and am not to be disturbed.'

At five minutes till nine Evelyn emerged from the doorway, having avoided contact with the hotel staff or guests in the nearly empty lobby. As she glanced nervously down the street, she heard the sound of an approaching vehicle. She could see that the driver was a black man, alone. Flashing a quick smile as he pulled over, Carter said, 'Evenin', Miz Shawcross.' She climbed in the back and, as Carter started off, slumped down on the seat. 'That's the idea,' he said, with a glance in the rear-view mirror. Carter drove through town to the highway out to Cable Beach, speeding along in the dark night while frequently checking the mirror. Within fifteen minutes he turned into the drive at Eves. Sitting up, Evelyn loosened her scarf and shook out her hair.

'Thank you,' she said as Carter switched off the ignition. 'That was very well done.'

'My pleasure. Tom said to tell you he's waiting in the living room.'

As Evelyn hurried up the flagstones, she struggled to overcome her guilty feelings about the night-time rendezvous. With a sharp intake of breath, she turned the knob and quickly stepped inside out of the glare of the porch light. The house was quiet and dark, except for the light from the hallway. Relieved that Sir Philip and Marnie had turned in, she was walking through the panelled den when a voice said, 'Hello, darlin',' in a soft Southern drawl. 'Marnie?' whispered Evelyn. Peering in the darkness, she discovered the African grey parrot on its perch.

'God,' muttered Evelyn, as she continued down the hallway. Tom was alone on the far side of the living room. At the sight of Evelyn, he began walking toward her, meeting her halfway and taking her into his arms without a word. For a moment they simply embraced. 'Why is it,' she finally said, 'each time I see you, I feel it's going to be the last?'

'Probably because,' he said, pulling away and looking in her eyes, 'I've dragged you into something I never should have.'

'Oh, Tom,' she murmured, rising on tiptoes to kiss him. Feeling suddenly embarrassed, she abruptly broke away.

'It's OK,' he said, gently touching her chin. 'Philip and Marnie have gone to bed.'

'Did they know I was coming?'

'Yes.' He studied her pale, anxious face, thinking she looked no less beautiful but more fragile than before. 'What can I get you?' he asked.

'Water would be fine,' she said, remembering her determination to control her feelings.

'All right,' he said with mild surprise. 'But I'm having a drink.'

As he turned toward the bar, she said, 'On second thoughts, I'll have a whisky.' As Hamilton went to the bar, she slipped off her coat and draped it over a chair.

'How did you get to the hotel?' he asked, as he took two glasses from the shelf.

'Samuel drove me. In Father's old Buick.'

Hamilton dropped several cubes of ice in one of the glasses and reached for a crystal decanter. 'No one saw you?' he asked, as he poured, topping off the whisky with water from a pitcher.

'I was flat on the back seat,' she said as she accepted her drink. 'Samuel was certain no one followed us.'

Hamilton took a sip and said, 'Why don't we sit down, and let me explain.' Settling in the corner of the sofa, Evelyn crossed her legs as he sat down beside her. He gave her an encouraging smile, staring into her eyes and thinking back to the first night they met.

'You said you need my help,' she began.

'What I really wish,' he said with a grimace, 'is that we could just forget the damned war and go away to some quiet place....'

'Don't be foolish, Tom,' she interrupted. 'Now what is it you want from me?'

He took a sip and said, 'Ericsson's construction project is almost finished, and my instincts tell me the Germans are planning an attack. Soon.'

'And you want me to plead with David, or perhaps Wallis, to do something, or at least to warn them.'

'No.'

'I won't do it! They'll think I'm mad. You haven't any proof. It's just your word, your conjecture, really. I know David. He'll simply pick up the phone and call Ericsson.'

'Listen to me,' said Hamilton. In the ensuing silence she stared into his grey eyes and then lifted the glass to her lips. 'I'm not asking you to call the duke or the duchess,' he said calmly. 'My government's convinced that Nils Ericsson, at the very least, is aiding and abetting the enemy. And we're planning to intern him, for the duration of the war.' She nodded, holding his gaze. 'The problem is that

Ericsson is a resident of a British Crown Colony, where we can't get at him.'

'What do you intend to do?'

'If we can entice him away from Nassau, we can grab him. Before the Germans attack. Publicly declare him to be a threat, aiding the Nazis, which will shame the British into moving on Hurricane Hole.'

'Hurricane Hole,' she whispered.

'The U-boat base.'

'And how do you intend, as you said, to entice him away?'

'With your help,' said Hamilton flatly.

Evelyn started to protest, but willed herself to stay quiet. After taking another sip, she said, 'What can I possibly do?'

'The best way to lure Ericsson away from Nassau is tempt him to go after something, or someone, he wants.'

Fascinated, she said, 'Such as...?'

'Me.' Hamilton leaned forward. 'Ericsson wants me out of the way. He's smart enough to guess that I'm the one who reconnoitred the construction site before Christmas and killed one of his men.'

'You did?' Evelyn's eyes widened.

'Yes,' said Hamilton with a nod. 'And Ericsson needs that strip of land on Hog Island to finish his canal.'

Evelyn stared impassively at him, fully aware that Ericsson knew even more than Tom realized. 'But you told me,' she said, 'that he thinks you're in Texas.'

'What if he discovers I've come back? That I'm staying in an out-of-the-way place up in the Abacos, let's say. If someone can show him where to find me, I think he'll take the bait.'

'But surely he'd come with his armed men.'

'We'll be ready for them. It's a trap.'

Evelyn gazed into his eyes. 'Tom, what is it you want *me* to do?'

'He knows you were seeing me before Christmas.' She nodded. 'So you tell him that I've come back and want to see you. That you know where I'm staying, where I can be found.'

Her mind racing, Evelyn thought ... just as Ericsson demanded.

'The idea is that you're coming to be with me, a discreet weekend together on one of these tiny cays. What you'd expect of two people having an affair.' Evelyn nodded. 'And Ericcson insists on coming with you. Right into the trap.'

'But Tom,' – she searched his eyes – 'why? Why would I betray you?'

'Betray me?' He gave her a puzzled look.

Suddenly reddening, Evelyn quickly said, 'Well, not betray you, but tell Ericsson where you are and that I was planning to see you?'

'The way I see it, you just casually let it drop that you've heard from me; that you're planning to see me again. You're friends, right?'

'Yes.'

'And when he hears I'm in the Bahamas, and you know where to find me, I'm betting he'll insist on knowing where, or even going with you. You may have to do a bit of improvising ...'

Oh, my God, she thought, staring into the distance. He was asking her to do precisely what Ericsson, with his threats, had demanded. Notify him the minute she heard from Tom. And, of course, Ericsson would jump at the chance to go after him. If Tom's scheme succeeded, Ericsson would be gone, locked up in an American jail. And Tom was right about the duke: he'd have no alternative but to send in the Royal Navy once the Americans made their sensational announcement. The German take-over would be scotched, the duke and duchess spared. It was her only chance. 'Oh, Tom,' she sighed, putting her glass aside. 'Of course I'll help you.' Leaning over, she threw her arms around his neck and kissed him.

'Mmm,' he murmured, caressing her through the sheer fabric of her blouse. 'I've been dreaming of holding you.'

'Hush,' she whispered, as she leaned over to switch off the lamp.

Sir Harry Oakes sat at his desk in the Westbourne library, his face obscured by the newspaper. 'Goddamn Germans,' he muttered, as he scanned an article about the losses in the Atlantic to hunting parties of U-boats. 'Wolf packs,' he said aloud, tossing the paper aside. He reached for the telephone, quickly dialled a number, and said, 'Miss Taylor, where the hell is Pemberton? Oh, he is ...' Looking up as he placed the receiver on the cradle, he observed a tall, ascetic looking man in a three-piece suit standing in the doorway. 'Pemberton,' he said. 'I've been expecting you.'

The tall man approached Oakes, taking a worn leather case from under his arm and opening the clasp. 'Good morning,' he said pleasantly, sitting down and removing a folder from his case. Reginald Pemberton spoke with the mild British accent of a Midlands-born solicitor, diluted by years in the Bahamas.

'You've got the papers?' asked Oakes.

'Indeed,' replied Pemberton, tapping his folder. 'The promissory note and mortgage.'

'Here,' said Oakes brusquely, reaching across the desk. 'Let me have a look.' The lawyer handed him the file and Oakes extracted several typewritten sheets. A small, satisfied smile curled his mouth. 'Twenty thousand pounds,' he said, as he fastened the pages with a paper-clip. 'Hah! The dough Hamilton paid those chumps is money down the drain as soon as we foreclose the mortgage.' Pemberton nodded in agreement. 'When can you get started?' asked Oakes.

'With the foreclosure?'

'Goddamn right.'

'As soon as there's a default.'

'Default?'

'Yes. May I?' He gestured to the file, which Oakes handed him across the desk. 'Let me see,' said Pemberton. 'Just as I thought,' he said after a moment. 'An instalment of principal and interest is payable on the 31st of May. Two months hence.'

'What?' said Oakes. 'I can't possibly wait that long. We need to call that note.'

'But, Sir Harry, the payment's not due till the end of May.'

'Goddamn it, Reggie, it was supposed to be a demand note! Payable on demand.'

'I have no such recollection—'

'Well, we'll just have to change it.'

'Change it?' said Pemberton timidly.

'You heard me. Substitute a different page with the note payable on *demand*. What the hell difference does it make to Jennings and his Bay Street pals? They've got their cash.'

'True,' said Pemberton with a nod. 'And considering the fact that the mortgage was never recorded, no one's likely to notice. A bit irregular, but we might do as you suggest.'

'Send out a written demand,' said Oakes, 'for payment in full, immediately. Then foreclose on that miserable piece of swampland.' Rubbing his hands together, he said, 'We'll see what kind of stuff Hamilton is made of.'

'Will there be anything else?' asked Pemberton, rising from his chair and returning the file to his case.

'No,' said Oakes. 'Just get to work. Oh, one last thing. I assume this foreclosure is a matter of public record. They'll pick it up in the papers.'

'Yes, I should think so.'

'Good. You get a call from a reporter, refer him to me.'

Within days of the interview with his solicitor, Oakes, relaxing in his study, was informed by the butler that the editor of the Nassau *Daily Tribune* was on the line. 'Sure, I'll talk to him,' said Oakes. He picked up the phone and said, 'Hello?'

'Sir Harry? Etienne Dupuch here. Mr Pemberton suggested I give you a call.'

'Yeah, right,' said Oakes. 'What can I do for you?'

'When we saw the notice regarding the foreclosure on Hog Island, we contacted your attorney.'

'Right.' Sir Harry smiled inwardly.

'I gather Lake Shore Mining is in some fashion affiliated with—'

'Right. One of my companies.'

'I see. And the gentlemen who own the property, I gather that they—'

'Yeah, I loaned them the money to buy it. My company did. And they owe me. It's that simple. If they can't pay, we foreclose. And that's what we're doing.'

'Isn't this the same property these gentlemen have agreed to sell? I assume you saw the recent announcement?'

'Sure, I saw it. Some fellow says he's gonna buy it and build a hotel.'

'And a casino.'

'Right. Listen, Mister, ah, Dupuch. Let's just say he made a poor decision. He'll have to pay off my mortgage to get clear title. And, quite frankly, I doubt he'll do that.'

'So you expect to foreclose?'

'Absolutely.'

'And what, if I may ask, are your intentions? Will you negotiate with the buyer, with Hamilton?'

'No,' said Oakes. 'If anybody builds a hotel and casino on Hog Island, it's gonna be Sir Harry Oakes.'

'Oh, I see.'

'And you can print that.'

CHAPTER SEVENTEEN

LUXURIATING UNDER THE quilt, Evelyn was vaguely conscious of a feeling of well-being, as though a great burden had been lifted. A shaft of sunlight shone through a crack in the chintz curtains, just enough to get her bearings in the strange room. She stretched out under the covers, aware that for the first time in weeks she'd awakened to a feeling other than despair. The door to the bathroom opened quietly, and Tom appeared, wearing only his striped pyjama bottoms and giving her a tender look. Returning the look with a smile, Evelyn yawned and said, 'Good morning, darling.'

Walking over to her bedside, he leaned down and kissed her lightly on the forehead, and then on the lips. 'It's early,' he said, sitting down beside her. 'I was hoping you'd sleep.'

Propping herself up, the covers modestly drawn up to her chin, Evelyn said, 'I've been sleeping late for weeks. Today I want to be up, to seize the day.'

'*Carpe diem*,' said Hamilton with a smile.

'Yes, *carpe diem*.' As she looked at his handsome face and bare torso in the dim light she suppressed a wave of desire, a reminder of the end of the evening. To her relief, she saw that her clothes were folded on a nearby chair and her shoes on the floor beneath them. The thought of making love in Marnie's house provoked a stab of guilt, though in the same instant she realized she was feeling guilty for the wrong reason. 'Tom,' she said. 'I should get dressed and go. Before the Sassoons are up.'

'Don't worry about them.'

'I'd prefer they didn't see me. Do you have a robe?'

'Sure.' He opened a louvred closet door, took out a plaid cotton bathrobe and handed it to her as she sat up and threw back the covers. For a moment he allowed himself to look at her, aware that he was only a heartbeat away from losing his self-control. Turning away as she slipped on his robe, he said, 'I'll get dressed and see if I can find us a cup of coffee. Then we'll decide how to get you home.'

By the time Evelyn emerged from the dressing-room, looking remarkably fresh in her clothes from the previous evening, Hamilton had returned from the kitchen with two steaming cups of coffee. 'Milk and sugar,' he said, handing her a cup, 'if I remember correctly.'

'You do,' she said with a happy smile.

'And I thought you'd be wanting those,' he added, pointing to her coat and scarf on the end of the bed.

'Oh, yes.'

'Carter can drive you to the hotel,' said Hamilton. 'I assume your man can meet you there and drive you home.'

'Yes, of course,' said Evelyn, feeling oddly let down, like Cinderella, she supposed, when the ball was over. 'And then what should I do?'

'Get in touch with Ericsson.' Hamilton took a sip of coffee and walked over to draw back the curtains, revealing the pale blue sky over the even bluer water. 'Invite him for cocktails.'

'Assuming he accepts, then what?'

'Casually mention that I've contacted you. That you're planning to see me.'

'Just where I am supposed to be meeting you?'

'There's a tiny cay up in the Abacos, about a hundred miles north of here, called Hope Town. It's easy to find because of its famous lighthouse, one of the old oil-burning variety.'

'I see.'

'Tell Ericsson I'm holed up in Hope Town and want you to spend a weekend with me. And then ask if he could provide you with a boat. My hunch is he'll follow you.'

'In his yacht?'

'The *Northern Lights*?' Hamilton shook his head. 'The water's too shallow in the Abacos. He'll take one of his speedboats.'

'When?' Evelyn sat on the end of the bed and sipped her coffee.

'If it looks like he's game, tell him you're planning to meet me Friday night.'

'Well,' said Evelyn. 'That's easy enough. Hope Town. With its famous lighthouse.'

'If he goes for it,' said Hamilton, walking over to her and placing his arms around her, 'we'll work out the details.'

She gave him a kiss. 'Tom,' she murmured, 'if we get through this ...'

'Yes,' he said, stroking her hair.

'I love you,' she whispered. 'I want to be with you.'

'What about your husband?'

'It's over. I'm asking for a divorce. Tom?' She gazed in his eyes. 'Will you have me?'

'God, Evelyn, I'm crazy about you. Now, I'm afraid Carter's waiting.'

Evelyn placed the call to Ericsson from the living room at Greycliff. 'It's Mrs Shawcross,' she said to the servant who answered.

'Why, Evelyn,' said Ericsson after a brief delay, 'what a pleasant surprise.'

'I have some information for you.'

'What sort of information?'

'I'd prefer to discuss it in person. Could you come by for a cocktail?'

'Well, that's very kind, but I'd have to know what this concerns.'

'It concerns the matter you were so anxious about.'

'There's something to report?'

'Yes. I should think you'd want to know right away.'

'Undoubtedly. I'll see you at seven.'

'I'll be expecting you.' Gently hanging up, she took a deep breath and slowly exhaled. Now she would simply have to wait.

*

Charley Katz studied the photograph on the front page of the newspaper. It had to be a stock photo, he reasoned, for he'd never seen Oakes in that Homburg nor the plaid suit that was way too heavy for the tropical climate. Jesus, he thought as he tossed the paper on the car seat. Katz could scarcely believe that Oakes had given the newspaper an interview. He could imagine Meyer Lansky's reaction when he read that quote, bragging that if anybody built a casino on Hog Island it would be Harry Oakes. Maybe you could have so much money it made you stupid. The thought was strangely depressing.

Fidgeting in the cramped seat, Katz wondered how much longer he could stand keeping watch on the Shawcross mansion to see if she came out, which was almost never, or if she had any callers. So far she'd had none. Just that man of hers driving around at night in the old Buick. And now that Lansky would be steamed at the article in the paper, things might get a little dicey. Maybe it was time to move on. In the gathering dusk he was aware of the deep, throaty exhaust of a large car and caught a glimpse in the side-mirror of headlights swinging onto the street. Slumping down, he listened to the vehicle's approach. A black Jaguar saloon, polished to a mirror finish, rolled by slowly and came to a stop in front of Greycliff. Hmm, thought Katz, peering over the dashboard. A burly man in a light-coloured suit, with a head of silver hair, emerged from the back seat and started up the path. Before he reached the front door, someone inside switched on the porch lights. As soon as he rang, the green door swung open, admitting the silver-haired man. When the door closed behind him, the Jaguar pulled out from the kerb and sped away, red tail-lights vanishing in the gloaming.

Evelyn waited nervously as Samuel showed Nils Ericcson up the stairs. She was wearing her blue chiffon dress and a stole over her bare shoulders, with a sapphire and diamond pendant on a gold chain. Squaring her shoulders, she smiled bravely as Ericsson came up.

'Good evening, my dear,' he said in his thick accent, as he took her hand and lightly kissed it. 'You look marvellous.'

'Thank you,' she said with forced politeness, as Ericcson gazed around the handsomely appointed room. 'Let's have our cocktails on the veranda,' she suggested. 'It's quite pleasant this time of the evening.'

'Very well.'

'Samuel,' said Evelyn to the servant. 'Would you get Mr Ericsson a drink? I'll have champagne.'

'Vodka,' specified Ericsson. 'Over ice.'

Evelyn led the way to the open veranda. 'This is fantastic,' said Ericsson, surveying the lawn and gardens, enclosed by tall tropical trees. 'I'm an admirer of good horticulture.' Samuel appeared with their drinks. When they were alone, Ericsson raised his glass and looked at Evelyn. 'Now,' he said after taking a sip, 'what do you have for me?'

'He called.'

After a fruitless surveillance of the Shawcross house for over a week, Charley Katz was intrigued by the arrival of the older gentleman in the Jaguar. As dusk settled over the quiet neighbourhood, he climbed out of the car, crossed the street, and approached the house. Lights were burning on the second storey, while the rooms below were dark. Peering into the twilight, he noticed a gate on the left. Hoping to get a closer look, he tried the gate, found it unlocked, and entered the garden. Carefully making his way along a flagstone path, he was aware of muffled voices. Katz looked up, where he could see an open veranda and hear a man and woman engaged in conversation. He grasped a sturdy branch of a banyan, swung himself up and, with infinite care, silently ascended until he was within five feet of the railing.

'Hamilton?' said Ericsson, arching his eyebrows.

'Yes,' said Evelyn. 'He called yesterday.'

'From America?'

'No. From the Bahamas.'

'Ah,' said Ericsson with a smile. 'I was sure he'd come back.'

'He wants to see me.'

'Well, well. I'm pleased you took our conversation to heart.' Ericsson leaned over the railing, peering out into the darkness.

'You must promise me,' said Evelyn, 'that no harm will come to my husband.'

He turned around and stared at her. 'You have nothing to fear so long as you co-operate. I assume Hamilton is staying with his friend, the Jew Sassoon?'

'No. He's staying on one of those tiny islands – cays I believe they're called – north of here. He wants me to join him for the weekend.'

'Ah,' said Ericsson, 'a romantic getaway. What could be more perfect. You shall lead me there.'

Oh, my God, thought Evelyn. It was exactly as Tom had predicted. 'If you like,' she said, sipping her champagne.

Katz clung tightly to the tree trunk, desperately trying to remain still and to concentrate on every word of the peculiar conversation.

'Where, exactly, is Hamilton staying?' asked Ericsson.

'A place called Hope Town. He said it's famous for its lighthouse.'

'Hope Town,' repeated Ericsson. 'I'm sure my men can find it.' He swirled his glass. 'Well, Evelyn,' he said, 'this could not have come at a more opportune moment.'

'Why is that?' she said, as casually as she was able.

'The Germans are preparing to strike. You see, I've built them a base for their U-boats at my marina. In a matter of days, they'll assault the island, seize Oakes Field, and place the duke under house arrest.'

'Oh, my goodness,' said Evelyn, feigning shock. 'Will the duke and duchess be all right?'

Ericsson smiled indulgently. 'They'll be treated with the greatest consideration. The duke could be very useful, you know, in bringing your countrymen to their senses.' Evelyn nodded. 'My only fear,' continued Ericsson, 'was that this American might spoil our plans. But thanks to you' – he looked in her eyes – 'we have nothing to worry about.'

From his perch on the sturdy bough, Charley Katz's mind was spinning. Germans, he thought ... a goddamn U-boat base! And she's obviously in on it....

'When is he expecting you?' asked Ericsson.

'Friday evening. I'm waiting for him to call with the specifics. And I'll have to arrange a boat. I was hoping you could help.'

'Naturally, my dear,' said Ericsson in an avuncular tone, reaching over to pat her arm. 'We'll take my motor-launch, with my best men.'

'When you find Hamilton,' she asked, looking Ericsson in the eye, 'what will you do?'

'Kill him,' replied Ericsson. 'We haven't any alternative.'

Shivering with a sudden chill, Evelyn said, 'Let's go to the living room. We can get you another drink.'

Once their voices faded away, Katz slowly and carefully made his way down, dropping onto the damp soil as silently as a cat. After resuming his vigil in the car to see if any other strange visitors arrived, he would report his amazing discovery first thing in the morning.

Standing at the window in Sir Philip's study, Hamilton watched the sunset, bands of gold and orange streaking the horizon, and the lights along the pier glittering in the dark water. At the sound of the lift, he turned as the door opened and Sir Philip propelled himself forward. 'There you are,' said Sir Philip with a smile, rolling up and giving Tom a firm handshake. 'Marnie should be joining us. I thought that while we have a moment you might share some of the details.'

Hamilton followed Sir Philip to his accustomed place in the study and sat down next to him. 'After tonight,' he said, 'we should be set.'

'I gather Evelyn was co-operative?'

'To be honest, I was surprised by her enthusiasm. Once I explained that it was a way to get Ericsson behind bars, she came right around.'

'Interesting,' commented Sir Philip. 'She's seeing the man this evening?'

'Yes, she phoned to say he accepted her invitation. She's planning to tell him I'm holed up on one of these cays and invited her to join me.'

'Do you suppose he'll fall for it?' asked Sir Philip.

'I'd lay ten-to-one odds.'

Sir Philip smiled, but then fixed Hamilton in his gaze. 'You're no doubt aware,' he said, 'that he'll come with a body of well-armed men. How do you plan to handle them?'

Leaning forward, Hamilton said, 'The navy's agreed to provide me three of their UDT men. One of our destroyers will be standing offshore.'

'UDT men?' Sir Philip arched his eyebrows.

'Underwater demolition teams,' explained Hamilton. 'Popularly known as 'frogmen'. They're trained like your SOE commandos. Experts in hand-to-hand combat.'

'I see.'

'Evelyn will tell them she's meeting me after dark at a café in town. Once they're on their way, she'll head for the lighthouse and wait for me at the lighthouse-keeper's shack. Carter knows the man. In case something goes wrong, he can look after her.'

Sir Philip sat silently in his cane-backed wheelchair, giving Hamilton an appraising look. 'A sound enough plan,' he said at last. 'But its success largely hinges on Evelyn. Either she's very courageous ... or very much in love.'

'Don't let me interrupt,' said Marnie, as she appeared at the top of the stairs. She stopped and stared at Tom with one hand on her hip.

'Not at all, darling,' said Sir Philip cheerfully. 'We were just finishing our, ah, official chat.'

Walking slowly over to Hamilton, Marnie said, 'I hope you got Evelyn fixed up with a ride home.'

'Now, how would you know—?' said Hamilton.

'I don't suppose that was *your* lipstick on the coffee cup.'

'Now, now,' objected Sir Philip. 'Leave poor Tom alone. He was merely—'

'I know,' said Marnie. 'Doing his duty.'

'If it weren't for Evelyn,' said Hamilton, 'we'd be in a real jam.'

'Tom's right,' said Sir Philip. 'Mrs Shawcross has agreed to help with the plan to detain Ericsson.'

'Well,' said Marnie, 'you'd better be careful. I warned you not to fall for that woman, but you wouldn't listen.' Taking a step closer, she said, 'There's something about her I don't understand.' Both men gave her a questioning look.

'Call it female intuition,' she said. 'But promise you'll be careful.'

CHAPTER EIGHTEEN

S LAPPING A MOSQUITO at his neck, Charley Katz flung open his
cheap canvas suitcase and rapidly began emptying the
contents of the chest of drawers. In a matter of minutes the
suitcase was bulging as he forced it shut and fastened the clasps.
Slipping on his fedora, he briskly walked to the telephone on the
bedside table. On his two previous attempts to contact his employer
he'd been curtly informed that Sir Harry was not to be disturbed.
Well, it was almost noon, and if he couldn't reach him on the phone,
he'd drive over and demand to see him. He dialled the number,
impatiently gave the operator his name, and to his surprise, she put
him through.

'Hello, Charley,' said Oakes. 'What's up?'

'Say, Harry. We need to talk. Not over the phone,' said Katz in
almost a whisper. 'I've got somethin' big.'

'Maybe later. I'm busy—'

'No, it won't wait. This is serious, boss.'

'Oh … Well, come on over. But it better be good.'

Hanging up, Katz wiped the sweat from his brow and lifted the
heavy suitcase. With a final glance around the squalid room, he was
out the door. After tossing the suitcase into the trunk of his car, he
jumped in and sped out the road to Cable Beach. Within minutes he
arrived at Westbourne and hurried inside, where the archly superior
butler led him to the library. Rapping lightly, Jenkins swung open
the door and announced, 'Mr Katz.'

Katz stepped past him, nervously clutching his hat.

Glaring from behind his desk, Oakes leaned forward and said,

'OK, Charley. What's so important you can't spill it over the phone?'

Glancing over his shoulder to make sure the door was shut, Katz said, 'I was keeping a lookout at the Shawcross place last night, and this big British sedan pulls up.' Katz began pacing. 'And this heavy-set fellow gets out – an older guy with silver hair – and goes straight in. It's getting dark, so I figure I might as well try to get a better look.'

'Get to the point,' said Oakes. 'And stop that pacing.'

Halting abruptly, Katz stared for a moment. 'Well,' he said, awkwardly immobile, 'I went around to the back. I could hear 'em talking on this upstairs balcony so I shinnied up a tree, just below where they was talking.'

'They? Who?'

'The Shawcross dame and this guy. Anyways, Harry, you're not gonna believe this.'

'Goddamn it, Charley, get to the point!'

'The guy had an accent. He's asking her about Hamilton, and she tells him Hamilton called her. Like she's reporting it to him. He thinks Hamilton's in the States, like we figured, but no, she says, he's in the Bahamas, but not Nassau. Up at some little island.'

'It had to be Ericsson,' said Oakes thoughtfully.

'Yeah, I guess so. So she tells him she can lead him to Hamilton's hideout. Jeez, some friend, right? And the guy, Ericsson, is dying to get his hands on him.'

'Let me get this straight,' said Oakes, narrowing his eyes. 'Evelyn Shawcross was offering to lead Ericsson to Hamilton, so Ericsson could—'

'Kill him.'

'What?' Sir Harry's eyes opened wide.

'Said it just like that, like he was gonna pluck a chicken. But that's not all.'

Taking a deep breath, Oakes sat up straight and said, 'What else?'

'He sort of bragged to her that he'd built the Germans a U-boat base at his marina.' Oakes slumped in his chair. 'Get this,' said Katz, leaning on the desk. 'He tells her the Germans are gonna take over the island and put the goddamn Duke of Windsor under arrest!'

'Oh, my God,' said Oakes. 'Charley ... are you sure? You hadn't been drinking?'

'Why, no. Not while I'm on duty. And I heard every word.'

'So,' muttered Oakes, 'Ericsson's working for the Germans....'

'And the Shawcross woman is working for Ericsson,' said Katz. 'The way I got it.'

'Hamilton must be on to them,' said Oakes, his eyes growing even wider. 'So Mrs Shawcross betrays him when she learns where he's hiding out.'

'And Ericsson plans to knock him off. To keep him from causing trouble.'

'A U-boat base,' said Oakes. 'My, God, Charley, we've got to stop this!'

'Yeah, but how?' said Katz glumly. 'We don't have any proof. Just my word. And I might have a problem explaining what I was doing up in that tree.'

'Yes. Yes, you might...'

'Listen, boss, things are getting too hot around here. This guy's not our only problem.'

Oakes gave Katz a curious look. 'What do you mean?'

'I got a call this morning from one of Lansky's boys. He says, you don't listen too good. You got concrete ears. He was really steamed.'

'What? What for?'

'For the goddamn article in the paper is what for. He says, "So Oakes is gonna open a casino in Nassau? We warned you," he says, "but you didn't think we was serious. If you know what's good for you, clear out of town. We're gonna have to teach Oakes a lesson."'

'He said that?'

'That's exactly what he said.'

'Charley, this is no good. We've got to come up with a plan....'

'Sorry, boss.' Katz slipped on his fedora. 'I'm leaving. It's too dangerous, what with the Germans and the mob.'

'I won't allow it,' said Oakes with a thump of his fist on the desk.

With a tight-lipped smile, Katz raised a finger to the brim of his hat. 'Good luck, Harry,' he said. 'You'll think of something. I'm on the next flight out.'

Carter knelt beside the gleaming bow of the Chris Craft, working polish into the grain with a chamois as a group of gulls floated overhead, almost motionless in the steady breeze. Carter rose to his feet as Hamilton started down the pier, lugging a wooden box. 'Let me give you a hand,' said Carter. The two men carefully lowered the box next to the stern.

'Whew,' said Hamilton, wiping sweat from his eyes. 'That's the last of it.'

'Will these Navy frogmen have their own gear?'

Hamilton nodded. 'We'll just take what we'll need, the 45s, ammo, and those knives.'

Carter reached into the box for one of the K-bar battle knives and inspected its twelve-inch blade. 'Plus the extra fuel,' he said, gesturing at the jerry cans lashed to the transom.

'And my little secret weapon,' said Hamilton.

'Right,' said Carter with a knowing smile. He looked up at the pale sky, noticing a faint ring of clouds that encircled the sun.

Hamilton's eyes travelled upward after him. 'What do you make of that?'

'They say it means a storm's coming.'

'Have you heard a weather report?' asked Hamilton.

'Miami radio says a cold snap's on the way. Warning about frost on the orange groves and heavy thunderstorms.'

'When?' A worried look crossed Hamilton's sun-tanned face.

'Later tonight.'

'Well, we'd better shove off....'

'Tom!' called Marnie from the terrace. 'You have a phone call.'

'It must be Evelyn,' he muttered. He trotted down the pier.

Taking the call in the study, Hamilton said, 'Evelyn? Are you all right?'

'Yes, I'm fine. Everything went just as you predicted.'

'He went for it?'

'Hook, line, and sinker, as you Yanks would say. When I mentioned that you were staying on a small cay, and that I was planning to see you, he insisted on coming along.'

'How did you handle that?'

'Well ... he acted the gentleman, offering to accompany me, to ensure my safety.' God, she thought, how easily the lies came.

'And naturally you accepted.'

'Of course. Tom, how soon...?'

'Tonight, if that's possible.'

'Yes, I think so. I told him I was planning to leave today.'

'Great. We're all set. We're headed for Hope Town this afternoon. It's just a tiny settlement, with a sheltered marina. There's this one café, in the middle of town. That's where we'll be waiting. Tell Ericsson you're meeting me there after dark, as late as midnight.'

'When we get there, what should I do?'

'Once Ericsson knows where to find me, you'll have to think of an excuse to stay behind. He'll buy it, because he won't want you getting in the way. When they've gone, make your way to the lighthouse. You can't miss it.'

'The lighthouse.'

'The lighthouse-keeper will be expecting you. Wait for me there. I'll come just as soon as we've taken care of Ericsson.'

'What will you do to him?'

'Turn him over to our navy. I'll have a destroyer waiting offshore. Evelyn, no matter what, stay with the lighthouse-keeper.'

'When are you leaving?'

'As soon as we can get underway.'

'Oh, Tom, I don't want to say goodbye.'

'It's just for a few hours. By tomorrow this will all be over.'

'Goodbye, Tom. And good luck.'

As he hung up, he turned and saw Marnie in the doorway.

'I wasn't eavesdropping,' she said. 'I just happened to come in as you were telling her goodbye.'

'I'm in love with her, Marnie.'

'What about her husband?'

'She's divorcing him.'

'I see,' said Marnie sceptically.

Sir Philip managed to propel himself in his wheelchair all the way to the end of the long pier where Hamilton and Carter were preparing to cast off. Marnie stood beside him, the breeze furling her yellow cover-up. Standing at the wheel, Carter turned the ignition and listened with satisfaction to the deep thrum of the engine. '*Bon chance*,' called Sir Philip.

Hamilton waved and said, 'If we're not back by noon tomorrow, you'll know what to do.'

'Be careful, Tom,' said Marnie. 'Carter,' she added, 'you look after him.'

'Yes, ma'am.'

Carter slowly backed the boat away from the pier, turned north, and the sleek craft surged forward, knifing into the swells. Holding Marnie's hand, Sir Philip shaded his eyes and watched until the boat was no more than a speck on the horizon.

Looking old and worn, Sir Harry Oakes walked slowly to the bookcase and bent down to examine a photograph in a tortoiseshell frame. He smiled wistfully at the family portrait: his handsome wife Eunice beside him, flanked by young Nancy, Sidney, and the other children on the front porch of their beautiful cottage on the rugged Maine coast. He felt a deep pang of yearning, like homesickness, for his beloved Maine and his family, even Nancy, who had gone away to boarding-school in Vermont, temporarily leaving the dreadful de Marigny behind. Pushing aside the unhappy ruminations, Oakes walked to the trolley and selected a bottle of aged Scotch. As he reached for several ice cubes from a silver bucket, he noticed the slightest tremor in his hand. With a sharp intake of breath, he dropped the ice into a glass and poured a drink.

He began pacing the faded Persian rug in front of his desk, pausing periodically to sip his drink, deep in concentration. In whom could he confide? He'd considered calling the duke, but the duke was a great admirer of Ericsson and terribly fond of Evelyn Shawcross – he would think him a raving lunatic. Contacting the authorities would be equally futile. What evidence did he have? Only Charley Katz's improbable story, and besides, Katz was gone, on a plane to Miami. My God, he thought desperately, was he simply to wait until the Germans attacked? Every British subject would be treated as the enemy, subject to internment and confiscation of their assets. With a base for their U-boats, and the Spitfires at the airfield at their disposal, it could alter the strategic balance of the war! He had to do *something*, call *someone* ... An idea suddenly flashed into his mind. Of course. Why hadn't he thought of it sooner? It would be risky, no doubt about that.

Unsure what he hoped to achieve, Oakes lifted the telephone and instructed the Westbourne operator to place a call to Greycliff. When Evelyn's Bahamian servant answered, Oakes calmly said, 'Is Madam Shawcross in? You may tell her Sir Harry Oakes is calling.'

Evelyn had spent the afternoon sequestered in the house, trying, without success, to sleep; every nerve on edge with the awareness of the extreme danger of the mission that lay ahead and its promise to free her from an otherwise inescapable trap. Finally, she had gone for a walk, to Government House, where she gazed out to the distant sea, imagining she could see the boat with Tom speeding northward to their rendezvous. She had just returned home when the phone rang, causing a flutter in her chest. As Samuel approached her, she said, 'Who is it?'

'Mister Oakes, ma'am.'

'What on earth,' she said softly as she walked across the room and picked up the receiver. 'Hello?' she said warily.

'Ah, Mrs Shawcross,' said Oakes pleasantly. 'Good afternoon.'

'Good afternoon,' repeated Evelyn, sitting down at the desk.

'Mrs Shawcross, there's some information that's come to my attention I'd like to discuss with you. About your friend Nils Ericsson.'

Oh, my God, thought Evelyn, her heart beating wildly.

'And his project on Hog Island,' Oakes continued coolly. 'Hurricane Hole.'

'I'm sorry,' said Evelyn firmly, 'I can't imagine what this has to do with me.'

'I have it on good authority,' said Oakes, 'that Ericsson's co-operating with the Germans. That he's built them a U-boat base, and they're planning an attack on Nassau.'

'An attack on Nassau?' said Evelyn with a weak attempt at a laugh. 'I don't know what you're talking about, or why you're telling me—'

'Because,' said Oakes, 'I know you're in on it, helping Ericsson keep an eye on that American fellow, Hamilton.'

Her mind racing, Evelyn raised a hand to her mouth. Stay calm, she implored herself, and find out exactly how much he knows. 'That's utter nonsense,' she declared. 'You've obviously been listening to some absurd rumour.'

'Oh, yeah?' Oakes paused to take a swallow of whisky. 'I'm on to your game. I know you're planning to lead Ericsson to the place where Hamilton's holed up.'

'What in heaven's name are you talking about?'

'Don't think I'm gonna stand by and let it happen. Not after everything I've done for this Colony. Oh, no, Mrs Shawcross.'

'No one would possibly believe you!' blurted Evelyn. In the ensuing silence, she perceived she'd struck a nerve. 'If you're so certain of this ridiculous tale, why don't you tell it to the police? Or better yet, to the Governor?'

'Maybe not,' said Oakes. 'But I'm not gonna just sit back and let the Germans take this island. I'll think of something. Such as getting word to Hamilton, to tip him off.'

'Hamilton? I hate to disappoint you, but he's safely at home in Texas.'

'Oh, really?' said Oakes sarcastically. 'Well, maybe I'll just pass the word to his friend Sir Philip Sassoon. Something tells me he'd know where to find him. And Sassoon would find it very interesting to learn you've been working for the Nazis!'

'It's a lie,' said Evelyn in a voice just above a whisper. 'Goodbye.' Gently hanging up, she slumped down on the desk, cradling her head on her arm. After a minute the panic subsided and her rational mind took command. Anyone might have heard the rumours about the U-boat base at Hurricane Hole, but the only way Oakes could possibly know she was planning to lead Ericsson to Tom's hideaway was if someone had overheard their conversation. Someone working for Oakes, skulking about her house. There was no other explanation. But if that were the case, he *didn't* have any proof … And what difference would it make after tonight, after Ericsson was in American custody? For a moment, she felt enormously relieved. And then it struck her: if Oakes told Sir Philip that she was co-operating with Ericcson and the Germans … that she'd betrayed Tom….

Startled by another phone call, she sat up and brushed back her hair. Was it Oakes calling back, with some new threat? She impulsively reached for the phone and said, 'Hello?'

'Ah, Evelyn,' said Nils Ericsson. 'I trust you're ready for this evening's expedition?'

'Well, yes, I suppose so.'

'Here are the particulars. If we're to arrive at the rendezvous by midnight, we should be underway at ten o'clock. Meet me at the public dock. Be there no later than nine forty-five.'

'All right,' murmured Evelyn. 'At nine forty-five.'

'Very well,' said Ericsson. 'Until then, goodbye.'

'Goodbye.' As she hung up, the kernel of an idea began to form. Opening the desk drawer, she searched among the odd papers and objects that had accumulated there. Finally, she found what she was looking for: a single-shot derringer, so small it could be easily concealed in the palm of her hand, and a box of cartridges. With a heavy sigh, she took them from the drawer and pushed back from the desk.

CHAPTER NINETEEN

Standing in the open cockpit of the Chris Craft with one hand on the wheel and the other on the throttle, Carter gazed out at the waters of North-east Providence Channel, occasionally glancing at the binnacle, maintaining a heading of due north. Running flat out in the glassy seas, the sleek powerboat traversed the fifty-miles to Great Abaco Island in just over an hour. Carter pointed into the glare of the afternoon sun. 'There,' he said. 'See that town?'

Hamilton shaded his eyes and studied the shoreline.

'Hole in the Wall,' said Carter.

Hamilton stared at the collection of tumbledown shanties and the masts of a few fishing boats amid the pale green vegetation.

'From here we run right up the coast.' Carter glanced over the side, where the water had turned from deep blue to pale turquoise. 'Till we raise the lighthouse.'

'How much further?' asked Hamilton.

Carter consulted the chart. 'We cruise across Conch Sound for thirty miles or so,' he said, 'to Little Harbour, and from there it's twenty miles to Hope Town.'

'Fifty miles,' said Hamilton. 'Another hour and a quarter at this speed. That should leave just enough time to get things ready.'

The minutes passed slowly in silence as the boat planed across the gentle swells, not more than a mile from shore. As they rounded the point, the great expanse of the Caribbean stretched to the horizon, while a necklace of coral cays separated them from the Abaco coastline. A thin layer of clouds obscured the sun, foreshadowing the coming storm. As they drew closer to the largest of the barrier islands, Carter pointed and said, 'There, can you see it, Tom?'

Hamilton stared into the gloom, and then a bright light flashed, the lighthouse beacon as it made its rotation. 'They built the lighthouse,' said Carter, 'to drive off the wreckers.'

'Wreckers?'

'Folks made their living by luring ships onto the reefs at night with a lantern on a mule, then plundering the wrecks.'

After another twenty minutes, Hamilton could make out the peppermint stripes of the Hope Town lighthouse in the gathering dusk. As they headed for the small, protected harbour, he gazed at the blood-red sun hanging above the horizon through a thick veil of clouds. The lighthouse beacon flashed out to sea as they passed beneath the tall, conical structure, an unmistakable landmark to mariners. Carter idled the engine as he steered into the marina, choosing a vacant slip among the fishing boats, which had been battened down or hauled up in preparation for the storm.

'We don't have much daylight,' said Carter as he killed the engine and reached for a length of rope. 'We should pay a call on the lighthouse-keeper.'

Standing on a steel platform below the upper chamber of the lighthouse, Hamilton studied the mechanism that rotated the beacon, a complex assembly of gears, springs, and rods the lighthouse keeper was obliged to wind with a long brass crank like some giant Swiss watch. Though the gears turned without a sound, the oil pumping into the lamp above them hissed noisily, fuelling a wick that burned with a brilliant white light through a heavy lens.

'She's one of the last of her kind,' said the keeper, a man in his 40s, as he checked the pressure gauges. He turned to Hamilton and asked, 'When are you expecting your guests?'

Hesitant to disclose their plans, Hamilton said, 'The man we're after should arrive by midnight. We'll be waiting in town. But, as I explained, a woman will be with him.'

'And she knows to find her way here?'

Hamilton nodded. 'I'll come for her as soon as we're finished. But no matter what happens, keep her with you, until I come for her.'

'And what if you don't come?' asked the keeper.

Hamilton glanced briefly at Carter. 'If we don't come,' said Hamilton, 'see to it she's kept out of sight until Carter's boss sends someone for her.'

Leaving the lighthouse, Hamilton and Carter retrieved the wooden box from the boat and then made their way to a small café in the centre of town. Hamilton explained their unusual request to the café owner and slipped a thick wad of bills into his hand. They stowed the weapons and ammunition in a storeroom next to the greasy kitchen and sat with cups of coffee at a table near the window. They had the café to themselves, except for the cook, who agreed to stay long enough to serve them coffee and supper.

'So when are your navy friends due?' asked Carter.

Checking the clock over the cracked linoleum counter, Hamilton said, 'Any minute. I told them to be here by nine.' Both men glanced out the window at a sudden flash in the black sky, followed after a few moments by a reverberating clap of thunder.

They stood up at the sound of men's voices. The door swung open, and three men walked in, wearing black oilskin jackets, denim dungarees, and heavy sea boots. One of the men was carrying a canvas bag.

Glancing around the small, spare room, the man with the bag said, 'Lieutenant Hamilton?'

Hamilton reached out and took the man's hand. 'I'm Hamilton,' he said. 'And this is my partner, James Carter.'

After giving Carter a questioning look, the sailor turned to Hamilton and said, 'I'm Petty Officer Watkins. And this is Konarski and Ford.'

'Pull up a chair,' said Hamilton, 'and we'll get you some coffee and a sandwich.'

'We're in for some heavy weather,' said Watkins, as he stripped off his oilskin and hung it by the door. 'Are you sure our guests can make it in?'

'These men are tough,' said Hamilton. 'And they think I'm the one being ambushed. I'm sure they'll make it.' The UDT men nodded and pulled up chairs. Glancing at the clock, Hamilton said, 'they should be here by midnight. So let's use the time to work out a detailed plan.'

Stifling a yawn, Sir Harry Oakes absently rearranged his cards, forcing himself to concentrate on the after-dinner game of bridge. 'Two hearts,' said the attractive woman on his left, Mrs Dulcibelle Henneage, a wartime evacuee from London and occasional dinner guest at Westbourne.

'OK, Harry, what's it gonna be?' asked the middle-aged man seated across from Oakes. Harold Christie, a successful Nassau real estate speculator, was a regular companion of Sir Harry's.

Oakes frowned as he distractedly studied his hand. His mind wandered to the call he intended to place to Sir Philip Sassoon in the morning and the reaction the news would elicit.

'C'mon, partner,' said Christie encouragingly.

'I don't know,' said Oakes with a yawn. 'I pass.'

'Aw, Harry,' complained Christie, 'you gotta bid!'

'Sorry,' said Oakes, who was still wearing tennis whites from a late afternoon doubles match. Rubbing a hand over his careworn face, he placed his cards on the elaborately inlaid table and said, 'I hate to be a party-pooper, but I'm gonna call it a day.'

'Dammit, Harry,' said Christie. 'We can't quit with them so far up on us.'

'Now, now,' Mrs Henneage chided Christie. 'Don't be a sore loser.'

Charles Hubbard, a retired, silver-haired Englishman with a home on Cable Beach who was Mrs Henneage's companion for the evening, smiled pleasantly and said, 'Well, Dulci, my dear, we'd best be on our way.'

'Need a lift?' asked Sir Harry.

'No, thank you,' said Mrs Henneage as she totted up the score. 'Charles is driving me home,' she added, intending to dispel any impression of a romantic liaison.

'Blasted rationing,' grumbled the Englishman. 'I've got just enough petrol to get me to town and back.'

After seeing his guests to the door, Oakes turned to his old friend and said, 'What do you say, Harold? How about a nightcap?'

Christie hesitated, listening for the sound of human activity in the mansion. 'Sure,' he said after a moment. 'And if it's OK, I was planning to spend the night....'

'Why not?' said Oakes, feeling his anxiety beginning to subside. 'I insist.'

As Oakes was finishing his drink, the clock over the mantel in the spacious study chimed a quarter past the hour. 'That's it for me, Harold,' said Oakes. 'I'm turning in.'

'Go right ahead,' said Christie. 'I think I'll read for awhile.' Both men looked up as a faint flash of lightning illuminated the curtained window, followed by an answering rumble of far-off thunder. 'Storm's on the way,' said Christie, in reply to which Oakes merely grunted.

'Night,' said Oakes with a yawn.

'Night, Harry.' Christie watched as Oakes walked slowly from the room.

One after another, the downstairs lights blinked off, leaving only a solitary lamp in the study and the lights in an upstairs bedroom. The quarter moon had risen, only to be swallowed up by a swiftly advancing line of menacing clouds, leaving the grounds surrounding the mansion in utter darkness. Concealed behind a thick tree trunk at the verge of the lawn, a dark figure carefully watched as Oakes trod up the open staircase to the master bedroom. The still, oppressive air was disturbed by a distant boom, and flashes of lightning blossomed in the dark clouds. After another ten minutes, the light in the study winked out, and moments later Harold Christie appeared on the stairs and upstairs gallery before entering the bedroom adjoining the darkened master suite.

With a cool breeze stirring the treetops, the black-clad figure moved swiftly across the lawn and disappeared beneath the staircase. Thirty minutes after the guest bedroom window went dark, the figure silently crept up the stairs and, as the tropical rain began to pour, moved furtively along the gallery, stopping at the door to the master suite. The doorknob turned silently, without resistance. The intruder stepped noiselessly across the threshold, holding a length of pipe and a tin of kerosene, and paused to study the dim outline of the bed, draped in mosquito netting, and listen to Oakes's laboured breathing. Moving quickly to the bedside, the intruder gently placed the kerosene on the carpet, drew back the mosquito netting and, with a grim smile, slowly raised the pipe and then delivered a crushing blow to the old man's skull, like a hatchet on a stick of firewood. Uttering a deep groan, Oakes somehow managed to sit up, clasping his hands to his bloodied face. A second blow, with a two-handed grip, brought him down again, silencing his groans. As a flash of lightning briefly illuminated the scene, the assailant grabbed the kerosene and doused the body and blood-soaked bedcovers, setting them ablaze with a single match. As macabre shadow-men danced on the walls, the figure backed away from the flames, taking a Chinese screen that stood next to the bed and placing it against the window. Pouring out the remaining kerosene, the killer struck a second match and tossed it on the floor.

As rain poured down in sheets and wind swayed the trees, a second figure crouched behind a tree, maintaining a solitary vigil. When bright light suddenly flashed in an upstairs window, the observer dropped to one knee, fascinated as an eerie, orange glow flickered in the window and then was abruptly blotted out. In the next instant, the door flew open, momentarily revealing the flames blazing inside. In the darkness and pouring rain, a figure could be seen dashing from the burning room before disappearing in the shadows. And then, in an arc of silvery lightning, the pale face and dark hair of a fleeing form were etched for a moment on the lawn, racing away from the mansion into the stormy night.

*

In her haste to make up time, Evelyn jammed down on the accelerator, glancing at the speedometer in the faint light of the dashboard. She entered the curve going much too fast, struggling to maintain control as the rear end of the car drifted onto the gravel shoulder. She eased off the accelerator and slowly exhaled, willing herself to be calm as she listened to the slap of the wiper blades. In a few more minutes she would be there. With the storm and petrol rationing, the town was empty. She parked at the end of the street and switched off the ignition. Two men appeared in the headlamps: one wearing a hat and long coat, the other in a uniform holding open an umbrella. Evelyn reached for her purse and let herself out.

'You're late,' said Nils Ericsson in the dripping rain.

'Yes,' said Evelyn, trying to calm her racing heart. 'I, ah, got caught up …' She froze as a bolt of lightning struck a utility pole, followed by an earth-jarring crash.

'It's past ten,' said Ericsson, glaring at her. 'But let's go onboard before we're electrocuted.' The uniformed man ushered her down to the dockside where Ericsson's forty-foot motor launch was waiting. Another uniformed man, a carbine slung over his shoulder, came to rigid attention as Ericsson stepped across the gangway. Evelyn could see two more men bending over a chart-table inside the cabin. The guard helped her across the gangway to the deck. As she alighted she turned to Ericsson.

'Can we still go,' she asked, 'in this weather?'

'Of course,' he replied, 'though I assure you the seas will be rough.'

Evelyn walked past him into the brightly illuminated cabin, panelled in gleaming walnut with polished brass fittings. Following behind, Ericsson barked a command in Swedish to the men by the table and then turned to Evelyn.

'Look at you,' he said, examining her drenched coat and tangled locks. 'You're soaked through.'

'Yes, well … I was having trouble with Father's car, and the rain began pouring.'

'I see,' said Ericsson with a frown. 'Let's get underway,' he said to the captain. Quickly saluting, the officer called out commands to the deckhands. A shudder passed through the boat as the powerful engine came to life.

'I suggest we go below,' said Ericsson, shrugging off his raincoat. Evelyn made her way down a steep, narrow staircase into a small but elegant salon furnished with a sofa and armchairs. A well-stocked bar was built into the bulkhead. As Ericsson appeared behind her, she removed her rain-soaked hat and shook out her hair.

'Let me get you a towel,' said Ericsson, as he helped her out of her coat. 'And something to drink.' Evelyn planted her feet apart to compensate for the rocking motion as the boat gathered speed. 'What will you have?' asked Ericsson, when he returned with the towel. She gratefully dried her face and patted her damp hair. The boat lurched violently and seemed to buck, causing Evelyn to stumble sideways, though Ericsson remained stolidly in place. 'Don't worry,' he said with a smile. 'The sea will smooth out.'

Feeling a bit queasy, Evelyn said, 'I'll have a whisky and soda.'

As he turned to pour the drinks, she peered out of a porthole into the blackness, listening to the vibration of the powerful engine and the pounding waves. 'There you are,' said Ericsson, handing her a crystal tumbler.

Accepting the drink, Evelyn sat in an armchair, aware that the boat was moving very swiftly, easing the pitching and rolling. Ericsson, standing with one hand on the sofa, raised his glass and said, 'Skaal.'

Evelyn took a sip, which seemed to calm her nerves. 'How fast,' she asked, 'is this boat?'

'Sixty knots, seventy perhaps. But not on a night like this.' His sentence was punctuated by a flash outside the portholes and a clap of thunder. 'I should imagine,' he continued calmly, 'the captain is making fifty knots. You see, Evelyn, this boat was built by a highly successful rum-runner from Miami. Fastest in the Caribbean.'

Sitting comfortably on the arm of the sofa despite another violent lurch, Ericsson sipped his vodka. 'The poor fellow lost everything with the end of Prohibition, and I picked up the boat for a song. Well, not quite a song.'

Hoping to draw him out, Evelyn feigned interest in the particulars of the vessel. Like most yachting enthusiasts, Ericsson never tired of the subject, and happily obliged her with a detailed description. After more than an hour had passed, Evelyn yawned and said, 'I assume you have accommodations for your men?'

'For the Germans, you mean?' he asked, as he walked over to pour another drink. 'My crew are all Swedes and have their own berths.'

'Yes, for the Germans,' said Evelyn as casually as possible.

Ericsson smiled and said, 'We've converted the cargo area – where the rum was hidden – into rather cramped sleeping quarters.' Evelyn merely nodded and sipped her drink. 'I assume Hamilton will be alone?' asked Ericsson.

'Oh, yes,' replied Evelyn, 'though it's possible Sir Philip's servant may be with him.'

'Hah,' said Ericsson derisively. 'I assure you they're no match for my men, and we'll have the advantage of surprise.'

'I see,' said Evelyn quietly. She tried to imagine the café where Tom would be waiting and the trap he was preparing. She intuitively believed that Tom would succeed, that within a few short hours the nightmare would be over.

Ericsson walked around the sofa and stopped to fix Evelyn in his pale-blue eyes. 'Can you imagine Hamilton's surprise,' he asked, 'when I explain that you're working for our side? That all along you've been helping the Germans?'

Staring back at him, she could feel her heart pounding, and her mouth was almost too dry to speak. In her desperation, she had failed to consider what Ericsson might say to Tom. If Tom were planning to kill him, it wouldn't matter … but he'd distinctly told her they were going to take him alive. And so now, after all that she'd risked, in the end Tom would know.

Ericsson gave her a curious look. 'Evelyn,' he said, '... is something the matter?'

Pressing her lips tightly together, she slowly exhaled and said, 'Perhaps I'm a bit seasick.'

'Pardon me, sir.'

Both turned to the first officer. 'We're within sight of the lighthouse,' he reported. 'I suggest you come on deck to observe our approach, as conditions are quite marginal.'

'I'll be right up,' said Ericsson, placing his glass on the table. 'Evelyn, I want you to stay below.'

CHAPTER TWENTY

THE POWERFUL STORM raced across the narrow coral island, leaving the settlement of Hope Town in blackness, with lingering flashes of lightning, and awash in churning rivulets. Seated at a table in the small café, Hamilton listened to the rain on the corrugated roof as he sipped black coffee. Ten minutes earlier Carter had reported from his lookout that a large powerboat was docking at the marina. Hamilton glanced at his reflection in the window in the glare of the overhead light and checked the time on the clock. Ten till one. As the minutes slowly passed, his mind was beginning to play games – imagined voices in the back room amid the sounds of the storm, visions of men moving along the street in the darkness. Hamilton laid his palms flat on the table, straining to detect the slightest sound above the steady drumbeat of the rain.

Ericsson had chosen a team of three of his best men, with a fourth left behind to guard Evelyn. He'd considered sending her alone to the café, with his men following behind, but rejected the scheme as too risky, as Hamilton might try to use her as a hostage. She was better off out of the way, to be used as a bargaining chip if the situation required it. He observed the efficiency with which the Germans blackened their faces and donned their gear: black sweaters, pants and boots, knives strapped to the ankles, and pistol-grip Schmeisser sub-machine-guns slung over their shoulders. With the advantage of surprise, the raid should be over within seconds. Nor would they have any difficulty locating him, as the lights burning in the café above the waterfront were visible even in the pouring rain. Before heading out, Ericsson took a few steps down the staircase, pleased that Evelyn was comfortably on the sofa where he'd left her.

'We're off for your friend,' he said with a smile. 'It appears that he's waiting up for you.'

Evelyn nodded, clutching the derringer concealed under her purse. 'How long will you be?' she asked, willing him to descend the rest of the way.

'Thirty minutes, I should think.' With his hand on the railing, Ericsson took another step.

'Where are the crew?' she asked, stalling for time, her finger on the trigger-guard.

'I've sent them out to check on the storm. But don't worry, I'm leaving Heinrich to look after you.' A tall man in a khaki uniform with a peaked cap appeared on the stairs behind Ericsson and descended quickly into the salon, his hand on the grip of a sub-machine-gun. 'Goodbye,' said Ericsson as he started up the stairs. 'I shall return shortly.' Biting her lip, she relaxed her grip on the pistol and watched him disappear into the wheelhouse.

Slipping on his coat and hat, Ericsson hurried onto the deck where the commandos were waiting. With a glance at the sky, he turned to the leader and said, 'Everything's ready?' When the man nodded, Ericsson said, 'All right. You know what to do.' They crossed the lurching gangway and headed for the humble collection of buildings ringing the waterfront. When they reached the first building, the point man turned and said, 'I'll reconnoitre. Stay here with the others.'

Within minutes he returned, darting around the building where the others were sheltering under the eaves. 'Well?' asked Ericsson impatiently. 'Is he there?'

'Yes,' replied the man in a whisper. 'I could see him in the window. And he's alone.'

'What about the back of the café?'

'All quiet. The only light is in the front room.'

'Excellent. You know the plan.' The men nodded and moved out in a crouch.

*

Hamilton glanced at the clock as the minute hand clicked. Instinct told him that the action would begin within minutes, in all likelihood an assault through the unlocked front door. He reached for the cigarettes on the table and extracted one, briefly examining it before placing it between his lips and picking up a nickel-plated lighter. He started at a brilliant arc of lightning that coincided with a deafening crash, plunging the room into darkness. Damn, he silently cursed. A power outage, the one thing he hadn't planned for.

'Tom,' whispered Carter from behind the counter. 'Light this.' He tossed a candle in the dark, which luckily landed at Hamilton's feet.

Crouching along the side of a building, Ericsson and his men froze at the errant lightning strike. Staring ahead into the next block, they perceived that the light in the window had been suddenly extinguished. Each of the low buildings looked just like the others in the darkness and steady rain. 'What now?' asked the leader.

'We wait,' whispered Ericsson, 'to see if another light comes on.'

Hamilton reached for the candle, feeling oddly relieved, no longer a sitting duck under the bright light. Though his plan assumed Ericsson's men would storm the building, there was always the chance he'd make an easy target for a sniper. He flicked the lighter and held the flame to the candle's wick. Propped in the coffee mug, it cast a flickering light across the room. They would know where to find him, but he would have the advantage of the dim and irregular illumination.

'Just as I predicted,' Ericsson said confidently when the flickering light appeared in the window. The commandos moved quickly toward their target, in single file in a low crouch with hands on the grips of their Schmeissers.

*

Evelyn sat facing her guard with her hands on the purse in her lap. As her fingers traced the outline of the tiny pistol she bitterly considered that she'd forfeited her one chance. Either way now, if Tom succeeded in capturing Ericsson, or the other way round … she was doomed. Her only hope to avoid exposure had been to shoot Ericsson before he left the boat.

'Pretty,' said the guard unexpectedly.

'What?' said Evelyn, raising her baleful eyes.

'Pretty,' he repeated with a smile, motioning toward her with the barrel of his gun. '*Niedliche mädel.*'

Averting her eyes from his gaze, she realized in an instant what she had to do, an absolute imperative arrived at without rational deliberation. Looking back up at the man, she smiled suggestively, which evoked an expression of pleasurable surprise. He took a step closer, allowing the gun to hang from its strap, removed his cap and smoothed his short, blond hair. Opening her purse, Evelyn reached for her lipstick. Holding the man in her eyes, she took off the cap and made an elaborate display of applying it. As she pressed her moist, red lips together, she slowly eased her hand under her purse. She smiled at the guard, who was watching her with an amused expression, his weapon pointing uselessly to the side. Holding the man in her gaze, she suddenly raised the derringer and jerked the trigger. With the sharp report, the man toppled backward, a strangled cry in his throat, as a puff of smoke curled from the squat barrel. Evelyn sprang to her feet and examined his motionless body. With lifeless eyes staring up at her, a crimson stain slowly spread across his khaki shirt. With her heart pounding, she seized her purse and coat and bounded up the stairs, praying that the sound of the pistol had been muffled by the downpour. A glance confirmed she was alone. Pulling on her coat, she hurried onto the deck and across the gangway. She looked into the town and then at the bright beacon of the lighthouse, flashing out to sea through the rain.

Bathed in the flickering candlelight, Hamilton placed the cigarette between his lips, holding the lighter in his right hand and listening for the slightest sound. Vaguely perceiving motion outside the door, he flicked the lighter and lit the cigarette. In the same instant the door flew open and three black-clad figures burst inside, training their guns in all directions.

'Jesus!' cried Hamilton, instinctively pushing back.

'Hands up!' screamed one of the commandos, as all three crouched with their Schmeissers aimed at Hamilton. 'Drop your weapons or we shoot!'

Standing up with his hands raised, Hamilton stared coolly at the men. 'I'm unarmed, understand?' he said. '*Verstehen*? No weapon.'

Glancing nervously around, the apparent leader barked a brief command. Hamilton stared at the man, smiled and lowered the cigarette to his lips, took a drag and then casually tossed it away. The cigarette struck the linoleum floor with a loud *pop* and simultaneous explosion of brilliant white light. One of the men fired a wild burst, ripping into the wall, while the others staggered blindly. Rising up from behind the counter, the UDT men fired a short volley with their Thompsons, instantly dropping one of the commandos. Vaulting over the counter, they quickly disarmed the others, who were stumbling with their hands to their eyes. Hamilton, who'd managed to close his eyes just before the explosion, called to Carter behind the counter: 'Toss me a .45! I'm going after Ericsson.' Carter flung the weapon to Hamilton, who raced out the door.

Glancing down the empty street, Hamilton thought he saw movement, a dark shape disappearing into a doorway. He gave chase, sprinting recklessly down the rough pavement, keyed up from the brief but violent encounter. The figure fled from the doorway, moving with surprising agility and vanishing down a narrow alley. As Hamilton rounded the corner, he lost his footing in the gravel and sprawled on all fours with the handgun clattering on the pavement. When he looked up, his breath caught in his throat. Not more than twenty paces away stood Nils Ericsson, holding a pistol aimed at Hamilton with a grim smile visible even in the darkness. Hamilton blinked, heard a loud *crack*, and watched in astonishment as Ericsson shuddered, dropped to his knees and crumpled to the ground. Turning to look over his shoulder, Hamilton saw Carter at the corner, arms extended with his .45 in a two-handed grip. Hamilton slowly got up. 'Nice shot,' he said in a trembling voice. 'I thought I was a goner.' The two men cautiously examined the form on the pavement. Carter felt for a pulse at Ericcson's carotid. 'Dead,' he said as he stood up and dusted his hands. 'I'd better get down to the boat and take care of the crew.'

'Take two of the frogmen,' said Hamilton. 'And be careful. He may have left another man behind. I'm heading for the lighthouse.'

Feeling a surge of elation, Hamilton started jogging toward the lighthouse. Though the rain abated, a hard breeze was blowing out of the north-west, cold on his wet face. In less than a minute he reached the lighthouse-keeper's shack, relieved to see a lamp burning in the window. Trotting up, he rapped on the door. Within moments it opened a crack.

'Is she here?' asked Hamilton.

With a look of relief, the man pulled open the door. 'No, I ain't seen her.'

Hamilton could hear a door blowing open and shut in the steady breeze. He glanced at the nearby lighthouse, where, in the darkness, he could just make out the door at the base swinging back and forth. 'Thanks,' he said to the perplexed lighthouse-keeper. 'I'll be back shortly.'

Thinking Evelyn had misunderstood, Hamilton ran to the light-house, which was perched on a rock and concrete base at the water's edge. Stepping inside, he peered up the winding staircase, suffused with faint yellow light from the upper chamber. He listened to the hissing of the oil pump and the wind shrieking through the windows. 'Evelyn!' he shouted. 'It's Tom!' He ran part way up the stairs, paused to listen, and then shouted to her again. When she failed to answer, he surmised there'd been trouble at the boat and hurried down the narrow stairs. When he reached the waterfront, gasping for breath, Carter and two of the navy men were standing guard over a group of men on the dock. Racing up, Hamilton blurted, 'Where is she?'

'She's not at the lighthouse?' said Carter.

'No,' said Hamilton, fighting despair.

'I thought for sure she'd be there,' said Carter. 'She got clean away from here.'

'How do you know?'

'Ericsson left a man behind to keep an eye on her. We found him dead, a bullet right through the heart. Below the wheelhouse,' Carter added, pointing at the boat, 'lying in the cabin.'

'What did the others say?' asked Hamilton, pointing to the crew.

'They don't speak much English, but the captain says they left the boat, and when they came back the guard was dead and Evelyn gone.'

Hamilton quickly crossed the gangway and bounded down the stairs to the salon. The lights were burning and the guard was sprawled on his back, a look of surprise frozen in his wide-open eyes. Hamilton stooped down and picked up Evelyn's lipstick case. He hurried back on deck and said to Carter, 'I'm going back to the lighthouse. Wait for me here.'

Hamilton ran all the way to the keeper's house, where the man informed him for a second time that he'd seen nothing of Evelyn. Where else on the tiny island could she have gone? He walked wearily to the lighthouse and stood on the rocks, listening to the crash of the waves and gazing out at the storm-tossed sea. For an instant he thought he saw a far-off light that blinked and disappeared in the murk. Looking up, he waited for the lamp to complete its rotation and watched as the bright shaft of light shone far out to sea, a beacon that surely she could see, no matter where she might be. He turned and walked inside the conical structure, slowly ascending the winding staircase. When he reached the machinery below the upper chamber, his heart was pounding, either from exertion or his growing sense of panic.

Maybe, he considered ... somehow they'd missed one another in the darkness, and now he'd find her, waiting in the safety of the chamber atop the old lighthouse. Hamilton ascended the last flight and shoved open the rusty iron door. He briefly studied the brightly burning lamp in the glass enclosure, turning in a slow, steady ambit. Aware of the rush of wind, he dashed to the other side of the chamber. A large, rectangular window had blown open. Hamilton peered out in the darkness and then looked down at the black water surging against the rocks. Fighting vertigo, he dropped to the floor, resting his back against the wall with his arms clasped around his knees.

He stayed there all night – dreaming he could hear her voice, that she had suddenly appeared through the doorway – not stirring until the first light of dawn. Hamilton slowly stood up and looked out the open window. The sky was deep blue, without a trace of cloud, above the rim of the rising sun, and a cold, steady breeze was blowing. He stared at the vast, empty sea, with jagged whitecaps, and then lowered his gaze to the foaming waves that surged on the rocks. No one could survive a fall into those waters. With a deep sigh, he walked slowly around the turning beacon and started down the staircase, every muscle and joint aching. When he reached the bottom, he noticed a small envelope partially hidden beneath the last stair. Stooping to pick it up, he saw the single word 'Tom.' He tore it open and read Evelyn's simple, farewell note:

> Dearest Tom,
> You will never know how much I love you, or how much I regret what happened. The simple truth is, I could never be worthy of you. Please promise me that you will try to forgive me and think only of the happiness we had.
> Evelyn

For hours, Hamilton and Carter slowly patrolled the Hope Town harbour and the waters surrounding the lighthouse in an inflatable boat, searching for some clue – an article of clothing, a scrap of paper – to Evelyn's mysterious disappearance. As the warming sun rose in the sky, Carter finally spoke up: 'Tom, do you think we ought to head back?'

Hamilton stared into the clear water, seeming to ignore the question. 'I've got to believe,' he said finally, 'that maybe … with that storm, the way the wind was blowing …' He lifted his eyes and gazed at the horizon.

'Tom,' said Carter firmly, 'those navy boys will be wanting to get underway.'

Looking toward the stern, Hamilton shielded his eyes and nodded. Carter turned the handle on the outboard to steer back to the marina. As they approached Ericsson's cruiser, two of the navy men were standing on deck, waiting with their arms crossed.

'Any luck?' one of them called out. Hamilton grimly shook his head as Carter brought the boat up to the stern ladder. Climbing on deck, Hamilton could see that everything was ready for an imminent departure, with the Germans and Swedish crew locked up below with the bodies of Ericsson and the two dead guards.

'Time to shove off?' he said, as he shook the petty officer's hand.

'Aye, aye, sir.'

'Thanks for everything,' said Hamilton. 'Tell your skipper to take these prisoners in right away. I'm cabling my report as soon as we're back in Nassau.' Crossing over to the dock, Hamilton and Carter watched as the boat passed beneath the lighthouse and out to sea.

'Tom,' said Carter quietly, 'there's nothing more we can do.'

'OK,' said Hamilton, running a hand over his stubble of beard. With a final glance at the red and white lighthouse, gleaming in the bright sunlight, he said, 'Let's go.'

Despite his total exhaustion, Hamilton stood at the dash of the Chris Craft, holding on to the windshield, for the entire two-and-a-half hour run, never uttering a word. When the pier at Eves finally came into view, Hamilton gave Carter a weary smile and said, 'Go get some rest while I report in.'

As the minutes ticked past, Sir Philip positioned himself in the living room with a clear view of the pier, maintaining a solitary vigil, as Marnie had chosen to wait, and pray, in her bedroom. When at last the boat came alongside the pier, and Sir Philip saw both men standing in the cockpit, he offered a silent word of thanks to God, though not a praying man. 'Philip,' said Marnie, appearing suddenly and rushing to her husband's side. 'Thank God.' But as Hamilton and Carter began walking up to the house, it was obvious that something was wrong. When they reached the terrace, Marnie was waiting at the door. 'Tom,' she said, shocked by the dark shadows under his eyes and his dazed expression. 'Are you all right?' Unable to answer, he looked from Marnie to Sir Philip, who was watching impassively.

'Maybe,' said Carter, making eye contact with Sir Philip, 'it would be better, Tom, if you wash up and let me explain.'

'We got Ericsson,' said Hamilton unexpectedly. With a deep sigh, he added, 'Dead, but we got him.'

'Excellent,' said Sir Philip in a strong, reassuring voice. 'Why don't you do as Carter suggested...?' Glancing uneasily at her husband, Marnie took Hamilton by the arm and walked with him toward the bedroom hallway. When they were out of earshot, Sir Philip turned to Carter and said, 'What's happened to the man?'

'It's Miz Shawcross,' Carter said quietly. 'We lost her.'

'Lost her? She was killed?'

Carter shook his head. 'Don't know. She disappeared. Tom's, well ... he's pretty bad off.'

Despite Marnie's insistence that he lie down, Hamilton politely refused, anxious to explain to Sir Philip what had happened and initiate the sequence of events that would expose Ericsson's treachery and shame the British into seizing Hurricane Hole. Resting his arms on the basin, he cupped his hands and splashed hot water on his face. After towelling off, he examined his bloodshot eyes in the mirror. With a growl from his stomach, he felt a sudden craving for food and coffee.

'I wonder,' said Hamilton as he strode into the living room, 'if I might get a cup of coffee and a piece of toast.'

'Darling,' Sir Philip called to Marnie. 'Please tell Henry that Mr Hamilton is ready for his breakfast.'

'Well,' said Hamilton as he slumped on the sofa, 'I suppose Carter filled you in....'

'Not entirely,' said Sir Philip. 'Though he briefly described the action at the café.'

'The café,' said Hamilton, thinking back to the scene which, in the light of day, had a surreal quality. He glanced up as Henry entered the room with a tray of eggs, bacon and toast and a steaming cup of black coffee. 'Thanks,' said Hamilton, lifting the cup to take a sip. 'At any rate,' he said, 'everything went pretty much according to plan.'

'The Germans were utterly disabled by that device of yours?' said Sir Philip. Hamilton nodded, pausing to take a bite. 'Very ingenious,' Sir Philip continued, 'a tiny canister of white phosphorous concealed in a cigarette.'

'It made one hell of a flash,' said Carter, who looked rested after a shower and change of clothes. 'Those Dutchmen were blind as bats.'

'Anyway,' said Hamilton, 'it was over before you could say Jack Robinson. That's when I went after Ericsson, and unfortunately—'

'Yes,' said Sir Philip. 'A pity Carter had to shoot him. Even so, with the two Germans you captured, your government has more than enough evidence. I've taken the liberty of telephoning Colonel Donovan.' Hamilton gave him an expectant look. 'He asked me to convey his congratulations,' continued Sir Philip. 'Your government will announce that Ericsson was caught aiding and abetting the enemy. So far as the public will know, he was lost at sea in the storm.'

Hamilton stared at Sir Philip and slowly exhaled. 'And what about your government?'

'Donovan is sending a cable to the Foreign Office, demanding the immediate seizure of Ericsson's holdings in the Bahamas. The duke won't have any alternative. The Royal Navy will send in that gunboat, and so much for Hurricane Hole.' Sir Philip gave Tom a look of almost paternal pride. 'Tom,' he said, 'following the incident in the alley—'

'I went to the lighthouse,' said Hamilton. 'Evelyn was supposed to wait for me there.'

'I gather she escaped from Ericsson's boat.'

'They left a man behind to guard her,' said Carter. 'We found him dead, shot right through the heart. Don't know where she got the gun.'

'And you found nothing?' asked Sir Philip. 'Not even a note?'

Hamilton stared off into the distance. 'I waited at the lighthouse all night,' he said quietly. 'She must have gone before I got there. And then I found her note.'

Carter looked at him with surprise.

'It didn't say much. Just that she was sorry and, in so many words, would never see me again.'

'Utterly baffling,' said Sir Philip. 'How she could have vanished without a trace. It's not the only mystery that last night yielded, nor was the death of Ericsson the only sensational death.'

Hamilton and Carter exchanged puzzled looks.

'Sir Harry Oakes,' explained Sir Philip, 'was found murdered this morning.'

'Murdered?' said Hamilton, his bloodshot eyes open wide.

'In his bed during the night, bludgeoned and set on fire.'

'Good Lord,' said Hamilton.

'Harold Christie found the body. He was staying over at Westbourne, sleeping in the room next door. The duke has assumed personal responsibility for the investigation,' said Sir Philip. 'He's flown in the chief of homicide from the Miami Police Department.'

'Miami?' said Hamilton. 'That's a bit irregular.'

'Highly. Rumour has it, they're interrogating Alfred de Marigny.'

'De Marigny,' said Hamilton. 'I knew there was bad blood between those two, but I would never have thought de Marigny the type to commit murder....'

'Nor I. But the duke detests de Marigny.'

'Oakes murdered,' muttered Hamilton. He closed his eyes, fighting a powerful wave of drowsiness.

'Tom,' said Sir Philip, 'you should rest.' Hamilton looked up wearily. 'You're devastated about Evelyn, we all are. In all probability, we'll never know what happened, but the operation could never have succeeded without her. If she died, she died a heroine.'

As Hamilton loaded the last of his things for the trip to Oakes Field, Marnie sat at Sir Philip's side in the living room, her arm around his shoulder. 'I can't believe he's leaving,' she said. 'After all these months.'

'Yes, darling,' he agreed. 'But the war's far from won, and I'm sure he's needed elsewhere.'

'Philip …' She paused. 'Is there anything you've learned that might help explain what happened?'

'Nothing,' he said after a moment, 'that would be of any comfort to him.'

'But what?' Marnie persisted. 'What *have* you learned?'

'Very little, I'm afraid, that sheds any light on her disappearance.' Marnie narrowed her eyes. 'Only that her husband was detained in Cairo, suspected of spying for the Germans.'

'Oh, my God,' said Marnie. 'How long have you known?'

'I received a telegram,' said Sir Philip, 'the very day Tom departed on his mission.'

'I wonder,' said Marnie, 'did she – Evelyn – know?'

'If she did,' said Sir Philip as he stroked his chin, 'we'll never know.'

Hamilton strode into the room, looking to Marnie exactly as he had the first night she met him, wearing a blue blazer and gray slacks. 'Time to go,' he said. 'The plane's waiting.'

'Oh, Tom,' said Marnie, throwing her arms around him. 'If only you could stay.'

'I'll be back, though I can't say when.'

'Who knows,' said Sir Philip, 'perhaps you'll come back some day to build that hotel and casino.'

'Where are you going?' asked Marnie. 'What's next?'

'I'm headed to Washington. But I'm planning to quit the OSS.'

'Are you serious?' asked Sir Philip.

Hamilton nodded. 'I've got my commission in the navy.'

'Well,' said Sir Philip, 'Colonel Donovan may have other ideas. Good luck, Tom.' He warmly shook his hand.

'Goodbye,' said Marnie, leaning over to kiss him on the cheek. 'We'll be waiting for you.'

Hamilton quickly glanced around the sun-filled room, as though he wanted to remember the smallest details. With a smile, he said, 'Goodbye,' and then turned and walked to his waiting car.

EPILOGUE

THE TRIAL OF Alfred de Marigny for the brutal murder of Sir Harry Oakes captured the attention of the English-speaking Press like no other, dominating daily headlines from Miami to New York and London despite the fact that the story was competing with the breathtaking events of the Second World War. Apart from the well-known antipathy between the accused and the deceased, the prosecution's case hinged on a single piece of forensic evidence: a fingerprint attributed to de Marigny lifted from the Chinese screen at Sir Harry's bedside the night he was bludgeoned to death. The accused maintained that he'd spent the evening in question quietly at home playing cards with the Marquis Georges de Videlou and his girlfriend, a story which de Videlou corroborated from the witness stand. In his skilful cross-examination of the homicide detective summoned by the Duke of Windsor to conduct the murder investigation, de Marigny's Nassau lawyer demonstrated that the fingerprint had in fact been fraudulently obtained during the police interrogation of de Marigny from a water glass he'd been offered, a revelation so stunning it prompted the chief of the Miami Homicide Division to bolt from the packed Nassau courtroom and become violently ill on the sidewalk, to the horror of the large crowd gathered outside. At the conclusion of the six-week trial, the jury returned a unanimous verdict of not guilty. De Marigny's joy was short-lived, as the jury, in an act unprecedented in Bahamian law, also voted to deport de Marigny and his young wife Nancy forthwith from the Colony. The murder of Sir Harry Oakes has never been solved.

Following the sensational Oakes murder trial, the Duke and Duchess of Windsor were largely absent from Nassau for the duration of the war, pleasuring themselves in the United States, where they would eventually take up permanent residence at the Waldorf Towers in New York. The duke never fully recovered from the blow to his prestige caused by his role in the botched Oakes murder investigation and the public exposure of the pro-Nazi activities of his Swedish friend, on whose innocence the duke would insist to his dying day.

The notion of opening a resort hotel and casino on Hog Island also died with the murder of Sir Harry Oakes. Meyer Lansky continued to enjoy a monopoly on casino gambling in Havana under the watchful eye of the corrupt Batista regime until its violent overthrow by the young Fidel Castro in 1958. With Havana suddenly off limits to American tourists, a wealthy American by the name of Huntington Hartford persuaded the Bay Street regime in Nassau to pass legislation authorizing casino gambling in the Colony. By the early 1960s, Hartford had acquired Hog Island, which he re-christened Paradise Island, connected it to Nassau with a bridge, and opened the first resort hotel and casino in the Bahamas, which thrives there to this day. Shangri-La, abandoned since the war, was renovated by Hartford into the world-renowned Ocean Club, along with its famous marina: Hurricane Hole.